Wekiva Winter

FREDRIC M. HITT

Indian River County Main Library
1600 21st Street
Vero Beach, Florida 32960

This book is a work of fiction. Any resemblance to actual events or persons, living or dead, is entirely coincidental.

"Wekiva Winter," by Fredric M. Hitt. ISBN 1-58939-759-2 (softcover); 1-58939-760-6 (hardcover).
Published 2005 by Virtualbookworm.com Publishing Inc., P.O. Box 9949, College Station, TX 77842, US. ©2005, Fredric M. Hitt. All rights reserved. No part of this publication may be reproduced, stored in a retrieval system, or transmitted in any form or by any means, electronic, mechanical, recording or otherwise, without the prior written permission of Fredric M. Hitt.

Manufactured in the United States of America.

3 2901 00436 9808

To Linda,

Whose love sustains me,
Whose spirit delights me,
Whose discipline drives me.

Lexicon of Timucua Words and Phrases

Anacotima -   Counselor

Atichicolo-Iri -   Spirit warrior

Chulufi-Yuchi -   Crying Bird

Holata -   Chief

Holata aco -   Chief of chiefs

Huque -   Hurricane

Inija -   Chief's next in command

Isucu -   Herbalist, medicine man, sorcerer

Itori -   Alligator

Jarva -   Shaman, spiritual person

Nariba -   Old man, term of respect

Niaholata -   Woman chief

Paracusi -   War chief

Paqe-Paqe -   Forgive, forget

Tacachale -   Fire that cleanses and purifies

Yaba -   Wizard, witch

Wekiva -   Waters of the spring (Seminole-Creek)

PROLOGUE

13th day of September, 1597
Franciscan Mission at Tolomato
Guale Province

Had he not tripped on the hem of his robe, the priest might have saved himself by hiding in the shadows of the blackened church. So close he was to the safety of the sacristy door that could have afforded time for his screams to bring rescue, yet here he lay helpless at the foot of the altar. His shrieks and upraised bony arm were no defense to the heavy club arching downward.

The last thing he saw was the hate-filled visage of his murderer, the Indian Juanillo.

* * *

Fray Pedro de Corpa, Doctrinario of the Mission at Tolomato, awoke with a start. He lay in his bed in the friary. His heart pounded in his chest and cries of terror still echoed in his head.

He had sweated during the night. The cotton pillow was soaked through and his nightshirt clung to him wherever it touched his skin.

Father De Corpa rolled to his side and placed his bare feet on the clay floor. Frightful specters of dissolving dreams fled his consciousness like quail spooked from their nests. The door of the tiny windowless apartment was closed and bolted from the inside. Not even a breath of fresh air had afforded relief from the stifling heat throughout the fitful night.

Early morning light seeped under the door and through the tiny cracks of the daub and wattle clay walls. This had been his home for two years, since the time in 1595 when the Governor and his military escort had accompanied de Corpa and his fellow Franciscans to their mission stations, spacing the eight brown-frocked priests at major Indian villages ranging sixty leagues to the north of the mission called Nombre de Dios at the Spanish settlement of St. Augustine.

The pomp and ceremony had impressed and attracted the curiosity of the natives. They knew the power of the soldiers, had heard the bluster of cannon and had witnessed the deadly consequence of the arquebus fired at close range. The fearful Indians fled the advancing procession and hid in the marshes and reedy swamps among the coastal islands where they made their home.

Music had been the key to their curiosity, and upon approaching each village the Spanish formed a parade. The military tambourines, drums, bugles and flutes were less intimidating than gunfire, and gave the march a pleasant Sunday-outing quality.

Leading the procession was Governor Domingo Martinez de Avendano, turned out in his finest green, red and yellow silk finery, his copper helmet glinting in the sunlight.

The priests followed along. Fr. Francisco Marron carried a large wooden cross; another held a gold leaf engraving of the Virgin Mary and the others were close at hand, proudly displaying icons of the Church. One father carried a smoking censer, swaying along in a moveable mass. Following behind, as if an afterthought, two platoons of well-armed Spanish soldiers marched in straight lines.

The process had been the same, first at the Missions of San Juan del Puerto and San Pedro de Mocama where the Indians spoke the tongue the French had called Timucua, and further north they entered the land of the Guale. In less than a fortnight missions were established at Ospo, Asao and Tupiqui and on Guale Island. Fray de Corpa was placed last and farthest to the north at the village of Tolomato.

At each village Indian scouts and unarmed soldiers herded the Indians out of their hiding places in the woods and swamps and into the village center where music and chanting and singing greeted them. A prayer was offered by the Franciscan leader, Fray Marron, aided by an interpreter. Gov. Martinez spoke eloquently of the Christian God who had come to bless the village with the peace and justice of the Spanish.

He promised the listeners that their village leaders and customs would be retained and respected and even protected by the Spanish military should they be threatened by their enemies. A mission was being established in the village to serve the Indians, he said, and a holy man would live among them, teaching them Christianity and serving them in every way.

Finally, the Governor kneeled before Fray de Corpa as he had the other Franciscans and kissed his hand and blessed him to his duties, cloaking him with all the power and authority of the Spanish military and civil government.

Then Martinez de Avendano and his entourage left Tolomato, going back the way they had come, again to the accompaniment of music, leaving Fray de Copa to his fated duties. A small detachment of Spanish engineers and soldiers remained with him for five days, marshalling and directing the Indians in the construction of the mission church and the small friary that was still his home.

Father de Corpa arose from his cot and moved to the door. He released the lock and cracked the door enough to peer into the sandy mission yard. His view was toward the east, and the golden globe of the sun balanced on the ocean surface under a cloudless cerulean sky.

Cautiously, he opened the door wider and looked out. The plaza was empty. By sunup he would have expected the women of Tolomato to have stoked the fire in the open-air kitchen, and the older children to be attending to the sweeping of the grounds. Instead, there was no one in sight in the mission yard.

The young friar closed the door and leaned against it. Curious, he thought, that no one would be about; as curious as it had been the day before that only a handful of Guale had attended mass, where the church was almost always filled to capacity.

This was Juanillo's doing. A protest, nothing more.

Juanillo, the moody son of the Chief of Tolomato. Juanillo, who had readily converted to Christianity and been baptized, but who clung stubbornly to his polygamous ways. He had thus far ignored de Corpa's entreaties to renounce any of his wives other than his first.

Otherwise, the successes with the villagers had been heartening. Once the chief, Juanillo's father, accepted Christ the rest of the village leaders followed. Fully two-thirds of the adults of Tolomato had been catechized and instructed in the tenets of the Church, and they now taught what they knew to their children.

In two short years God had performed many miracles in this place. Graven images had been destroyed and replaced by the cross. Superstitions and mystic beliefs once taught by the elders were being forgotten as the children learned stories of the Sermon on the Mount, and the birth of Christ and His marvelous resurrection. The genuine enthusiasm with which the natives embraced their new religion was a blessing for which de Corpa thanked his Father daily.

Yet, with all the successes, challenges were common, and Juanillo and his obstinacy had become the source of much worry and frustration for the beleaguered priest. Private talks with the future chief had availed nothing. Scriptural proof of the sinfulness of polygamy were never refuted by Juanillo, but never accepted in practice.

Father de Corpa had finally consulted with his friend and mentor, Father Blas Rodriguez who served the nearby mission at Tupiqui. Fr. Rodriguez had been adamant: Polygamy was insidious and difficult to eradicate. If the future chief were allowed to flaunt the teachings of Christ then the village would be scandalized, Fr. Rodriguez had counseled. Soon other teachings would be questioned and the mission effort would be undermined not only in Tolomato but throughout the other missions and villages of Guale.

Rodriguez urged a firm response. At Sunday Mass the issue was addressed publicly. Fathers de Corpa and Rodriguez stood together and again denounced the sin of polygamy. All eyes were on Juanillo who stood quietly and implacably in his place of honor near the altar, his muscular arms across his chest.

Father Rodriguez spoke eloquently of the blessed nature of Christian marriage, and of the scriptural prohibitions against having more than one wife. De Corpa studied the faces of the congregation, and in particular the countenance of Juanillo. It came as a surprise when Fr. Rodriguez went well beyond the denunciation the two priests had agreed upon. Swept along by his own eloquence, Rodriguez intoned dramatically that no practitioner of polygamy would be qualified for any position of leadership within the tribe.

Juanillo's reaction had been sudden and emphatic. He cursed the priests in the Guale tongue, and accused them of interfering with matters that were none of their concern. He stomped out of the church. In his wake many of the others followed. Only a handful of nervous worshipers remained for the benediction, and even they slipped out immediately thereafter.

Father Rodriguez assured de Corpa that they had been as true to the scripture as had Saints Peter and Paul, and ultimately they had made a necessary point. Rodriguez then counseled de Corpa to be careful until Juanillo's anger and embarrassment ebbed, and left immediately to return to the mission at Tupiqui.

A tension gripped Tolomato for these last days. Juanillo and the other leaders stayed out of sight, and it was rumored that strangers had been seen in the village. Only two of the mission cooks continued to work, and none of the workers who maintained the church, friary and grounds.

Fr. de Corpa earnestly believed that Juanillo would eventually accede to the clear dictates of the scriptures, and that this crisis would evolve into a closer understanding on the part of the natives of the Word of God. Still, the isolation and loneliness of living among the Indians wore upon his spirit. He prayed daily for the courage and strength to meet the challenges to which God had called him.

As was his custom every day of his adult life, Fr. de Corpa prepared for his morning prayers. He stripped off the damp nightshirt and relieved himself in the chamber pot and bathed himself from the basin of tepid water on the stand in the corner of his room.

He kneeled next to his bed, his eyes closed and his fingers working the beads of the rosary. His lips moved inaudibly as he recited the Apostles' Creed, the prayer the Lord had taught and the Hail Marys. He asked forgiveness of his Father for his doubts and his lack of steadfastness. He prayed that God's hand strengthen and direct his mission, and he prayed for the soul of the son of the chief, Juanillo.

So engrossed was he in his supplications, Father de Corpa was not aware that the unlocked door behind him had opened. His tightly closed eyes failed to alert him of the sunlight that suddenly flooded the room. He took no note of the fresh early morning air that touched his bare skin. His eyes flickered briefly at the sound of the thin whistle of the war club as it arched above his head and came crashing down.

* * *

Three days later ...
Franciscan Mission at Tupiqui
Guale Province

Four days had passed without word and Fr. Blas Rodriguez was worried. At first it had been just a feeling of unease. The distance between Tupiqui and Tolomato was only four leagues, a day's round-trip travel by the native messengers who were regularly dispatched between the missions so that the Franciscan priests might feel less isolated and vulnerable.

Yesterday morning Fr. Rodriguez had sent a letter to Fr. de Corpa, hoping for a response and word that the dispute with Juanillo had dissipated if not completely resolved. The messenger had not returned.

Adding to his sense of foreboding, Fr. Rodriguez noted the absence of the chief of Tupiqui for the past two days. By itself this was not unusual. Chief Tupiqui often left the village for a day or two to visit relatives up and down the coast. It was unusual that the chief's second in command, his *inija,* was also nowhere to be found.

Just an hour ago Father Rodriguez had heard the loud, chattering greetings of the women in the village as their chief returned, and word was soon delivered to Fr. Rodriguez that Tupiqui wished an audience at the mission church, and it was there the priest waited.

Fr. Rodriguez heard the approach of the chief and his entourage and stepped from the darkened church into the sunlit mission yard. With the chief were his *inija* and the other senior advisors. And there were others: three men who were strangers and dressed differently than the Guale.

One was very tall, and wore his long hair loose and below his shoulders, instead of knotted high on his head as was the custom. Another, who appeared to be the leader, was powerfully built, with tattoos running down his arms and thighs. The third man was also Timucua like the other two, but dressed differently with his hair embroidered with shells of the sea and the feathers of wading birds.

Fr. Rodriguez pronounced the traditional greeting in the Guale tongue, and awaited a reply that did not come. Chief of Tupiqui did not step forward to introduce the visiting dignitaries, but instead remained in his place, unsmiling. His face, like the other Guale, was painted with red and black pigment. And there was yet another. Juanillo, the son and heir of the chief of Tolomato stood to the side, his arms crossed over his chest.

The priest saw that the men, both the Guale and the Timucua, were armed with darts and knives. One stood to the side, slowly swinging a war club called a macana. Another man held a battle axe, a weapon so lethal it had been forbidden in the village.

As terror took hold the priest trembled and his knees shook and knocked together beneath his long robe. His darkest fears and those of all his brothers who had placed their lives in the hands of God in this dark land were to be realized. The death of a martyr was to be his fate. Escape was impossible. He knew that the day for which he had prepared all of his adult life was at hand.

Fr. Rodriguez asked Chief Tupiqui that he be allowed to celebrate a final mass, and his wish was granted. Only a handful of villagers were in attendance, and they wept openly throughout the service. Chief Tupiqui, Juanillo and the others sat on the chapel floor and waited.

When the mass was done, Fr. Rodriguez divided his scant personal belongings among the worshipers. He charged them to be steadfast and to obey God's law, and to bring up their children as good Catholics.

When there was nothing more to be said he walked out of the darkened sanctuary. He lifted his eyes for the last time to the brilliant blue sky above. Then he nodded to Chief Tupiqui that he was ready.

* * *

On the third day thereafter ...
Franciscan Mission on Guale Island (St. Catherine's Island)
Guale Province

Father Miguel de Aunon and his lay brother and friend, Antonio de Badajoz, awaited their fate. They had known for four days of the attack at Tolomato. The messenger was certain that Fr. de Corpa had been slain but did not know if it was an isolated event, or part of a wider rebellion.

That question had been answered the previous night when a Christian trader from the north came with news of the tragic happenings at Tupiqui.

Fr. de Aunon celebrated a special mass at daybreak, and noted to his discouragement that it was sparsely attended. He gave Holy Communion to Brother Antonio. There was left only the waiting.

Scouts had been placed at the portages at both ends of the island. A band of Indians had landed at dawn to the south, established a day camp and showed no sign of approaching the village or mission.

By mid-morning another war party landed in the north and moved through the tidal marsh. From an overgrown hillock of shell and bone which commanded an excellent view in any direction, the missionaries watched. The marsh grasses swayed to and fro signaling movement.

Father Aunon knelt with Brother Antonio and heard his last confession. The men embraced as their executioners approached

* * *

The following day...
Franciscan Mission at Santo Domingo de Asao
Guale Province

The Catabrian Giant moved swiftly for such a large man. Although a man measuring six and a half feet tall and weighing close to two hundred and fifty pounds might find sheer size a detriment to moving through the thick coastal swamps, Fray Francisco de Verascolo, Doctrinario of the mission located at the Guale village of Asao, experience no such handicap.

Long, well-muscled legs under the tattered brown Franciscan robe propelled him along at a swift pace. Through fields or open woods he loped with long strides. When he encountered swamps he removed his leather sandals and cinched his robe hem around his waist, and proceeded on his calloused feet, slowing his pace not for comfort but to avoid the occasional sunning alligator or water snake.

On earlier journeys to St. Augustine for supplies the priest had traveled with guides from the village, but that was in the early days of the mission when he was unfamiliar with the Indian trails and with the landmarks along the way. For this trip he had chosen to go alone. It was not that his guides could not move as swiftly as he, but that they chose to enjoy the forty league journey, stopping to fish at every stream, camping early each night, and visiting relatives and friends in villages along the way. Whereas it would take a full six days each way with guides, Verascolo could make it in five days alone and unencumbered.

Even so, Verascolo had stayed overnight at the missions at San Pedro and San Juan on each leg of his journey. It was good to rest for the night and visit with fellow Franciscan priests.

The return trip was more difficult with no one to share the load of supplies, vestments, tools, cloth for the women to sew, wheat flower that was needed for the host, salt and sugarcane. He shouldered it all, taking care to keep his cargo dry when he crossed small streams along the way.

At major crossings he would load his arquebus with black powder and discharge it into the air, scattering the gulls, terns and other shore birds. In a short time an Indian in a canoe would appear and for a small price provide him safe transport to the other side.

Verascolo had been away from his post for too long. The journey to St. Augustine had been easily accomplished. The illness he contracted on the way, however, had delayed his return.

When Father Marron noticed the younger man suffering fever and chills he immediately ordered him to bed at the convento, where he was well fed and medicated with herbs, and caused to sweat until the poisons had left his body. Three days passed before Father Marron consented to his return. During the illness other priests had collected and packed the supplies for the Mission at Asao.

When at long last he was within sight of Asao, the burden seemed lighter. The priest's love for the people and his natural energy and exuberance moved him swiftly toward the village where he would be welcomed back with great excitement.

The population of Asao was no more than one hundred, with a like number of Guale scattered through the outlying villages that Verascolo sought to serve at the mission. Thus it was a surprise to him that he did not recognize the first group of men who greeted him as he entered the village. Two of the party did not appear to be Guale at all, one being taller and thinner, and the other powerfully built and heavily tattooed.

But there was the chief of Asao and the other principal men, holding back a bit with typical Guale reserve. The first man smiled and took the supply burden from the priest. The second man, a Guale, greeted him warmly and reached out with a strong welcoming embrace. A third man had moved behind Fr. Verascolo, who soon sensed that the Guale had no intention of loosening his powerful hug.

* * *

October 4, 1597
Mission at San Pedro de Mocama
Mocama Province

It was sunrise of the Feast Day of St. Francis. Father Francisco Pareja busied himself in preparation for the mass that would be celebrated at nine o'clock and last throughout the morning, followed by a feast that would be attended by three hundred Indians from the mainland and coastal islands.

Timucua-speaking natives from as far away as Inihiba and Colomato arrived the day before, some having traveled for two days to attend, and visited with relatives and fellow clan members, while others slept in the village council house.

Chief Tacatacura, the paramount chief of all Mocama, had sent word that he and his entourage of twenty advisors, their wives and children, would attend the celebration and cross from the mainland early in the morning. Father Pareja had sounded the church bell every quarter hour to stir the air of excitement and anticipation that spread across the island.

Only the recent fragmentary and inconsistent reports of trouble among the Guale to the north dampened the mood of the visiting priest, but he knew the tendency of these simple and excitable people to exaggerate. When the rumor spread that one of the priests had been attacked, as disturbing as that was, Fr. Pareja reasoned that the other five priests in the province would have fled toward St. Augustine, or at least sent runners to notify the Spanish garrison here at San Pedro. *No news was good news.*

The fires were lit and the women of the village were busy preparing the stews of venison and fish and the breads and gaucha cakes of maize, hickory nut and a variety of berries that grew here in such profusion. The stimulating smell of roasting yaupon leaves permeated the mission yard, luring the Indians from their huts in the surrounding village.

Only those who attended mass were welcomed to partake in the meal that would follow. Fr. Pareja asked the village chief, whose Christian name was Don Juan, to order tribal leaders to police the rest to assure that no one ate who had not prayed.

As he worked to arrange the implements needed for mass, Fr. Pareja could hear the laughter of children in the mission square and the good natured sound of the cooks talking coarsely to each other, and occasionally joining together in hymns taught them by their resident priest, Father Lopez.

Pareja knew that Fr. Lopez had served his people well with his ministry of music, and although he recognized that he himself was tone-deaf, and his only real talent was in the area of languages, he resolved to do better upon his return to San Juan del Puerto.

Perhaps Fr. Lopez could be persuaded to send some of the singers with Fr. Pareja to teach the women of San Juan. These people were blessed with a natural musical talent that was obvious to anyone who had heard the sweet native songs and chants that they sang in the mornings and late into the evenings.

He would speak to Fr. Lopez when he returned from his journey to the west, where he was meeting with the tribes in that region.

Fr. Pareja had received reports that Fr. Lopez was in ill health, and his return had been delayed until he was able to travel. It was for this reason that Fr. Pareja had come to San Pedro to conduct today's celebration. In turn, a younger priest had been dispatched from the Mission Nombre de Dios in St. Augustine to cover Pareja's own responsibilities at the Mission San Juan del Puerto.

Alone in the church, Fr. Pareja knelt before the altar and prayed that Fr. Lopez be restored his good health and vitality. He thanked his Father for blessing his work among the wonderful people of San Juan del Puerto, and prayed that his words today would be a blessing to the people of San Pedro. He beseeched his Heavenly Father to be with the Guale and with the priests assigned to them, and that His word be taught them with such clarity and force that the people would put away their pagan beliefs and become true Catholics and believers in Christ, as had the Timucua at the missions at San Juan and here at San Pedro.

As he concluded his prayer, Fr. Pareja became aware that the sounds from the mission yard had changed. Laughter and singing had ceased, and in their place loud shouts of alarm could be heard. When he heard his name called he quickly ended his prayer, crossed himself and backed away from the altar.

"War! War!" people were shouting.

The sun had now fully risen, and the sandy mission yard reflected its glare as he stepped from the darkened church, partially blinded. Before his eyes had adjusted to make out the man waiting for him outside, he recognized the voice of the village chief, Don Juan.

"Father, you must come quickly. We are being attacked by the Guale," he said.

* * *

It was mid-day by the time the all-clear was given by the war chief. Fr. Pareja had spent the morning in the village council house, guarded by twenty men.

Most of the visitors were frightened and had gone home. For those who remained Pareja recited a short mass followed by a meal of over-cooked stew and cold and stale breads.

In the late afternoon Don Juan walked with Fr. Pareja and his personal guards to the south end of the island and told the priest what was known of the attack.

Before daybreak, in what appeared to be a diversionary attack, two canoes carrying approximately twelve to fourteen warriors came ashore near the home of Antonio Lopez, a village leader who lived on the north end of the island. The father-in-law of Lopez was severely injured by arrows, but the son-in-law escaped to raise the alarm.

"These Guale dogs are ignorant savages," Don Juan said. "They thought we would immediately send all of our men to fight a few cowardly attackers.

"Instead, I ordered most of my warriors to the south where we are more vulnerable. They were there, just off-shore near the embarcadero. We could count twenty four canoes. They had almost four hundred fighters but in their stupidity they had lost the value of surprise. Imagine, trying to sneak up on us in the daylight."

Don Juan spit on the ground. "By the time they approached shore we were ready for them. Our plan was to wait in hiding until they began to land their canoes. They had twice the number of warriors we had, so now we had to use surprise.

"We watched as they paddled back and forth in broad daylight. A Spanish ship was anchored at the bar, just there," he said gesturing toward the Spanish brig that was used to carry supplies between St. Augustine and the far-flung missions.

"We were so close to them we could hear their war chief shouting orders. He worried that the supply ship might have soldiers aboard with weapons. Finally, he sent one canoe ashore to see if the soldiers would show themselves.

"We could have killed everyone in that first canoe. We were so close we could smell them, but we knew the others would escape if we acted too soon. So we waited, and watched. They shot some arrows but did no real damage. Then they got back in their canoe and left immediately.

"Our scouts watched as they went back to the north, but before they made their escape two of their canoes began to leak and were abandoned. In one of the canoes we found this habit and cowl," he said, handing the clothing to the priest.

Fr. Pareja felt his heart sink. The Franciscans were sworn to vows of poverty. None of the priests had more than one habit and cowl, and none would give it up.

The Indian placed his hand on the priest's shoulder. "There's something you need to see," he said.

Pareja followed the chief down the hill toward the water. A large wooden cross erected by Father Lopez marked the embarcadero. Today the cross had been struck by five arrows.

Fr. Pareja guessed the meaning of the display. The Guale had announced that five Spanish missionaries had been killed. The Franciscan sank to the ground and sat in the dirt, his back against the rough timber of the crude cross. His hands covered his face but they could not staunch the flow of tears.

For an hour he mourned while the chief and guards, embarrassed by his pain, looked away. When he had no more tears Father Pareja blew his nose on his kerchief. Then he stood and asked the chief to have a search conducted to determine if perhaps another arrow had been shot but failed to lodge in the cross.

Don Juan argued that at this range not even a Guale could miss the target, but when Fr. Pareja insisted, a search was made. When no other Guale arrows were found, Don Juan looked questioningly at the young priest.

"There were six of them. Six who worked among the Guale, but only five arrows. God has preserved one of us," he said. He blew his nose again and as darkness fell they began the long walk back to the mission.

CHAPTER 1

May 12, 1601
Mission at San Juan del Puerto
Timucua Province

The old man was more comfortable on the dirt floor than on the deerskin covered wooden stool that was provided for his use, so he sat cross-legged with his back to the wall.

"There is a place on the river many days travel from here that was known to only a few. It is remembered now only by me," he began.

His audience, a boy of twelve with his hair cut short in the fashion favored by the Spanish, stood across the room leaning against a corner post, his skinny arms across his chest.

"The others are dead, as I will be soon", he continued. "Only in my heart such a place still exists and nowhere else. It can do no harm to describe the place to you, or to tell you its secrets. You could never find it on your own.

It had none of the gold or silver for which the Spanish lust, and no precious stones. There were freshwater pearls, but they were few and of such poor quality they would not be traded, even among our own people.

It was a place for catching fish, where snails and freshwater mussels were so plentiful in the shallows that the work of just a few of our people could feed the entire village. When it was discovered that the shellfish would feed on a deer carcass the way wolves attack a fallen deer, the catches were so abundant that the village had something to barter with the traders, when they visited with their canoes full of maize and beans and squash that would not grow in our poor soil.

Fish traps were built to catch the gar, catfish, mullet and bass. Occasionally an alligator wandered into the open and met an exciting death at the hands of the men. The drying racks were over-laden with fish, sweet turtle meat, birds of the swamp, snakes and every other imaginable gift of the river. The roasting pot for the shellfish was on the fire day and night.

Every few days canoes loaded with meat would leave for Ibitibi, to feed our people.

We had no name for this place, as a village has a name. We sometimes called it *'hachanamoyo-ibi-ca-re'* which means, in the tongue of the Acuera, 'where the rivers meet'. Usually we just said 'Wekiva.'

The camp was two days travel by canoe from our home at Ibitibi, and thus difficult to defend against our enemy, the Mayaca. The main village of the Mayaca was also at a great distance which made it difficult for them to defend also.

Either tribe could have sent enough warriors to attack the other and seize the camp. That subject was argued at council of the Acuera many times. Some of the lesser village chiefs and the war chiefs believed that the camp was vital to the survival of our people, so rich was the bounty the Spirit had provided there.

Chief Acuera and his advisors felt differently. They said the Mayaca could be tolerated because they lived near the great ocean to the east, and only came to the river for protection from the cold wind in the winter. Since the warm months produced a bountiful supply of food, less so in the winter, there was nothing worth fighting for.

No councils were held and no treaties were reached between our two peoples to share the camp. When the air warmed and the hickory showed its new green buds the Acuera moved into the burned-out camp of the Mayaca and re-built it with pine saplings and the abundant palmetto fronds.

Then, when the swamp mallow blossoms fell and the wind shifted to the north we would simply destroy the fish weirs and traps, pack the canoes, burn the camp and make our way downstream to Ibitibi. When we had rested a day, the entire village would canoe across the lake to Acuera where a great feast and celebration was held.

It was in my seventh year that I was first allowed to go with the men to the camp, and only because my mother, Acuchara, was going to prepare the mussels, snails and other meats for shipment home. She was heavy with my younger brother, but her time was not to come until winter.

I was in the lead canoe, sitting in front. It was a game, my father said, and the name of the game was 'Find the Wekiva.' If I won the game I would receive a wonderful prize, all the men promised.

I knew that the small, clear Wekiva River would enter the larger brown and green-stained River of the Sun on my right hand side.

All day I watched the western shore, looking for signs of another river. I saw banks of reeds, and of cat-tails. I saw swamplands stretching as far as the eye could see, then forests of giant cypress trees so tall that they brushed the clouds and so wide at the trunk that three men reaching their arms around could not touch each other's fingers. And more swamp . . .and more reeds.

The men tried to distract me. 'Itore! Itore!', they would shout, pointing toward the left bank, but I knew there was no alligator, and if there was, I had seen much larger ones every day of my life. I continued to watch without blinking until my eyes stung with my own sweat.

As the afternoon wore on the jokes and laughter were silenced. We were in Mayacan territory and since we were not there to trade with them, we might be welcomed with spears or arrows. It had happened before between our peoples.

After awhile the canoes began to slow. Whether it was because the river was narrower here and the current more swift, or because we were cautiously approaching our destination, I did not know. It was not that the men were tiring. Our braves can canoe steadily for three or more days without stopping, so strong they are.

I redoubled my concentration on the right bank but saw only more reeds, more scrub oak, more palmetto.

One of the men in the second canoe waded ashore into a hammock of willow and maple, and was lost from sight in the swamp beyond. The rest of the party huddled together where a stand of hickory hung out over the water providing shade and concealment.

Sometime later the man returned and told us the camp was empty of Mayaca, and was burned, so they would not return. We set out again and went only a short distance before we stopped once more in the shallows. One man from each canoe got out and pulled the canoe toward a solid bank of low-hanging willow trees. The only signs that there was a passage was the swift current and the clear water flowing from under the trees that quickly lost itself in the darker waters of the River of the Sun.

The mouth of the river was no wider than the length of the canoe, and the passageway was long, dark and sheltered by overhanging trees. The Wekiva current was swift, and the channel so narrow at its mouth that a strong brave pulling was the only way to enter.

Soon the river widened, and the current slowed. The men who had been pulling got back in the canoes and helped paddle. The water was as clear as the air itself, and clean. I could see all the way to the bottom. A school of brightly colored sunfish swam under the canoe.

The banks on one side were high and sandy and had been cleared of trees and brush. Only the filthy burned-out huts left by the Mayaca could darken our joy. Surely the Great Spirit intended that the Acuera stay in this place.

'Step out, my son, and walk ashore,' my father, Itoriibali, commanded.

I did as he said, but the bottom did not come up to meet my feet. I plunged into the depths, but was not afraid. I saw the beautiful white sand of the bottom, the remains of an old damaged and sunken Mayacan canoe, the bottom of my own canoe floating there above my head, and the azure beauty of the sky beyond. I knew then that when I die, it must be at this place.

But not this day! I surfaced to the joyful laughter of my mother, my father and the rest of the party. A kick of the legs and four swift strokes of my arms and I was ashore. Their cheers lifted me, and I stood there basking in love and the warmth of the sun flexing my puny muscles to show them my strength."

* * *

"Are you listening to me?" the old man scolded.

The boy slowly lifted his chin from his chest where it had been resting.

"I am listening, Nariba."

The old man leaned forward, hawked deeply into his throat and spit onto the dirt floor near where the youth stood against the mud-daubed wall.

"I suppose that closing your eyes and nodding your head is your way of remembering what is said. You must show more respect. Did you fall asleep when your uncles told you the stories of your childhood? I suspect not, or you would still show the marks of the willow on your back side."

"I do remember my uncles," the boy said, "there were three of them. But it has been so long ago, and I was so young that I don't remember their stories."

"You could not have been so young that you do not remember the Story of Fire and the tale of the Hummingbird and the Crane. And the Story of Bread? Are these not so familiar to you that you could repeat them yourself?"

The young man leaned his head back against the wall, his eyes closed, as if remembering, but made no reply.

"Tell me who you are," the old Acueran said.

Silence lingered, as did the heat. The old man endured both better than the youth.

The boy stirred. "I introduced myself yesterday. I am called Juan de Coya."

"I did not ask by what name you are known by the Spanish. You are who your mother said you were at birth, and any name later granted to you by your *holata*."

The boy collected his thoughts so that he could reply correctly.

"At my birth I was born a Timucuan, a pagan. By the grace of God I was delivered into the care of the Franciscans as a small child. I lived first in the village of Seloy near the mission called Nombre de Dios," he said.

"The same year Father Pareja came to this mission I was sent here to be educated. I have learned the teachings of Christ for these past five years. Only a month ago I was baptized into the faith, and I am now known by my Christian name. What went before is of no importance."

The old Indian snorted, but said nothing.

"What have I said to make you laugh at me?" the boy demanded.

"Every word you have uttered since we met has been the word of a fool. That nothing in your life is worth remembering is a ridiculous thing to say. When you say you are Timucuan you speak as an idiot. But I have manners, and would not show disrespect by laughing in your face," the old man said.

"But you did laugh, I heard you." The boy held his arms tightly at his sides, fists clinched.

The old man wrinkled his forehead and squinted his eyes, as if trying to remember a distant event. "You are right, my mother's teachings deserted me, and I have shown disrespect. For that I ask your forgiveness. *Paqe, Paqe*, but it is hard not to laugh when you claim to speak the language of the Timucua."

The youth stared at the old man.

The Acueran continued: "There are no such people as the Timucua. They never existed outside the crazy heads of the Spanish and their enemies, the French. There is no tongue for the Timucua, since they do not exist."

"What riddle is this, that I do not speak Timucuan? What language do you say we are speaking now?"

"It is the tongue of the Utina, your own people, which you now speak so poorly. You also understand Mocaman, since that is the language in this country. If you are more comfortable speaking Mocaman than your own tongue we can do that. I will not speak to you in the Spanish tongue in which you are taught to forget who you are."

"And I suppose you speak all of these and more?" the boy asked.

Now it was the old man's time to close his eyes. "I can speak as an Acueran, of course, and in the manner of the Mocama, and the Utina, but you already knew this. I also speak Potanan, Yuferan, Ais, Ocale... Tawasan . . .and Appalachee. . and others I can not recall. But I cannot speak as a Timucuan, since they do not exist."

"And do you also understand and speak the language of the Spanish?"

The old man cleared his throat once again, this time with a harsh growling sound. Juan did not flinch as the wad of spittle kicked up dust between his feet.

"I do not understand the Spanish, anymore than I do the whining of a camp dog or the chattering of a blue jay. I would cut out my tongue before speaking the language of these *Hiti*."

Juan moved to the door, opened it just enough to see whether a guard was within hearing distance. He closed the door and leaned against it.

"Mind your manners, old man. You laugh at me and spit in my direction but I forgive you because you are old and addle-minded. To curse the Spanish as devils is punishable by a public whipping by the soldiers, so I warn you to watch your words in whatever language you speak."

The old man stirred and struggled to his feet. "I do not fear the soldiers. They are pigs and not real men. Perhaps it is time for me to call them by name. They say 'puerco'. That is what I will call them," he said, moving toward the door.

Juan slipped out quickly, pushed the heavy wooden door closed and snapped the metal latch into place.

The sun had set outside the small window of the old man's prison, and it became dark. He nibbled at the maize cakes that had been provided as his meal, then relieved himself in the wooden bucket in the corner and threw what remained of the cakes into the bucket.

He could have waited for the guard to empty the bucket in the morning, but instead he sloshed its contents through the window. Spanish soldiers playing cards outside narrowly escaped the shower of urine, and their curses could be heard throughout the mission.

The old man lay down on his pallet and curled into the sleeping position. A smile crossed his face as he closed his eyes and slowly drifted back to the Wekiva and happier times.

CHAPTER 2

A lthough he had little in his experience with which to compare, Juan de Coya could not imagine a more splendid and beautiful place to live and study.

The Mission of San Juan del Puerto sat nestled on an island among the palm, palmetto and pine trees just north of the river the French had called River of May, and which the conquering Spanish later named San Juan, near where the river joins the ocean.

The mission shared the island with two villages, Alicamany and Hicacharico. Seven other villages on nearby islands and on the mainland were also served by the Doctrina under the inspired and benevolent leadership of Franciscan Friar Francisco Pareja.

The church was the largest of the mission buildings, a rectangular structure measuring twenty meters long and twelve meters wide, it's wooden front double doors facing the garrison house about half its size across a small plaza.

The walls of the church were wattle and daub, clay hand packed over latticework of narrow saplings and twigs. The inner walls of the church were smoothed and colorfully painted by the Indians under the close scrutiny of Father Pareja. The Saints, the Holy Mother and even the Baby Jesus in a manger were rendered in the available black, blue, red, brown and yellow pigments of the native soil and vegetation.

Father Pareja had said many times that if the Virgin Mary looked more Timucuan than Nazarene, and if St. Peter and the other disciples all stood more than six feet tall and had the hawk-noses and high cheekbones of tribal leaders, it was small sacrifice in ecclesiastical correctness to preserve the genuine enthusiasm of the natives for their new-found faith. Besides, the quality of the paintings, perhaps primitive by European standards, was quite good.

The nave, just inside the front door, was little more than a passageway into the sanctuary and thus remained unadorned. Only the font for holy water caused the natives to pause as they rushed to worship, called by the echoing tones emanating twice daily from the bell tower above.

The floor of the sanctuary where the congregants gathered, like the floor of the nave, was of hard clay. Unencumbered by pews or other furnishings, the sanctuary could accommodate more than two hundred worshipers, standing or kneeling at mass.

Below a portion of the floor, dug out and then covered over in neat rows, were the remains of two dozen or more baptized and saved souls who had put away their pagan ways and accepted Christ before their departure from this life.

The altar, where the priest stood and where the effigies of the saints and other religious icons were displayed, was slightly elevated on a floor of pine and cypress planks, hand-milled by the Indians.

No Indians were buried under the altar floor, as it was reserved for members of the Franciscan Order, senior military officers who might request it and members of the civil Spanish government. To date, as of the year 1601, the fourteenth year of the existence of the Mission of San Juan del Puerto, no one had yet been buried here.

The bodies of five martyred Franciscan Friars had been delivered here for burial years before, but on the order of the Governor had been sent on to the Mission Nombre de Dios at St. Augustine where they were interred. They were remembered on the first Sunday of each month at a special mass here, and at every mission church where mass was celebrated.

The garrison was the newest structure in the compound, having been built in 1597 after the priests were murdered in a bloody native revolt in Guale, to the north.

The barracks could accommodate up to thirty soldiers with their armament and stores, but the contingent of troops had fluctuated between three and twenty. There were now fifteen soldiers assigned to San Juan del Puerto, commanded by a sergeant.

One end of the barracks building had been designed for storage of munitions, and had been fortified with heavy timber to make it more secure. When Fr. Pareja learned that the soldiers planned to store gun powder within thirty meters of the church he successfully petitioned the authorities in St.Augustine and the military was required to construct a second magazine at some distance from the garrison and church.

When the sergeant got over his pique at having lost an argument with a priest he soon discovered that the old armory could be used as a prison cell. It was there that the old Acueran was now held.

It was a source of curiosity among the Indians, and perhaps a matter of contention among the Spanish, that the sergeant's personal quarters in the garrison were larger by half than those of Fr. Pareja who resided in the convento.

The convento housed, in addition to the mission stores and the friars personal apartment, classrooms and barracks for the half-dozen young Timucua in training as sacristan, chorister and catechist. Juan de Coya was the oldest of the group, at twelve years of age.

An un-walled outdoor kitchen served the residents of the mission compound. On feast days it also fed the natives from the surrounding villages. The roof structure of the kitchen was mounted on posts, and like the church, garrison and convento was fashioned of woven palmetto and palm fronds.

Cinders and embers from the cooking pit would light the dry roofing material from time to time, but a new roof could be constructed in a day with the plentiful materials available.

Father Pareja compensated for the relative lack of space in his quarters by having a sheltered porch constructed outside his private entrance to the convento.

In the quiet evening hours after mass, if time were available from his busy schedule, he enjoyed taking the air and watching the sunset. His chair was made of hickory, stuffed with moss and covered by deerskin, a gift from the chief of the village of Carabay on the day the chief was baptized.

It was understood by Timucua and Spaniard alike that unless invited to do so, no one was to approach the gentle priest during his private moments of meditation, reflection and prayer.

Juan de Coya had received such an invitation earlier in the day, but out of respect stood quietly some distance away until Fr. Pareja noted his presence and gestured for him to come forward. Juan waited for Fr. Pareja to speak first.

"Good evening, Juan de Coya," Fr. Pareja said.

"Good Evening, Father."

"What a beautiful vineyard God has provided in which we labor," Fr. Pareja exclaimed expansively, looking to the west where the sun was setting behind a bank of cumulous clouds shooting rockets of red, amber and gold light against the darkening blue.

De Coya did not know the meaning of 'vineyard', and was unsure of how he was expected to answer, so he smiled and turned his face toward the sunset.

"Ah, yes," Fr. Pareja answered his own question.

Father Pareja asked about the boy's studies, about the progress of two new students who had recently arrived from Tacatacura, and about a visit Juan had made at Pareja's request to the village of Emola where they were suffering an outbreak of illness.

This was familiar conversation for de Coya, and he was confident in his responses. He was doing well in his memorization of the catechism, and could recite the Seven Deadly Sins and the Ten Commandments. He had taken it upon himself to teach the Tacatacurans The Lord's Prayer.

When the conversation moved to the problems at Emola the priest was no longer smiling. There had been so many deaths in the villages his responsibility to perform Last Rights had overwhelmed Pareja. He had sent the boy to determine if he would need to plan another trip to Emola before Easter.

De Coya said that two women and one child in the village appeared to be near death. Nearly one in four people in Emola had died over the past two years.

"The village *isucu* has treated the ill with medicinal plants, with tobacco and willow bark and has administered curing ceremonies. He hopes that he may yet save the child and perhaps one of the women," de Coya said.

"Yaba! Sorcerer!" Fr. Pareja reacted. "When will these people realize that their salvation comes only through faith in the Father and his Son, and not through some fake shaman's magic?"

De Coya remained silent, shifting from one foot to the other, looking down.

"God has called for a great harvest of souls in this land," Fr. Pareja uttered almost to himself.

Both were quiet for some time, lost in thought.

The sun had fully set when Fr. Pareja spoke again. "And what have you to report about our Acueran guest? I trust he is comfortable. Have you told him that his apartment is more spacious than my own?"

De Coya was never good at answering so many questions at one time.

"He does not complain. His room is well ventilated and he is comfortable enough. The sergeant has provided a stool and a pallet on which he sleeps," de Coya said.

"Has he been eating?"

"No. He has not eaten but he does drink a lot of water, according to the guards."

"What do these people, these Acuerans, eat?" Fr. Pareja asked.

De Coya thought for awhile before answering. "They are river people. I believe they eat fish, manatee, snails, roots, berries and anything edible that grows wild. I don't know if they plant maize. The Acueran homeland is to the west and south of my own. The soil may be quite poor there. Perhaps they have no maize or squash."

"I believe he is well traveled," Pareja said. "My guess is that he will eat anything we serve when he becomes hungry enough. Ask the cooks to do what they can to make him happy."

"Yes, Father," de Coya said, hoping to remember to speak to the cooks first thing in the morning.

"Father, it might be good to let him outside for exercise. He has been locked up for three days and suffers cramps in his legs and back."

Father Pareja leaned backward in his chair and laughed, not an insulting laugh as de Coya had heard earlier from the Acueran, but a pleasant, mirthful chuckle.

"I first heard of the Acueran a year ago. He was staying at the island village of Edelano. It was reported that he had an amazing talent for language. Chief Edelano told him I wanted to visit with him, and the very next morning he had disappeared."

Father Pareja paused to fill his pipe with tobacco he carried in a pouch slung around his neck. Having no fire immediately available to light it, he went on.

"During the winter he reappeared at Chilili, apparently hungry and in need of medical attention. He was taken by the soldiers and brought here to Alicamany. He simply walked out of Alicamany while his captors slept. You can imagine the complaint I addressed to the sergeant!

"Now we have him again, but unless we keep him secure he may wander off once more. These old people sometimes forget where they belong. No, until I have determined that he can be useful in my studies of the Timucuan language, he will remain where he is."

De Coya stood quietly, looking at his feet.

"Were you able to speak with him? Did you and he understand each other?" the priest asked.

"Yes. We spoke in the tongue of my people, the Utina. He speaks very clearly. Sometimes he speaks in riddles, and his meaning is not clear."

"Go on".

"He speaks the Timucuan language. Then he denies that there is such a tongue. He even says that the people do not exist. It is very confusing."

The priest sucked noisily on his cold pipe. "Let me tell you a story. Unless the Acueran is trying to be difficult and deliberately confuse you, once you have heard it you may understand."

The young Indian looked at the priest and listened attentively.

"Years ago, before you were born, the French landed in La Florida not far from here. They viciously exploited your people. Their lust for silver and precious stones led them to do very bad things to the Mocamans.

"The chief of Saturiwa tried to befriend the French. He showed them a bar of pure silver, and they insisted that he say where he got it. The language skills of the French were so poor that when the chief waved his arm to the west and said that he got it from his enemy, using the word 'thimogona', they misunderstood and thought he was speaking the name of the people."

De Coya's brow was wrinkled, as he struggled to understand what the priest was saying.

"When the Spanish came to save your people from the murderous French, we were told that your people were called 'thimogona.' In our language that would be pronounced 'Timucua'.

"We Spanish, being more intelligent and observant, soon realized the French error. Our early priests knew that there were many different tribes here, each speaking tongues that were similar and yet different one from the other, but by that time the use of the name 'Timucua' was so wide spread it was impossible to correct.

"The Jesuits who preceded us met with your people, the Utina, with the Potano and the other tribes along the river and the ocean, and asked for the name, some general word by which we could describe your people.

"Each time the answer was 'We are the people.' We would be told the name of the village, which was sometimes the same as the name of the village chief, but the Indians never felt the need for a name to describe the society, if you can understand my meaning."

De Coya understood very little, but smiled and nodded.

Father Pareja tried again: "My people are the Spanish, your people had no name. Do you understand?" De Coya understood that much, and said he did. He also understood that the old man was right, that there were no 'Timucua.' He would need to think more about what that might mean.

"What tongues does the old man speak?" the priest asked.

"He speaks Utinan, of course, and Acueran, Mocaman, Yuferan and Appalachee."

"Appalachee, you say?" the Priest exclaimed, his eyes wide.

"And other tongues I do not remember," the youth said.

"But Appalachee is not Timucuan at all. This man is indeed well traveled."

By now it was full dark. Mosquitoes brushed against the boy's face but he did not move to swat them away.

"Father, the old man wants to tell me the story of his life, of the old ways, and he asks me about my childhood, when I was still a pagan before, by the grace of God, my soul was saved by Jesus Christ. You have taught us that the old ways are sinful, that we are commanded to put them away and put on the Gospel of Jesus and St. Peter."

The old Priest was silent for awhile, sucking thoughtfully on his pipe.

"You are a bright child. I think it would be possible for you to listen to his little stories without soiling your soul. If they disturb you, you can always come to me and we will talk. I see no reason why you should not tell him of your early life, that which you can remember."

The mosquitoes were getting more aggressive now, and the priest almost knocked the pipe out of his mouth with his swatting. "Find out for me if our guest speaks the Guale dialect," he said, standing up and moving toward the door of his apartment.

He paused before entering. "Does he, per chance, speak any Spanish?" he asked.

De Coya hesitated. "He may know a word or two."

"What words does he speak?" the priest asked.

De Coya considered his answer carefully. "I don't remember," he said.

"Good night, my son."

"Good night, Father."

CHAPTER 3

"There were twenty-five of us that first summer, maybe thirty. I do not recall, exactly. It is now more than fifty years past, and my memory is not to be trusted on such things as exact numbers, and the passage of time, for that matter.

"Until the Spanish came there was no reason for us to count. We knew what one was, and ten and all the numbers between, but the Spanish say 'How many are you' and we answer 'many', then they say 'How many', and they get angry. Of course, you know that about the Spanish."

The old man paused. He retrieved a leather pouch from the waistband of his pants and with two fingers extracted a wad of brown leaves and placed them in his mouth. It was the first time the boy had seen him use tobacco, although he had noticed the old man's brown-stained teeth.

The old Indian chewed pleasurably. Outside, the screech of seagulls could be heard, and in the distance the slapping of waves on the shore.

"Where was I?" he asked finally, breaking the silence.

"There were many of us in camp on the Wekiva. I was not the youngest. There were two children, a boy and a girl who were three or four summers and not yet weaned of their mothers. I, being older, had many responsibilities with them since their mothers were busy with work and because a camp can be a dangerous place.

A short distance upstream the river widened and became very shallow with a sand bar on the inside bend. It was there I

33

taught them to swim. They were well-coordinated and athletic, like all Acuerans.

The second day of my lessons I had the fright of my life, and at the same time made an important discovery that made me a hero to my people.

I was teaching the girl, Amita, to hold her breath under water, while the boy practiced his swimming on the downstream side of the bar. She and I were in shallow water, and on my word we both lifted our feet and bent our knees so we would sink to the bottom facing each other. Soon she would gesture that she needed to breath and wanted to stand up. I would shake my head 'no' and blow out a few bubbles of air until she remembered my instructions and did the same thing herself.

You know, of course, that when you feel your lungs will burst, if you blow out a little air you can stand it awhile longer.

When even I had no air left I would gesture and both of us would come to the surface, gulping in the sweet warm air. She was good, this girl. Maybe I feared that she might be better than the teacher. On our last time I deliberately stayed under until my lungs were screaming for air. Both of us might have drowned of stubbornness if she had not finally popped to the surface.

When I came up I felt dizzy and ill, with spots all around my head. I bent over with my head down, trying not to faint. What a joke it would have been in camp if I was saved from drowning by a three year old girl!

My strength and wits returned quickly, however, and I was soon able to stand. When I looked around the boy was gone and I almost died for the second time. The current on the downstream side of the sandbar was swift, and just beyond the water deepened into a hole many meters deep.

I have never run so quickly, swum so fast or dived as deeply as I did in the next few moments.

The water there, like all of the Wekiva, was perfectly clear, and the sun was high overhead and even at this depth I could see the bottom. There, floating motionless just above the bottom, I thought I saw the body of the boy.

I swam straight to the bottom, not waiting to get a breath. I prayed to the Great Spirit that the boy could be saved, or that this was just a dream or perhaps that I had drowned earlier trying to teach the girl a lesson and this was my punishment. An answer to any of those prayers would have been acceptable.

My first doubt was its size. It was at least twice as large as the boy. Then it moved. Just as I reached out my hand it swam a short distance and turned to face me. It had whiskers, and its flat mouth opened and closed as it studied me.

It was the largest catfish I or anyone else had ever seen.

When I came to the surface, again gasping for air, there were the boy and girl sitting together on the sand, playing with a baby turtle. The boy had gone into the woods to relieve himself earlier and had not drowned.

When we returned to camp the only part of the story I told was about the enormous fish, as large as an alligator. Only my father believed me. Oh, you should have heard the laughter when I told what I had seen.

My uncle speared the fish later that day and there was no laughter when one fish fed the entire camp. There were more of them too, each as fat and docile and easy to spear as the first. That evening the camp elder said that these fish would hereafter be called 'Marehootie-cuyu.'

I have never had anything else named after me.

During the days, from before the sun rose in the sky until it was dark there was work to do. The fact that I was a child was no excuse. My uncle said that if I wished to play instead of work, those who did my share of the work would eat my share of the food.

The hard work was left to the adults, but the children were all expected to help. The men did all of the hunting and the fishing and the transporting of the food and supplies between Wekiva and Ibitibi.

I liked to work with the women, as it is my nature. Even in the village I had shown a talent in making pottery. The Acueran pottery was sturdy and beautiful, much superior to the flimsy shards left behind by the Mayaca. In those days I hoped to become the village potter, as my mother was.

Of course there was no pottery oven in a fish camp. My first duty, after watching out for the younger children, was to keep a neat and clean camp. I fashioned a broom from a sapling and palm fronds and busied myself each afternoon sweeping inside and outside the five huts that the men had constructed for sleep.

I also carried water for the women's cooking and for all to drink. Of course this was a simple chore with the river so close to camp. At first the men would shout 'water boy!' and I would run fast to the river with the brave's cup, and return so quickly he would be surprised.

After awhile this was no longer fun and I stored a large amount of water in a deer-skin bag that was hung from a tree limb in the middle of camp. Because I was no longer running the men started helping themselves and I had escaped a hard job by thinking of a solution."

* * *

The old man dipped his drinking cup into the earthen pot the boy had brought him, smacking his lips appreciatively. "Spring water, not the rancid animal urine the Spanish drink from their well," he declared.

"There is a spring in Alicamany, and since I had to be there this morning I thought you might like the water," de Coya said.

"Not Wekiva water, but sweet and clean. Thank you. Should I consider it as a gift to repay me for the disrespect you showed me yesterday?"

"I meant no disrespect, Nariba, but much of what you told me was confusing. When you said there are no such people as the Timucua I did not understand. Father now says that you are right, that it was a stupid mistake of the French."

"*Yaca boho yaca*," the old man said in his own tongue. 'The stupid follow the stupid,' he explained.

"Father sends his greetings. He asks about your comfort, and what you would like to eat. I spoke to the cooks and they do not know what an Acueran would prefer."

"My needs are simple. Fish stew is good, along with maize or coontie. I do not eat much. Berries are tasty. I don't want to get too comfortable here or get fattened up like a Spanish pig," the old man said.

"Father Pareja hopes to meet with you when his work allows. He has asked me to learn about you, about your travels and about the many tongues you speak."

The Acueran was silent for awhile, his eyes closed. He finally spoke. "For what purpose?"

"Father Pareja is an educated man, what the Spanish call a scholar. He serves God and would teach the Timuc . . ." the boy paused.

"You may use the word if you wish, as long as we both understand it is wrong" the old man said.

"He teaches us of Jesus. He will write a book where all the words of our language are written down, and another book where the Gospel is written in our own tongue, and he would teach the people to read and understand the stories in our own language," de Coya said, leaning forward and handing the Acueran his catechism study book written in Spanish

"This is the text we now use, as the first thing we students do is learn the Spanish tongue, but the people in the villages are too ignorant to understand its meaning."

The old man slowly turned the pages. De Coya saw that he was holding the book upside down.

"And I can be useful in this? I can neither read nor write in any tongue."

"No, but you can speak in many tongues. I can interpret your words to Father Pareja, and he can write them down. Your words would live on in these books, even after you are dead."

The old man dipped his shell cup into the bowl of spring water the boy had brought with him. His hand shook slightly as he raised it to his lips and sipped slowly. "I will have to think on this. The Spanish kill us, steal from us, enslave us, violate our women and call us ignorant savages. Yet they would learn from us. This is very strange."

"Perhaps we can all learn from each other," de Coya said.

The old Indian chuckled. "We will learn little of value from the Spanish, and it will be difficult to teach them anything important. They ask many questions but ignore the answers. Tell me, what do the Spanish call this land?"

"They call it La Florida," the boy answered.

"*La Florida*! That proves what I want to say. Most of us call this land *'cautio,'* not all of us, but many do. Yet they make up a new word of their own for our land. Maybe they believe that if they name something, it belongs to them."

De Coya prepared to leave. He said he would return in the morning with fresh spring water and maize cakes. If he could find some blueberries he would bring them also.

"I have spoken to Father of your stories. He has said it is well that I listen to you, although you may be telling me the old ways. He also says that I should answer your questions about myself and what I remember of my life."

"Then since I am responsible for your education, as well as Father's, we should start with your poor manners. Among friends when one becomes insulting and rude and later feels badly about what he has said, it is a further insult to bring a gift. That would suggest that friendship can be bought. Gifts between strangers are expected. Between kin, just say *'Paqe, paqe'* and if said sincerely, all will be forgiven."

De Coya turned to face the old Acueran as he left. "*Paqe, Paqe,*" he said, before he shut the heavy wooden door behind him.

The old man waited until the boy was gone. He reached inside his tunic and withdrew the book of catechism the boy had forgotten to take with him, and he smiled to himself as he slowly turned the pages.

CHAPTER 4

"Life in the camp was not always easy. For a child it was an adventure, of course. Every day we played hide-and-seek in the forest, we could run and swim and canoe up and down the river as long as we did not go to the mouth of the Wekiva and risk disclosing our presence to Mayacan scouts.

For the adults, however, there were hardships. We lacked some of the comforts and conveniences of the village. We had no smudge fires under our beds and the swamp mosquitoes and bed bugs feasted on us making sleep difficult. We had no granaries or other storage for foods.

We ate only what we could find on the river, or what the canoes would bring from the village on their return trips. The men soon tired of eating fish and turtle, and alligator and snails and mussels.

Worst of all, there was no maize for bread. The elders of the village were unwilling to allow what little corn we had to be taken from the granaries. You should have heard the complaints by the middle of summer!

My uncle Apoholo, brother of Chief Ibitibi, was our leader, and called a council of the principal men in camp, including my father. It was no secret what was discussed. The camp was so small that everyone could hear what was said, and it was funny to the children to hear the adults fuss at each other.

The *isucu* was knowledgeable about plants, and spoke of a root he called *ache* which grew in the swamp. He said it made tasty bread when ground, soaked in water then buried in the warm earth for two days before baking. Swamps would not be hard to find. They were all around us.

The next morning the *isucu* and the women set out in search of *ache*. My mother was too fat with child to leave camp. She watched the younger children and I was allowed to go.

It was the hardest work I have ever done. *Isucu* would find edible swamp plants and he would say his prayers and blessings. Then we would dig out the roots, sometimes standing in water over our knees. Bending and standing up, bending again and standing up, always watching for snakes, and there were many of them.

Women are suited for this work. They are built closer to the ground, and do not have far to bend.

We also found the *coontie* outside the swamps in the hammocks. It makes tasty cakes when the root is ground just right, made into dough and cooked in the fire. You must take care to wash out the poisons, however. Before you prepare *coontie*, perhaps I can show you how it is to be cleaned.

It was a long day. When the sun was high in the sky the women rested for awhile. I wandered a short distance away and found some interesting plants with red berries I had never seen before. I picked some of the berries and put them in my basket with the *ache* and *coontie* roots.

We took a different trail back to camp, and passed through an area of oak trees that were dropping their last acorns. We gathered as much as we could carry while an army of squirrels scolded us from the trees.

Acorns of the white oak, as you know, are small and bitter, but when they are hulled and the meat is finely ground you have the makings of *ogacha*. Only the chiefs and their guests are served this delicacy. The *isucu* said it should be prepared by burying it in the warm soil then cooking it on a stick over the fire.

We would send the *ogacha* as a tribute to Chief Ibitibi on the next canoe going to the village. Of course *Isucu* sampled it when it was done late that night and blessed it with his prayers, announcing that it was worthy of a chief. No one else could taste it, or we would have very bad luck.

That evening I showed *Isucu* the berries I had picked and asked if they could be eaten. He became very excited when he saw the berries. He warned me that they would make a person vomit, and suffer diarrhea, but said that I must show him where I found them the next day.

We did not leave the camp the next day, because a very exciting thing happened late that night."

* * *

The Acueran rested for awhile, and drank a cup of the sweet spring water de Coya had brought with him, and nibbled on the cakes of corn and hickory nut. He stood and walked around, stretching his back. At one point he rocked onto the balls of his feet and looked out through the window at the courtyard where the people of the mission scurried about on their morning chores.

The window was at a level to allow in light, but too high for a Spaniard to look out. The Acueran, a head taller than most of the soldiers, had no problem seeing out. His hair grew long and was knotted on top of his head today, in the old fashion, making him an even more imposing figure.

The boy spoke before the old man resumed his story. "You say you speak the tongue of the Appalachee, which is different from what we now call Timucuan. Do you also speak Guale?"

"Why do you ask?"

"Because Father wanted to know."

"I have been told that Father Pareja once served among the Yammassee, and their neighbors, the Guale. If that is so, he must speak Guale himself," the Acueran said.

"But he wants to know if you speak Guale."

"I have never traveled to the land of the Guale," he answered, resuming his seat on the stool.

He reached inside his shirt and handed the boy the book of catechism from the day before. "You forgot this yesterday when you left so hurriedly," he said.

"Praise God," the boy exclaimed, "I thought I had lost it, and was afraid to tell Father Pareja of my carelessness. I would have been punished severely if it was not found."

"Could you just say '*Paqe Paqe*' to Father Pareja?" the old man asked.

The boy laughed out loud. "I don't think that translates into Spanish," he said.

The old man went on with his story.

* * *

"Two braves stood watch each night, alternating with periods of sleep so that someone was always alert to dangers. The penalty for falling asleep during watch was death. We had with us a deerskin full of black drink. Though we had no planned ceremonies for which the drink was to be used, it was well known that even a little would sharpen a person's wits, and make it impossible to sleep until the effects of the yaupon wore off.

We had good reason to remain alert. The Mayaca knew we used the camp in their absence, and knew its location. They could have attacked at any time. If they had spies watching us, they would know that our party included women and children.

We Acuerans were more civilized than the Mayacans. They would slaughter the defenseless along with the men. We would allow women and children to live and take them as slaves.

There was a breeze that night, and most of us slept outside our huts since mosquitoes would not be a problem. I was tired and slept soundly without dreams.

Mocochucu of the Earth Clan was on guard, along with his brother Nayo. I believe it was Nayo's sleep time, and Mocochucu who raised the alarm.

When I heard his shout I awoke and felt under my sleep-mat for my knife. So startled were we, and so frightened, we thought the arrows whizzing through camp were Mayacan. We soon realized that they were our own, as sleepy braves awoke and shot their arrows at shadows, and at each other.

'Stop shooting! Stop shooting,' Mocochucu shouted.

The intruder was not Mayacan, as we had feared, but a large black bear. The commotion had not driven him away. He was sitting near where the campfire had been, calmly eating the *ogacha* cakes that had been prepared for shipment the next day to Ibitibi.

It took four arrows to kill the bear. Prayers were said when he at last gave up the struggle. At this time sleep was impossible and much work to be done. This was the only bear killed that summer, and we were all excited and pleased.

The bear was first bled, skinned and then butchered under the direction of an elder. It was an old bear, he said, but he had not been run before death and there would be much tender meat. The heart and liver, along with the bearskin, would be sent as a gift to Chief Ibitibi. There were several *ogacha* cakes remaining, also.

Other than the bear there was only one injury that night. Alobo, of the Buzzard Clan, had stopped an arrow with his butt. He was very angry and demanded to know who had shot him. Apoholo told him to shut up, and that the only reason he was hurt was because he was on his hands and knees crawling into the safety of his hut.

Alobo recovered from his wound but not from the shame of his cowardice. No one respected him from that day.

This story would be told and retold by our people, as the night the Mayacans did not attack."

CHAPTER 5

Sergeant Jose Suarez sat at the crude wooden desk in his apartment and stared at the blank piece of parchment before him. He was a soldier and not a common scribe, he told himself, and yet this was the type of occasion and he was dealing with the sort of man where caution required such matters to be written down.

Suarez had been warned by his superiors in St. Augustine that there be no further conflict between himself and the mission priest. One more incident like the issue of the location of the powder magazine and the sergeant would be recalled to the Presidio. Since there were no additional billets he could fill, and because of his age, he fully expected to be retired from active duty with no pension.

How far I have fallen, he thought to himself, and a gloomy blackness of despair once again descended upon him.

Six short years earlier he had been made a company commander with the rank of captain, with one hundred fifty officers and soldiers under his command. He was stationed at the Presidio in New Spain, where the glory, the wealth and the opportunity for advancement were everywhere for his taking. But he had been impatient and as a consequence his career had taken a bad turn.

All around him officers of his rank and above dealt with smugglers and became rich beyond imagination. Gold and silver mined by the pagans became coin, or was smelted into ingots. Precious stones suitable for the crown jewels themselves were collected from mines hundreds of miles away and shipped northward from the Mexican coast, though the Straits of Florida and thence across the broad ocean to Spain. There was so much wealth it was only natural that some of it went unaccounted. Even the crown's own ships carried undocumented treasure. The footlocker of an officer, for instance, was not subject to search by the authorities either in the port of origin or at Seville. It was said that even ordinary seamen were skillful enough to retire after only one cruise.

There were limits, of course. French pirates and their agents would pay handsomely for manifests on outbound ships carrying bounty. One clerk received the equivalent of two years pay for information on such a shipment, and was later hanged at the dock when a pirate admitted the source of his information. It was ironic that the governor himself served as executioner, since he was reportedly the richest man in the Americas through his own smuggling activities.

Suarez knew this to be true, as he knew that Emilio Bartron, Sergeant-Major to the Governor, controlled the loading of all outbound ships and was possibly the second wealthiest man in the Americas.

"Crumbs from the King's banquet table," Sergeant- Major Bartron had once characterized it after Suarez had gotten him suitably drunk on rum.

Killing the sergeant-major would be risky business. Even if he succeeded it was doubtful that the governor would consider Suarez for the position of sergeant- major. The strict caste system among the military in Spain held sway even here on the frontier. Men who reached the upper ranks had all attended the best academies at Madrid or Seville and were from the most influential families.

Suarez had neither academy training nor influence in the homeland. What he did have, and what had propelled him from a simple soldier to a position of high command, was his self-discipline and single-minded purpose to do whatever was necessary to carry out his orders.

By the time the young Suarez arrived in New Spain the defeat of the Aztec Empire by the armies of Cortez was complete, and even the notorious Nuno de Guzman had carried out his pogroms of the western tribes that would not submit to slavery.

What remained to be done for Suarez was the pacification of the mountain tribes, the Tarascans, the Coyutec and the Chichimecs who for centuries had resisted domination by the Aztecs and continued to threaten Guadalajara and the other Spanish settlements. It was here Suarez found his calling and earned his reputation.

For twenty-five years Sergeant, then Ensign, then Lieutenant, then, finally, Captain Suarez pursued Indians through the central mountains of Mexico, torturing those who refused to cooperate, burning villages and destroying the enemy. He was good at what he did, and he eventually attracted the attention of Spanish ranchers and farmers who themselves had problems with the Indians. Suarez always made it a point to accommodate their needs, to rid them of their problem for which he was generously rewarded.

Like Nuno de Guzman before him, Suarez eventually attracted the attention of the Archbishop of New Spain who complained to the Governor that even converts to Christianity were being victimized by Suarez' unrelenting attacks.

The governor recalled Captain Suarez and gave him the option of surrendering his command and leaving New Spain or facing an Audiencia convened to determine criminal charges against him.

Suarez appealed to his old friend, Bartron, to intercede with the governor in his behalf. Bartron had grown fat over the years, and had announced his intention to retire. Bartron's own son had already been named as his successor.

"Very well, Sergeant-Major, you may report to His Excellency that I have refused to resign," Suarez said after it became clear that he would get no help.

Bartron looked at Suarez, surprised. "You understand, of course, that your decision requires me to place you under arrest until the court is convened."

Suarez nodded. "And you understand that as an officer in the Army of Spain it will be my duty to report irregularities of which I have knowledge," he said.

"Such as?" the sergeant-major asked.

"Many things I have observed and documented over the years," Suarez said, "including crumbs that fall and are gathered up by the servants."

The following day the governor relented, and in consideration of Suarez' long and faithful service, agreed to his transfer to the Presidio of San Augustin de la Florida.

Thus it was that in the winter of the year, 1595, carrying with him military transfer papers and a sealed personal letter of introduction addressed to Domingo Martinez de Avendano, Governor and Captain General of Florida, the forty-two year old Suarez disembarked a Spanish galleon on its way to Spain, and set foot in this new land.

The letter from the Governor of New Spain never reached the hand of Governor Martinez. Captain Suarez had develop many talents in his years of service to the King, one of which was the ability to unseal documents, view their contents and repair the seal so that it's violation could not be detected.

For that purpose, and others, Suarez carried with him a stiletto, a sharp-edged dagger whose keen blade was hardly thicker than the leaf of a tree.

The night before his arrival at St. Augustine, after all of his shipmates other than the guards on deck had retired for the night, Suarez lighted a lamp in the galley. The seas were almost calm, and the wooden beams of the ship barely creaked as he heated the blade until it glowed, then made a parallel cut through the paraffin seal as if it were through butter.

With a steady hand, his wrist firmly braced on a hard surface, Suarez avoided contact between the blade and parchment, assuring that the document would not be charred or scorched. The base of the wax seal could then be sliced open, disclosing the contents of the document.

Once he was done, it was a simple matter to reheat the seal and melt it into place. He would then, ordinarily, strike the seal with the heel of his boot, marring its surface and causing tiny cracks, but disguising the fact that the seal had been broken.

The knife, itself, had other less subtle uses. It could easily be concealed in the sleeve and in one move slice the throat of an enemy. It was also a useful tool for torture, for peeling off skin, or for scalping an Indian who refused to answer questions.

"Your Excellency, and my good friend, Domingo." the letter began:

> *This may not seem an ordinary letter of introduction, written in my own careless hand and without the aid of a scrivener, and sealed as if it were some highly secretive military dispatch. Nor is it intended to be placed in the personnel records of the bearer, for reasons I am sure will be obvious to you.*

> *I present to you Captain Jose Suarez, late of my command, who after twenty-five years of service to the Crown has become a liability and an embarrassment to the Presidio of New Spain and to me, personally.*

> *When I have the pleasure of seeing you again, I will recount for you his many deficiencies and crimes. Suffice it now for me to say that he is not to be trusted, that he takes inordinate interest in the financial affairs of his superiors and threatens disclosure and embarrassment to those with whose affairs he has been entrusted. I'm sure nothing more on that matter need be said.*

> *What use you might have for such a man in your command I can not imagine. Perhaps you could send him to some dangerous post among the savages where he will have little contact with anyone of importance. I warn you, though, he will mindlessly follow orders to an absurd conclusion. If you charge him with reducing an insurrection among the Indians he may well burn them all, as he has here, much*

*to my embarrassment and to the annoyance of
the Church.*

*I might also suggest that when you are done
with him that he be retired to an inactive
capacity. I would prefer that he never be given
passage back to Spain, or to San Juan or
Havana, for that matter. In conclusion, I pray
that you will commit this message to your
indelible memory (an ability you so aptly
demonstrated at the Academy) and destroy its
contents.*

Suarez didn't bother to reseal the document. He tore it into
small pieces and leisurely strolled onto deck and scattered it off
the stern into the roiling waters of the Gulf Stream.

* * *

When he presented himself upon arrival at the Presidio he
was required to surrender his transfer documents to a clerk, and
then to wait in the courtyard outside the squat clay building that
served as military headquarters until he was summoned inside.

Governor Martinez was unavailable, he was told, and his
interview was to be conducted the following afternoon by
Sergeant-Major Vincente Gonsalves, a nephew of the
Governor.

Suarez occupied his time by walking around the village of
St. Augustine, the military fort and the mission. He had little
interest in visiting the Indian village that adjoined the mission
to the north.

The main street through St. Augustine spoke to the
poverty of the inhabitants. Ramshackle huts with dirt floors
were common. The road was narrow, unlike the wide
thoroughfares of the colonies in New Spain, and muddy with
accumulated rain. Buildings with foundations of coquina stone
were being constructed by black slaves and Indians under the
supervision of soldiers.

The people he passed were friendly enough, and recognizing him as a stranger greeted him and would have paused to speak had he not continued to walk straight ahead. They were a motley group, poorly dressed and even less well fed.

Suarez found his way back to the Presidio and sought out the Archives de Florida, where the governor maintained the historic record of general orders, ordinances and regulations, military engagement reports and troop deployment assignments. The records were available to civil officers and to military officers of the rank of Captain and above. When the clerk saw the insignia of rank on Suarez' tunic, he immediately granted access.

The rest of the afternoon and the following morning he sat at a small clerk's desk, reading military records, memorizing the names of officers and familiarizing himself with current issues of importance to the governor.

It was a habit he had developed in the early years of his career, when he could barely read. While other soldiers wasted their spare time drinking, gambling and sporting with Indian women, Suarez became self-taught. By studying the writing and penmanship of those high in military command he had learned to emulate them, and could now write as eloquently and clearly as even the best educated officer.

* * *

Shortly after noon the second day he was ushered into the second-floor Presidio office of the Sergeant- Major.

The men saluted and shook each other's hand. Sergeant-Major Gonsalves was a tall man, and light skinned. He seated himself behind a large oak desk and invited Captain Suarez to be seated in a low chair in front. Suarez respectfully declined and said that he preferred to stand.

"I have reviewed your transfer documents and your service records, and they appear to be in order," Gonsalves intoned in the crisp military manner affected by recent academy graduates.

"I am new to the frontier, and to this command, but I would have expected you to carry a letter of introduction from your last commanding officer," he said, more as a question than a challenge.

"You have before you the papers that were supplied to me when I left Mexico," Suarez replied.

"Still, as at least a matter of courtesy, when an officer is transferred in the homeland . . ."

"And this being my first transfer I did not think to ask for such a letter," Suarez offered quickly.

Sergeant Major Gonsalves pondered the matter for awhile, sorting through the papers. "I see that your service in New Spain was quite impressive. Your first rank was as a common soldier. You have no academy background, and yet you rose quickly through the ranks as a corporal, then a sergeant."

Gonsalves looked up, studying the dark leathery face of the man before him. Suarez, for his part, stared straight ahead, relieved that the conversation had moved beyond the missing letter of introduction.

"You received a field commission as an ensign, and three years later were elevated to a lieutenancy. Quite remarkable. And you were given your own command as a captain six years ago."

Suarez had seen this reaction many times. *These academy-bred blueblood cowards would never understand what makes a real soldier.*

"And you still hold the rank of captain?" Gonsalves asked, as if disbelieving the evidence before him.

"I look forward to serving the governor in whatever capacity is required," Suarez replied, squaring his shoulders and standing as tall as possible.

Gonsalves reached behind the desk and produced a packet of military forms. He thumbed through them quickly.

"Unfortunately, as much as we would benefit from a man of your talents, there are only two billets in this command for a rank of captain, and both were recently filled by men younger than yourself, both academy graduates."

"Sir, if it would please the governor I have many years of service as an adjutant and would be willing to fill a billet as a lieutenant until something more appropriate to my rank becomes available." Suarez could feel the sweat gathering under his mustache, but made no move to wipe it off.

"Hmmm . . ." the sergeant-major mused, still studying the papers.

"We are authorized only one additional lieutenant and one position of ensign. However, on the governor's order those billets have been transferred to the Franciscans. My uncle believes that saving the souls of the savages is almost as important as protecting the good people of St. Augustine," he said.

Gonsalves replaced the billet papers in their packet, and bound Suarez records separately. "Apparently we have no need for you here. I will speak to the governor about you. He should be here in a matter of days. Unless I am mistaken, all we can do is send you back to your last command in Mexico."

"But you could put me on a ship back to Spain," Suarez said.

Golsalves looked up sharply. "You have not been accepted here. Unless you have the means to pay passage home, I'm afraid we have no funds budgeted for that purpose." He stood a head taller than the former Captain of the Army of Spain. The interview was over.

Ten days later Suarez was summoned to the office of Governor Martinez who, along with the sergeant-major, said that there might be a need for Suarez, after all. Martinez had established a tribute requirement for the support of the colony of St. Augustine, assessing one arroba of corn per year from each married Indian male in the Christianized areas, and four arrobas from unmarried adult males.

The system had never worked as designed, the governor said, and because the land near St. Augustine was infertile and would not support a corn crop, the entire settlement was in danger of being starved. The village and regional chiefs, who willingly accepted tribute from the Spanish government on their visits to St. Augustine, were becoming less motivated to enforce the governor's orders.

"Your experience in dealing firmly with the Mexican Indians would seem to qualify you for enforcing my orders among the natives here," the governor said.

"You would command a squad and hold the provisional rank of sergeant," Gonsalves added.

If he accepted the position it would be his duty to distribute the quota orders throughout the civilized villages, from Santa Lucia to the south, to Guale, sixty leagues to the north, and to require that they be filled. He would also be responsible for the safe travel of Franciscan priests between their missions and St. Augustine. If he refused, he would be returned to Mexico.

Suarez had not eaten a full meal since he arrived in Florida. The commissary refused to feed him because he did not have a billet. The Franciscans at Nombre de Dios fed only themselves and the wretched Indians who lived at the mission. He might have starved were it not for the Indians in a nearby village who shared their daily portion of a bland, smelly fish stew.

Sergeant Suarez shook the hand of the governor and promised to carry out his orders. He did not reach for the hand of the sergeant-major.

* * *

Suarez' reverie was interrupted by the echoing commands of the corporal drilling the rag-tag assortment of misfits in the churchyard outside his quarters. It would be his duty to perform an inspection of the troops who were even now standing at attention under the hot noon-day sun awaiting his appearance.

Suarez wetted his quill from the inkwell and bent over the paper. He worked slowly and methodically making each letter just so. When he was done he read even more carefully than he had written. Finding no mis-spellings or errors in grammar, he was satisfied.

He carefully blotted the ink dry and waved the parchment back and forth to be sure. He folded it and placed it in his tunic before he walked out to view the troops.

CHAPTER 6

"Early the second morning after the bear attack *Isucu* shook me awake. It was still dark when we left camp in search of the plants and berries I had found while working with the women. Although we would search throughout each day for the flowers, roots, trees and lichens he sought, the leaves of the plant bearing the berries could only be harvested early in the morning, before the rays of the sun touched them.

As you may have guessed this plant was the sacred yaupon. From its leaves is brewed the black drink, which is made by the women for special occasions and ceremonies.

We found no yaupon that morning before the sun rose, but we did discover some of the bushes during the day. *Isucu* noted their location and we arose even earlier the next morning to complete our harvesting before dawn.

When we located the plants in the dark *Isucu* said his prayers and taught them to me. He would bless our hands, both his and mine, before we could touch the leaves, and he showed me how to remove the leaves cleanly from the stem, and not damage the plant.

Each day we discovered more bushes further from camp, and each new morning we would arise even earlier than the day before. Within five days I was exhausted from lack of sleep, but each evening the collection of leaves grew by more than a basket. *Isucu* was very proud of the yaupon harvest, and of me for having discovered the plants at Wekiva.

Yaupon was found to the north in the land of the Potano. The leaves were essential to the spiritual life of the Acuerans, the Utinans and many of the other people who lived near the River of the Sun. The Potanans were very difficult to deal with, insisting that an arroba of yaupon leaves was more valuable than the high quality deer skins we offered in trade.

Isucu said that we had collected a sufficient supply to serve the needs of all the Acueran villages, and perhaps even enough to do some trading, ourselves.

After sunup, when it was no longer permissible to gather yaupon, we searched for medicinal plants. *Isucu* taught me how to recognize each plant, the prayers to be said, and how it was to be prepared for use.

We gathered the bark of the willow tree that grew along the river bank of both the Wekiva and the River of the Sun. He taught me to prepare the bark into a powder that was very good to relieve aches in the head. He also told me to take only a little bark from each tree, since a tree that has lost its skin will soon die.

There were many flowers of different kinds along the edges of the swamp, and it seemed that each had its own purpose and name. One red flower could be wetted, and laid on the closed eyelids of someone suffering redness or burning of the eyes. Another flower with big petals of yellow could be prepared to stop coughing, particularly with young children suffering from croup.

There is a small red flower where the very center of the flower, and not the petals, can bring relief from the pain of burns.

There was still another plant with a very special use. I will not describe it to you for fear you may tell the Spanish, but when it is prayed over and prepared in a certain way as a poultice, it will cure serious wounds of those hurt in battle. I will tell you nothing more now. Perhaps some day I will teach you its use.

There were so many others. One plant would move your bowels that would not move on their own. Another would stop your bowels from moving. Some would darken your skin, others lighten it. I have no idea why a man would want to lighten his skin, but some women do. Some plants were very good for treating fevers.

55

Many of the women asked us to find particular flowers that they could rub on their faces to make them more beautiful, or on their bodies to make them smell like flowers. I myself wiped my body with a poultice. Uncle Apoholo said I smelled like a wolf after a rain storm, so I never tried it again.

One particular herb was much prized by the women. I was too young, they said, to understand its use. Isucu told me later that the women burned the herb in a fire and smoked their skirts that were made from moss of the oak trees. They believed that the sweet fragrance would make their husband faithful, and would also attract other men to them. *Isucu* said he believed the smoke would just chase the red bugs out of the skirt. I never really knew the truth.

Isucu was a kind man, and very knowledgeable of the swamp, the hammocks and the hardwood forests. He taught me many things that summer, some of which saved my life and the lives of others in years to come. I was very good at recognizing and preparing medicinal herbs, you know. Many of those lessons I may share with you some day."

* * *

Marehootie paused in his story telling, stood up and walked to the window, looking out on the mission yard. Presently, he resumed his seat on the stool and sipped a cup of spring water.

"Do you have a cure for the mosquito?" de Coya asked.

"Why do you ask? I thought only the Spanish and French resented the eating habits of our friendly mosquitoes. Did you know that the Spanish buried the French up to their neck in the sand and allowed the mosquitoes and crabs to feast on their ears, eyes and lips until they were dead? Even the Mayacans were never so cruel to their prisoners."

"Some of the other students complain of mosquito bites at night. Fr. Pareja has nothing to give them. The mosquitoes don't bother me that much, but some are suffering," de Coya said.

"If you were raised in your own village, instead of being sold by your uncle to the Spanish, you would know the answer yourself. Have you noticed this time of year that the villagers hang dried gourds from the trees?"

De Coya thought for a minute. "They cut holes in them, and then string them up for their pet birds to use as their nests."

"They are called purple martins, but they are not pets. Hardly! They won't eat out of your hand like the scrub jays, and you couldn't catch a martin if you tried. But they love to snack on mosquitoes so the mosquitoes don't snack on you."

"But the purple martins will be flying north soon, as they do every spring, and the hot weather is the mosquito's time to feast. Then they will be much more of a problem than they are now," the boy said.

"I can take out the sting or I can convince him not to bite me in the first place. Do you have the wax myrtle bush growing here?" Marehootie asked.

De Coya thought a minute. "I believe we do."

"Next time you come, bring a mortar and pestle, the wax myrtle leaves and oil that does not smell sweet. Bear fat will work, if you have any."

"That summer at the fish camp must have been a wonderful time for you," de Coya said.

Marehootie looked at the boy but did not answer immediately. He finally spoke. "I learned many important things that I needed to know to survive. It was a bad time in the end. My mother died, but Chulufi-Yuchi was born. I will speak more to you when I am rested tomorrow."

CHAPTER 7

Father Pareja was in the sacristy attending to the altar cloth and implements used at morning mass when he received the note handed to him by the aide. He pondered its contents, dismayed at the imprecise, tortured penmanship. His Timucuan students could write more legibly than a Spanish sergeant with a dozen men under his command.

He deciphered the note:

> *My Dear Father Pareja,*
>
> *I request the honor of your presence at my quarters at 3 o'clock today, after your siesta. We have several matters to be discussed and hopefully we can agree without the necessity of referring these matters to our superiors in St. Augustine.*

It was signed *"Respectfully, Sergeant Jose Suarez."*

Fr. Pareja folded the note, and then folded it again before slipping it into the pocket of his robe.

"Tell your sergeant that I will receive him after evening mass, at 6 o'clock on the porch of the convento."

The young soldier silently mouthed the words of the message, bowed as he backed out of the sacristy and scampered out of the church.

'Several matters', Pareja mused. One matter would probably concern the quality of the evening meals prepared by

the cooks. That subject had been discussed before, but never resolved to the satisfaction of the sergeant.

Native tastes were not agreeable to the Spanish soldiers, neither to their palates nor their stomachs. They preferred heavy stews of meat, corn, rice and beans and the fresh fruits and vegetables that were sometimes served at the garrison at St. Augustine.

The thin, fishy stews preferred by the Indians were both smelly and bland. The wheat-less unleavened breads of hickory nut and acorn meal were un-filling and generally unsatisfying and bitter to the Spanish taste.

Pareja had accepted the responsibility to adequately feed the soldiers upon whom the mission depended for its survival. If the matter were referred to St. Augustine the sergeant would prevail on the issue and Fr. Pareja would have to explain his actions to Fr. Marron, the Custudio of Franciscan Missions. It was an experience Pareja preferred to avoid.

He had repeatedly instructed the women from Alicamany, who cooked for the mission, in the proper preparation of civilized food. Unfortunately, the necessary herbs and spices were rarely available. Even the wild onions were bitter and a poor substitute for the onions grown at St. Augustine. He believed the women cooked to please the forty Timucua and Tacatacuran men who daily took their meals at the mission.

In the end, he gave up and the women continued to cook as they had for centuries.

Fr. Pareja believed that differences in diet might account for the difference in physique of the races. The Indians were taller, leaner and more athletic than the soldiers. The games once played between the two groups had been abandoned on the Governor's orders when so many soldiers reported injuries.

Pareja felt sorry for the young soldiers, many of whom were away from home for the first time. Occasionally a soldier or two would attend mass, and the priest had heard the confessions of many. Theirs was a hard life, and they marked the days, weeks, months and sometimes years left on their enlistments.

On the other hand, despite the privations suffered by the Indians they were a spirited people. Their sense of humor was infectious and their enthusiasm about their new-found religion was a constant source of joy to Fr. Pareja.

The priest was both annoyed and pleased when he found himself the butt of the Indians' practical jokes. They never showed personal ill will or disrespect, and they were careful never to do anything sacrilegious. The church bell, however, was too great a temptation to the children.

At anytime, day or night, the bell might be rung by a youth slipping into the church undetected and pulling on the long rope. It was a game, and the ringing always drew laughter from the adjoining village. Regardless of how fast Father Pareja ran to the church to catch the culprit, no one was ever there and the church would be empty.

Father Pareja tied up the rope so it could not be reached by a child. Within an hour the bell was ringing again. The ladder used in repairing the roof had been carried into the church.

It was a harmless prank and Pareja chided the congregation only mildly. He said that the bell was a reflection on the majesty of the voice of God, and as such was to be respected and not used for sport. It was an unconvincing argument. The unauthorized bell-ringing continued.

A hurricane had blown over the island in the fall, and when it was finished and it was apparent not much damage had been done, Father Pareja rang the bell to summons the Indians in nearby villages to a special mass of thanksgiving. When the mass was finished, and as the people left the church for their homes, the sun came out just before nightfall. In this land of beautiful sunsets, God put on his most glorious display. The island was bathed in gold and orange and brilliant pink hues. The clouds in the west were etched with a filigree of silver. A rainbow arched across the darkening sky. No one moved. Every eye looked up in wonder as the colors melded and changed and mutated to even more beautiful forms.

The five hundred pound steeple bell began to peal. Slowly and rhythmically, soft yet powerful and resonant the voice of God blessed his children. The bell rang until it was full dark and the brilliant stars shone. Father Pareja made no move to stop the ringing of the bell. He never asked if he had witnessed a miracle. From that time the ringing of the bell ceased to be a major problem.

The soldiers seemed to lack the good humor that was so evident among the Indians. The only games they favored involved gambling, and more often than not would lead to fights.

Even the *catecumenos*, the religious students, who lived in the convento seemed to share the joy of life of the Indians in the villages. As hard as they were driven by the priest in their study assignments and as exhausting as their physical labor was in working the mission gardens, their energies were unflagging and their spirits high.

The Indians were healthier and happier than the soldiers. Pareja thought that perhaps it was a matter of diet.

It might not do to suggest to Sergeant Suarez that his men would benefit from the Timucua diet, Fr. Pareja mused. It would undoubtedly ignite a blustering rage, the red-faced uncontrolled primal anger of the semi-literate sergeant.

Fr. Pareja had seen Suarez react that way in the past on other issues with him and with his own men. They were ugly scenes punctuated with vile language, totally inappropriate in a Franciscan mission where young people and villagers might see or hear.

Sergeant Suarez came to San Juan del Puerto in the winter of 1595, barely a year after Pareja arrived. Still insecure and fearful among the Indians, Pareja welcomed the military presence. Suarez' duties were to consist of the transport of corn from the Indian villages to St. Augustine, and to provide soldiers to accompany the priests of Mocama and Guale on their travels to St. Augustine for supplies and meetings with church leaders.

As it turned out, Sergeant Suarez never offered to accompany Pareja to St. Augustine and Pareja found Suarez such disagreeable company he never asked for an escort.

There came a time, however, in the summer of 1597 when Father Pareja could no longer tolerate the sergeant's treatment of the people in the villages surrounding the mission. The Indians, not understanding that the priests and the military were very different in their approach to the Indians, were at first fearful and reluctant to complain.

What became clear to Pareja, however, was that Suarez relied on fear and threats against the village chiefs to insure that the corn tributes were filled. Frankly, the first complaint he heard, that Sergeant Suarez had threatened to cut a chief with a knife for his failure to produce the correct number of arrobas of corn, was unbelievable to the priest.

Soon other complaints surfaced. The village of Chinysca had experience a terrible plague in the winter, and many men had died. Only thirty men survived, and many of them were sickly. Father Pareja visited the village many times performing last rites and burying the dead.

The chief of Chinysca was unable to produce the eighty arrobas of corn required by the sergeant, who solved the problem by the simple expedient of raiding the village granary of the entire crop, leaving the village with barely enough corn for planting.

When the village of Napuyca was ten arrobas short of the levy, its chief was tied to a post in the center of the village and whipped by the soldiers. So great was his humiliation, the chief forbade his people from attending mass.

Father Pareja resolved to bring these complaints against the sergeant. Father Marron offered to intercede, and spoke to the governor. An order was issued that military officers first obtain consent of the mission priest before beating any village chief or chief of higher rank.

Pareja did not think the order went far enough in curbing abuse, and would have done more if it were not for the terrible happenings in Guale.

In some unfathomable way, the fortunes of Father Pareja and Sergeant Suarez were bound together by that terrible event. The revolt had occurred within the sergeant's military jurisdiction, but at a time when he was accompanying Father Lopez on a visit to the Potanan tribe in the west.

When the governor's messenger found the sergeant's party, and delivered the terrible news and the governor's orders, Sergeant Suarez ordered a forced march back to San Pedro. Day and night for four days, with little time for rest or food, he drove his party. Exhausted and already sick, Father Lopez was unable to keep up. Suarez left him beside the trail with a flask of water and some cakes.

Sergeant Suarez had been ordered to report to San Pedro with his squad of soldiers and to protect it from further attack. He was forbidden from entering Guale until the governor and his command of one hundred fifty soldiers arrived in a week or ten days.

Don Juan, the chief at San Pedro, informed Suarez that there had been no attacks by the Guale after the first day, but that his scouts told him that a Guale war party was gathered on an island only two leagues to the north.

Suarez allowed his men to rest for a day, and then ordered Don Juan to accompany him in an attack on the Guale island. Two canoes with Indian guides and arquebuss armed soldiers set out, accompanied by four canoes of Don Juan's warriors.

The skirmish that day cost the lives of three of Don Juan's men, cut down by a fusillade of arrows before they could make land. The Spanish never came under fire and never saw a Guale that they could recognize among the heavy marsh grasses.

When the new governor, Mendez de Canzo, arrived with two ships full of Spanish soldiers, he convened an inquiry into the events that had occurred. Sergeant Suarez volunteered to serve on the inquiry board because of his knowledge of both Guale and Mocama. Angered that Suarez had directly violated his orders causing the death of three Indians, Gov. Canzo rejected the offer and ordered that Suarez have his rank reduced to private, and that he be imprisoned until his superiors decided whether he should be court-martialed.

Fr. Pareja, as depressed as he was at the terrible loss, thought he would be rid of Suarez, once and for all.

Within a week a retaliatory raid went out from San Pedro, led by Sergeant Major Vincente Gonsalves. Every important Guale village, including Tolomato, Tupiqui, Asao, Guale Island and Ospo, were burned to the ground and their wells poisoned and their maize fields destroyed.

The remains of all of the priests, other than Father Francisco de Avila, were recovered, along with their personal effects. The arms and legs of Father Aunon and Brother

Badajoz had been broken, and Aunon's head had been severed. Father Rodriguez' head had been split. The others had suffered similar injuries.

Other than a battle at Ospo in which three Spaniards were killed and a dozen Guale, and occasional sneak attacks that injured some of Don Juan's warriors, there were no major battles. Their villages destroyed, their crops burned, the Guale simply disappeared rather than fight. Those who were captured knew very little about the events that had occurred, or freely accepted torture rather than tell what they knew.

No one offered any information on the whereabouts of Father de Avila.

When the Guale incursion was complete, Gov. Canzo ordered the remaining priests to return to St. Augustine. He asked Chief Tacatacura to remove his people to the south, possibly to San Juan del Puerto where they would be safe.

Finally, he released Suarez from custody when the sergeant offered to remain in Guale with a group of volunteers to fully investigate the causes of the revolt and to look for what was left of Father de Avila. Gov. Canzo imposed no restrictions on Suarez in carrying out his mission. He did not reinstate his rank.

Since that time Suarez had made it his calling to punish the Guale who were responsible, and to hunt down and kill the leaders of the revolt. The missions among the Guale had not been rebuilt.

Nine months after he had disappeared into the Guale swamps, Father Francisco de Avila was returned, barely alive, to St. Augustine by Suarez and his men. Suarez reported to the governor the miraculous events that led to Father de Avila's rescue from the armed and hostile Guale.

Suarez was richly honored by the governor. He received a distinguished medal for bravery, and his rank of sergeant was restored.

Father de Avila recovered from his illness, but never to the point that he could be sent to another mission. He assisted Father Marron at Nombre de Dios. When he was summoned before the governor to testify as to the cause of the Guale revolt and the names of the instigators, he declined to speak. Father

Marron spoke in his behalf, and said that Father de Avila was forbidden by his oath as a priest from testifying if his words could be used to punish the Indians.

Governor Mendez de Canzo's investigation concluded that the revolt was sparked when a priest interfered with chiefly succession and refused to recognize the authority of the new chief. Neither Pareja nor the other Franciscans believed that was the full story. It might explain the slaying of Father de Corpa by Juanillo, they argued, but not the sudden deaths of four other priests in such a coordinated manner.

In the aftermath, the Franciscans returned to their missions at San Pedro and San Juan del Puerto, but not to Guale. Chief Tacatacura and his people who spoke the Timucua language but who had been friendly with the Guale had been moved to the south. Tacatacura's people now inhabited the old village of Potoya that had been decimated by a plague two years before. Father Pareja established a *visita* at the village, and served them through the mission at San Juan del Puerto.

The results of what had happened in Guale were devastating. Five priests were dead and a Christian province was destroyed. Pareja and the other Franciscans would carry the pain of that loss to their graves. Yet one of their number, Father de Avila, had been saved, a source of great joy, but Sergeant Suarez had been rehabilitated in the eyes of the governor and remained a thorn in the flesh of Fr. Pareja.

* * *

The sun was three fingers above the horizon when Sergeant Suarez joined Fr. Pareja on the porch, where he had been waiting half an hour past 6 o'clock.

Suarez had carried his own shopkeeper's stool from his quarters, and set it next to Fr. Pareja's low chair on the porch. The stool was too tall for the Spaniard, and his feet hung an inch above the floor. Nevertheless, he towered a foot above Father Pareja as he sat down and loosened his collar against the oppressive heat.

As was his custom, Suarez went straight to what was on his mind, with no cordiality or greeting. "Did you sample the swill your cooks provided for the evening meal?" he asked.

"I did, and I would like to apologize. I found it extremely unappetizing and have complained to the cooks again. We have received a bushel of maize, and they have promised tortillas in the Spanish style tomorrow evening. I have further instructed them not to serve that particular stew again."

Father Pareja knew that the sergeant could not argue against an abject apology. It was a technique that left the sergeant floundering for something else to say. Of course, on important matters the friar was well able to hold his ground against the bullying tactics of the military.

Suarez complained next that he needed his storage room, and wanted to know how long Pareja would need it to house the old man.

"Only until I determine if he can and will help me with my study of Timucuan dialects," Pareja promised. "If he is not useful I will have no reason to detain him. If it will help I will make arrangements for him to stay at the convento. It will just be a few days more."

"Is this the same Indian, the Acueran, we caught for you last year, the one who escaped us at Alicamany?" the sergeant asked.

Pareja wondered after all this time if the sergeant still felt the sting of criticism be had gotten when the old man walked away from his sleeping guards.

"Yes, it is the same man," he said.

"I would like for you to find out for me if he speaks Guale," the sergeant said.

"I have already looked into that matter. I'm told he has never been to Guale," the priest said.

Suarez considered what he would say next. "As you know, I always wish to accommodate you in every way. Perhaps it would be easier for me if you could explain by what authority you detain the Acueran. I have assigned my own men to keep him confined at your request and unless there were some legal justification for his imprisonment . . ."

"The man is not a prisoner. He is my guest, but as you know he is old and ill, and tends to wander off," Pareja said.

"Still . . ." Suarez paused. "Perhaps we would both be justified in keeping him if I were given access to him for questioning about his knowledge of the Guale massacre."

Father Pareja looked out to sea as he chewed the stem of his pipe. "Do you have reason to believe this man was at Guale?"

"There were reports that two Acuerans were seen at Tupiqui in the days before the first killing."

"That is a weak reason to hold a man against his will. There must be hundreds of Acuerans scattered about," Father Pareja replied.

"No weaker than holding him because he is addle-minded. I feel it is my duty to release him, and since he has been held a captive in a military facility at your request, perhaps this needs to be reported to our superiors."

Father Pareja looked at the sergeant. Were he not a man of the cloth he would have taken pleasure in wiping the smugness from his face.

"As long as there is no torture and no beatings, I see no reason why you should not satisfy your curiosity by asking him simple questions," Pareja said.

"Very well," Suarez said, climbing down from his stool and preparing to leave. "I have many duties that are more important than talking to that old man. Tomorrow I travel to the presidio to collect the corn requisitions, and it will take three weeks to deliver them to the villages throughout the provinces. I will interrogate the old man when I return. Do you have an interpreter who can assist me?"

"My altar boy, Juan de Coya, communicates well with the Acueran. He can help you when he is not engaged in his other duties," the priest said.

Suarez stepped off the porch, and turned to address Pareja one more time.

"Exactly what was that meat in the stew tonight, or was it fowl?" Suarez asked, his lips pursed and the pudgy nose above the bushy mustache wrinkled in disgust.

"I believe it was lobster," Pareja replied.

CHAPTER 8

Two days later Juan de Coya returned to the storage room that served as Marehootie's prison. He said that his studies had been neglected and that Father Pareja had required the attendance of all the students at lessons that lasted from morning to night, interrupted only by mass and vespers.

Fr. Pareja traveled frequently to visit the nine surrounding villages served by the mission, two of which were a full day's travel from San Juan del Puerto.

"He asked me to express his regrets for failing to meet with you thus far. He believes that his work will allow a visit with you in three days, and wonders if that will be convenient."

Marehootie laughed aloud. "You may tell Fr. Pareja that if I am still here, I will be honored to meet with him in three days."

De Coya brought with him the myrtle leaves he had picked that morning from trees growing in a thicket on the west side of the island. The plant was one common to the coastal area, but one that de Coya had not previously noticed or identified. He also brought the grinding implements and a portion of bear oil secured from the kitchen, as well as a small Spanish glass bottle and cork stopper.

Marehootie pronounced a short prayer in the Acueran tongue, and set about his task. He sat on the floor cross-legged and leaned forward working on the pallet upon which he had laid a wooden plank. He produced a tiny shell cutting blade from inside the waistband of his loin cloth and began to separate the leafy material from the stem and from the visible veins within each leaf. It was exacting work, but he worked deftly and quickly.

When he had finished the cutting he had two piles of material before him, the leafy part and the residual stems and veins.

He stood for awhile, stretching his back in a motion that was by now familiar to de Coya.

"I want you to coat the bottom of the mortar with a small amount of bear oil, just enough to make it shiny," he directed.

De Coya did as he was instructed, kneeling before the mat and spreading a thin coat of oil in the wooden bowl.

"You do that very well, this standing on your knees," Marehootie said.

"I learned it from the Spanish. They kneel all the time. It is part of the practice of the Catholic religion. It is not a position that is easy for the Indians. You can always recognize the new converts at mass. They try to kneel, but when they close their eyes they topple over. It is very funny to watch them, but Fr. Pareja says that if we laugh during mass we will be punished, so we look away when they fall."

Marehootie resumed his position on the floor, but this time he was on his knees bending over his work. He inspected the mortar and determined it had too much oil, and required de Coya to wipe out the excess with a rag.

When he was satisfied, Marehootie took the stone pestle in hand and began to grind the green material, a little at a time, until the plant oils separated. When he was done he gradually added bear oil, and stirred the mixture.

"Now we will leave this for awhile, and finish later," he said, resuming his customary place on the stool against the wall.

Outside, the wind had picked up and begun to whistle around the walls of the barracks. Dollops of rain kicked up dust in the mission yard. The rumble of distant thunder echoed across the island, and dark clouds to the east could be seen through the tiny window.

"Our afternoon shower is starting a little early today," de Coya said. It was much darker in the room now as the storm approached, and his eyes had difficulty adjusting as he looked at the old Acueran sitting quietly in the shadows.

A sudden crack of lightning flashed nearby, splitting a pine tree and making de Coya jump. Marehootie remained silent and unfazed. After awhile he began to speak, so softly that de Coya had to move closer to hear above the sound of thunder and falling rain.

* * *

"It was a day much like this, but worse. The sky was yellow in the morning, and the sun never showed his face. Our elders said it was *Huque*. In Utinan, you would say it was a hurricane.

None of the usual work would be done that day. Apoholo said that the canoes should be pulled from the water and tied to the strongest trees. Children were ordered to stay in the large hut in the center of camp. Nearby trees that might be blown down were felled, and their trunks dragged away. Another hut was built outside of camp, but no one would say why.

A story teller from the Earth Clan stayed with the children. We sang songs, and listened to the stories and played games as the wind tore through the camp. Later in the day, about the time the children were complaining about being hungry, the wind quieted.

I didn't know where my mother was and I worried. I had seen her earlier, before the storm struck. She had been crying, and bending over in pain. I went looking when we were allowed to get out of the hut but couldn't find her. My father told me she was with the women, and not to think about it. I continued to look for her. The men were cleaning up the damage caused by the wind.

When it was dark the wind still blew some more, but not nearly as much as earlier. Apoholo spoke to us and said that the worst part of the storm had missed us, and that we were very lucky. He also said that Acuchara, my mother, was being attended to. Again, no one would answer me when I asked where she was. I was ordered to bed with all the other children.

That night I slipped out of my hut and went in search of my mother. As I crept around the camp I might have been mistaken for a spy. Maybe the guards did not see me, or maybe they chose not to shoot me with an arrow.

I heard sounds coming from the hut outside camp, and crept closer to hear. I heard my mother crying softly, and then much louder. And again, soft and loud, loud and soft. I cried too, and my heart ached. There were other voices, too. The women of the camp were singing and chanting and speaking softly.

I am ashamed to say I fell asleep with my head cradled in wet pine straw. I was shaken awake while it was still dark. The guard said nothing but pointed toward my hut. I scampered back to my bed, happy not to have been hit by an arrow.

There was much shouting when I awoke for the second time. Everyone in the camp was gathered at the birthing hut. When I ran to the hut, there was my father holding a tiny, red-faced baby in a soft deer skin above his head. "This is my Son! This is my Son!" he shouted.

Apoholo was laughing, and stomping his feet and clapping his hands in celebration along with the other men and women. I was ashamed of my tears, and returned to my bed."

* * *

Marehootie paused, stood, stretched and walked to the window, as was his custom. He looked out into the yard for a very long time. The storm was beginning to subside and there were some cracks in the clouds where the blue sky shined through. De Coya was quiet, and asked no questions.

The Acueran resumed his seat, took a big drink of water, and began again.

"My mother did not do well after the child was born. She remained in the birthing hut for several days. This caused problems among the elders who insisted that the hut must be burned down in accord with our beliefs.

I was not allowed to see her until she was finally carried to our hut three days later. She was weak from loss of blood, and

71

could not stand. She was happy to see me, but her body was hot to the touch and her face shiny with sweat.

The women of the camp burned the hut and carried the ashes away.

The baby was cranky, and cried a lot. An old woman said it was because my mother did not have enough milk, or that it was bad for the child. Mother cried and prayed. The *isucu* said prayers and blessed my mother's breasts, but nothing helped. The baby cried and cried.

Apoholo's wife, Niho, had recently birthed a child and was full of milk. That made things better. The baby stopped crying all the time and my mother finally got to sleep. She must have needed a lot of sleep, because she slept most of the time we remained in camp.

Isucu asked me to go with him to look for a medicine that might break my mother's fever. He said comfrey root was good when made into a tea. There was also a tree whose bark could reduce a fever, but he had not seen any growing this far south. I knew he was worried for my mother. As we left camp early the next morning the women were already bathing her in the cold waters of the Wekiva.

We wandered far that day without finding what we sought, but we did find something that was very upsetting. There, in the middle of the trail, three Mayacan arrows were stuck in the dirt. They each had tufts of hair wound around the point. *Isucu* gathered the arrows and told me to run back to camp and not look back.

Isucu knew a quick way back to camp and we followed a trail used by the Mayaca which led from another of their villages.

Isucu was not an old man, as I am an old man now, and he proved that day that he could still run. I ran as fast and as long as I could, stopping only a few times to catch my breath. He jumped over logs, ran straight through briars that cut his flesh, waded where he could and swam where he couldn't wade.

I feared that if I could not keep up with him I would become lost in the swamp and end up as a meal for *Itori*, or if I was really unlucky a slave of the Mayacans. By the time we reached camp my side was aching just here under the ribs.

When Apoholo saw the arrows, he cursed and broke them over his knee.

Mayaca had declared war on us, he said, and leaving the arrows where they could be found was a bad sign. It meant that they would not ambush us one at a time, as they had done in the past, but would attack with their full force and kill all of us.

A camp council was held. Some of the younger men wanted to stand and fight, but Apoholo and the wiser heads won the argument. We had women and children, but the Mayacan hunting party would have only warriors of fighting age.

My mother's condition was also considered. If she did not get to Ibitibi for the proper medicines for her fever, she might soon die. She was only awake part of the time and could not defend herself.

We had all thought that *Huque* had been early in the season, but perhaps not. Maybe it was later than we thought and time to return to Ibitibi. The Mayacan threat was very serious. No one wanted to wait for them to attack during the night.

Apoholo ordered us to break camp immediately, although the sun was already moving toward its resting place. The canoes were loaded and the fish weirs destroyed. Two canoes were attached together side by side with a mat platform between them so that my mother could lay down for the journey. They were so wide that they barely cleared the mouth of the Wekiva as we entered the big river.

It was full dark as we headed north with the slow current. After awhile a full moon rose over the trees along the east shore. Over my left shoulder I could see the glow of the fires destroying our camp. I looked back for a long time until the fires were gone. I slept, and in my dreams Mayacans murdered us in our beds.

By morning we were out of Mayacan territory. We met one of our supply canoes on its way to camp, and it turned around and followed us for the rest of the day until we arrived at Ibitibi. We were not expected and there was no celebration or ceremony planned. *Isucu* said his prayers of thanksgiving for our safe return.

I must tell this quickly, or I may not be able to say it at all. My mother was speaking a tongue I did not understand. She did not hear me when I asked her what she meant by it. Apoholo took me to the side as they carried her from the canoe to our house.

'Your mother is speaking only to the Spirits, now,' he said. She never spoke again to anyone."

* * *

The old Acueran sat quietly, his head down and his arms crossed over his chest. He rocked gently. In a while his lips began to move, and in the soft tones of the Acueran tongue he sang an ancient chant of remembrance.

De Coya collected his things to leave.

Marehootie raised one hand, gesturing de Coya to wait. He did so, and presently the Acueran was again ready to speak.

"You must skim the green scum off the mosquito potion before you put it in the bottle, and throw the scum away. Keep the stems and veins. There are other uses for them I will show you someday."

De Coya did as he was instructed.

"This medicine is meant only for you and the other students. Do you understand?"

De Coya nodded his agreement, and prepared to leave. It was already dark in the small room, and in the mission yard also.

"Juan de Coya, there is one more thing I would like you to remember. You spoke of how the people fall over when they try to stand on their knees in church. The Spanish soldiers also ask the people to kneel. Then they cut off their heads with a sword. It saves gun powder."

CHAPTER 9

"My mother was given a chiefly burial upon the direct order of Chief Acuera. This is unusual for a woman, but she and I were of the White Deer Clan and therefore of the lineage from which chiefs are selected. It is the same among your people, the Utina.

At Cofahiqui, far to the north, there was a woman who ruled seven villages honorably for many years, and when she died her sister's daughter became *niaholata*.

I met this chieftess many years ago, but that is a story for another day.

Acuchara was respected deeply by all Acuerans, not just in Ibitibi where she was known for her talent with pottery and for her loving, sweet nature. They said I inherited her spirit. My brother was nothing like her, and he resembled our father only in his stature.

The night she passed into Spirit the news was sent to the main village, and Chief Acuera came immediately with his wife, his *jarva* and all of the principal men. They were such a large number they came in three canoes. Ibitibi is a small village but so profound was the grief no one complained about the lack of comfortable sleeping quarters.

The women cried and wailed for five day and nights. As is our custom, the men did not cry. I always thought that strange, that the men would cut their hair when someone died and would sit or stand around frowning, but would not cry along with the women. When a chief died, the men would cut their own flesh with sharp shells and sticks, but still would not cry. Perhaps they considered it a sign of weakness.

I was never afraid to cry, and it always made me feel better afterward. Of course it was a long time before I felt better after my mother's death. After almost a lifetime, if I think of her I am likely to lose some tears, so I don't dwell on it.

Prayers were offered up for her delivery into Spirit. It was decided that she would be buried without allowing her flesh to waste and separate from the bones, as is the custom when a chief dies. Acuera made that decision, but I believe it was because most of the village chiefs thought that honor should be reserved for them.

She was buried in the clan burial mound which stood on a hill outside the village.

Acuera ordered a canoe of ocher to be brought to the village and mixed with the white sand in the mound. This, too, is usually reserved for the burial of a chief, but no one complained.

Chief Ibitibi cut off all his hair, and I still remember the blood on his scalp. The *jarva* from Acuera led the procession to the mound. The ceremony went throughout the day and all night. She was buried with her most delicate and beautiful works of pottery.

There was talk of who should pay for her death. *Isucu* had treated her and his cures had all failed. I thought that the baby was responsible for her death, but no one asked me. In the end, no one was punished for my mother's death. Even *Isucu* was allowed to continue until I became *isucu* of Ibitibi much later.

My mother's burial brought all the village chiefs and their principal men together. Acuera declared that a council should be held to discuss many issues. The declaration of war by the Mayacans was not considered official, since no blood had been spilled, but the continued use of the camp on the Wekiva would have to be considered.

Of course, the council gave the men an opportunity to speak of who would succeed Acuera as chief upon his death. Chief Acuera was not a young man, but neither was he on death's door.

The council house in Ibitibi could seat no more than fifty men, and was not nearly large enough to accommodate the tribal council. Chief Acuera held the meeting outside in the center of the village, with the men seated on benches according to their rank. It was all very orderly, and everyone knew his place.

The women roasted the leaves and then prepared the black drink by boiling them in water, using the yaupon leaves we had picked at Wekiva. *Isucu* and I were both very proud to hear the men comment on the high quality of the drink. Of course, *Isucu* was seated with the men and I was in my hut peeking out the door.

When the brew had cooled sufficiently Chief Acuera took the first drink from a large shell drinking vessel. "Yeeeaaaauuuu", he roared his approval and passed the cup to Ibitibi who did the same thing, screaming even louder. It was passed down the line to the next village chief. Soon several cups were being passed to the other officials and principal men.

The shouting and hollering became almost deafening, and the men began to dance around, showing off.

Within a few minutes Chief Acuera was sweating profusely, such being the effect of the drink. All the men, in turn, began to sweat as the cups were passed around for the second and third time. Some of the men had foam on their lips. Finally, the chief of another village vomited and this was met with much laughter. Several others could not hold the drink down.

A war chief from the main village was seen to put his fingers down his throat, and his vomit was powerful, bringing much laughter from the rest of the council.

In Acuera vomiting is seen as purification of the body and mind. I know that it is seen as a sign of weakness and unfitness by your people. The Utina have always been too serious about such matters. They have no sense of humor. They need to laugh more than they do.

Chief Acuera had a very loud voice and he hollered "Shut up and listen, Shut up and listen", over and over again. One of my cousins who thought he might be selected as the next chief continued to talk loudly, showing the others the strength of his spirit.

Acuera walked over to him and slapped him across the face, sending him sprawling over a bench and into a cactus. There was much laughter, but no more loud talk.

Upon the death of Acuera the council of the principal men would select the next Acuera from among the chief's nephews. If there was no suitable nephew, a sister's daughter could be considered. If there were no respected nieces or nephews, any other member of the White Deer Clan could be considered.

Many of the principal men spoke, usually in support of themselves or a close kin. I waited for my uncle Ibitibi to mention my name, but he never stood to speak. I was the eldest nephew he had, and could be considered as the next chief of Acuera, or perhaps as the next village chief of Ibitibi.

Chief Acuera had four sisters, including Acuchara, and each had born male children. I thought that because of Acuchara's death they would honor her by mentioning my name, but it was not to be. Was it because of my nature that my name was not considered? I wondered. If I ever dreamed of being chief, my dream died that day. My new brother also was not considered.

Chief Acuera was strong and active and I prayed that he never die. None of the dogs that had been mentioned were fit to walk in his moccasins.

Every chief and principal man could speak. They were all respected and listened to unless they spoke too long. Some loved the sound of their own voice and if they began to repeat what they had already said the others would start to murmur and complain among themselves, until the speaker's words were drowned out and he would finally sit down.

One of the village chiefs asked if anyone had heard rumors or reports of the return of the people called the Spanish who had twice before invaded the land, killing and robbing and stealing. No one expected that there were any such reports. If the Spanish again set foot in Cautio, the word would travel faster than a fire in a dry field and it would not be necessary to ask. But by asking, it was an opportunity for the *inija* of Acuera to tell the familiar story.

This tale is told at every tribal council and at every festival and formal occasion. It is told to the children throughout childhood. So important is it that no child is deemed to have passed into manhood or womanhood until they could repeat the story perfectly. Each time the story is told the old men listen carefully and if even one word is forgotten or misspoken they will point out the error.

I will tell it to you exactly as it is told among the Acuerans, although I do not expect you will memorize it after only one telling.

'The great Acuera, the Children of the Sun, have inhabited the Kingdom of the Sun from the beginning days of the middle world.

Their leader, Chief of all Acuera, is a kindly, benevolent Holata. His wisdom and charity are known throughout Cautio by all peoples. He is loved and respected by everyone and his word is law.One day a dark cloud spread across the land from Tocobago and Pahoy in the west, but it brought no soothing rain. The thunder of cannon and the lightning of powerful weapons rolled across the land until it came to the village of Piliuco.

Murderous men in metal hats rode atop fearsome animals that breathed smoke and trampled the people into the dust. Weapons shattered the peace and struck down children in their play. Women were raped and taken as slaves. Old women were fed to the hounds of the devil and warriors were butchered for sport.

The men of Tocobago and Pahoy, chained by the neck together, no longer men but beasts of burden, looked on with sightless eyes and feared to cry out even a warning to their brothers of Acuera.

79

The storehouse was robbed and the winter's foods taken away without barter or trade. The people of Acuera had met the Spanish, but the Spanish were yet to meet the strength of the people, The mighty Chief of the Acuera. 'Bring me their heads that I might decorate the land,' He commanded it, and it was so. One by one, for fourteen days, fourteen heads in fourteen helmets were brought to the mighty Holata, and they were put on fourteen pikes and left for the Spanish to see.

'The devils have buried their dead,' the people said. 'Then dig them up, and butcher each carcass and decorate the trees,' Acuera said, and it was so.And when the Spanish saw that the Acuera were not Tocobago or Pahoy, And were not cowards, but men, the Spanish fled for their lives, never again to return to the Kingdom of the Sun.' "

* * *

The old man rested and sipped from the spring water. He smiled and looked at de Coya, sitting in the corner and leaning against the wall.

"Can you recite your catechism as flawlessly as an old man tells a story he has not told in forty years?" he asked. "It is written in no book, but it is forever recorded here," he said, tapping his chest with his fingers.

"There is more I could say about the time Acuera fell under the boot of the Spanish. You should know what the Spanish demanded of Acuera, and what our brave chief said that frightened them away. If you remind me, I will tell you later. There is more that you should know now about the council meeting that was held in Ibitibi, after my mother died."

* * *

"Chief Acuera invited Chief Ibitibi to account for the food transported to the village from the camp at Wekiva. Ibitibi announced that there were twice as many arrobas of foodstuffs produced than ever before, and of greater variety.

He asked *Isucu* to tell about the discoveries he had made of herbs and medicinal plants. To his credit, *Isucu* did not claim that he had found the yaupon. Even so, he did not give me the credit I was due.

Ibitibi interrupted and said 'I am told that the yaupon was found by Acuchara's oldest son, Marehootie.'

The men murmured their approval and appreciation. No one thought to summons me to accept their thanks in person, which I was prepared to do. I rolled over on my back and continued to listen.

Apoholo told the story of the bear's visit to camp, and presented the remaining ogacha cakes to Chief Acuera, who divided them among the village chiefs. No one under the position of chief would eat ogacha.

I waited for Apoholo to tell about Alobo getting an arrow in the butt, but he was too kind to say such an embarrassing thing with Alobo being present. Some of the other men were laughing among themselves, and I believed the story was already well known.

Apoholo finally showed the Mayacan arrows, and they were passed around among the war chiefs. He spoke of the early storm, the illness of Acuchara and the discovery of the arrows. No one said we should have stayed longer.

One or two chiefs suggested we not return to Wekiva, but they were shouted down by the rest. Chief Acuera listened to the advice of the war chiefs, his *jarva* and anyone else who wanted to be heard.

In the end Chief Acuera said that we would return next year in greater force, better armed, but without women or children. He also said that men would come from each village, so that the strain on the village of Ibitibi would be less. As we had come to expect from Acuera, he made a very wise decision.

The sun was four fingers above the horizon when Acuera and his people left. Flute players played a tribute to their chief.

Jarva from each village offered up prayers for his preservation, health and safe return. Other chiefs who had longer journeys to their villages remained in Ibitibi until morning but were gone soon after daybreak.

Our customs required that children without their mother be raised within her clan. Our mother's sisters and brothers were many. Apoholo, Ibitibi and Chief Acuera were her brothers. She also had three sisters who lived in other villages.

Acuera lived in the main village and was too old and busy with his duties as chief to take on two children. Ibitibi was our village chief, and though his duties were not great, his wife had died years before. He busied himself each day with building canoes and other woodwork.

I was asked by members of the clan where I wished to be raised. I did not know my mother's sisters well, and did not want to move to a different village.

Before I could decide, the decision was made for me. Apoholo's wife, Niho, had suckled the baby from the day of its birth, and would be its mother. Apoholo came to me and said he would be honored to raise the baby and me in his household, and to continue my education in the ways of the White Deer Clan.

I don't know if I could have objected. He told me that it had been my mother's wish that if she died that Niho be the baby's mother. I wondered if Apoholo would offer to raise me if there were no baby for Niho.

So the baby and I came to be raised by Apoholo and Niho. They had a three year old daughter, Amita, who became my younger sister. I love her as I would my own sister. Apoholo and Niho were good parents. I never felt that they loved me less because I was not their own child, nor that because of my nature they considered me as the lesser of their two sons.

Our father, Itoribali, had nothing to say about it since he was of another clan. He went to live with his own mother, which is our custom. He continued to live in Ibitibi and after awhile he meant nothing to me. I don't know if my brother ever knew his father, but he had a good uncle to raise him.

There was one other problem. The baby had no name. It was our custom that the mother should name her child. The chief had the right to give the child a name also, after the child reached manhood or womanhood.

Since my mother never named the baby, that duty fell to Niho, but she could not make up her mind. She wanted a name that was acceptable to Apoholo and to me. Each name she suggested did not fit the baby. She said '*Qiso*,' which means godchild, and '*Huque*' for the storm at his birth. Apoholo and I thought both names were dumb.

Within a moon of his birth, the baby named himself, and I shall tell you how the child got his name.

You will remember that the child cried at his birth, and afterward when it was hungry. This is not unusual. Babies cry. But this child never stopped crying except to eat and sleep. Every day and every night the same 'Yeoouing' and 'Yeoouing' until we all thought we would go crazy.

Isucu used all of his charms and herbs and prayers. He said that the child missed his real mother, and that with time he would learn to love Niho and the crying would stop. This made Niho feel very sad. She already loved the baby deeply.

There was something very familiar about the sound of the cry. 'Yeoouing!' We listened to it every night and day.

One night a hunter returned to Ibitibi after being gone a long time. He heard the sound of a wading bird of the swamp as he entered the village. This brown and white speckled bird is prized among hunters and is very tasty. As he followed the sound he came to our hut and pulled back the door-flap.

'Do you have a *chulufi-yuchi* in your hut?' he asked.

Apoholo and I both laughed out loud. We had heard that cry a hundred times at night at the camp on the Wekiva. It was the sound of the bird you would call the crying bird. From that night my brother was called Crying Bird. It was not a manly name, but it was the right name for him."

CHAPTER 10

Sergeant Suarez would have preferred to travel alone, were it not for the standing orders of the governor that forbade him to do so.

Orders requiring soldiers to travel in at least squad strength had been in effect continuously since the post at Santa Lucia was attacked by the Ais in 1566. Twenty two men were cut down by arrows that day.

During the decade of the 70's the savages repeatedly attacked St. Augustine, at the cost of many soldiers and civilians. The Englishman Drake burned St. Augustine in 1586, aided by Timucua-speaking Indians. Otherwise, and with the notable exception of the revolt at Guale, the Spanish colonies, and particularly the missions had been free from attack.

The ambush of travelers was another matter. Such attacks had been both chronic and episodic. Although the Indians feared the firearms carried by the soldiers, there was always the risk that an advance scout might be ambushed or that the last man in a formation might catch an arrow in the back.

Suarez had lost two men from his squad, one during a fact-finding trip into Guale and another near the river village of Tocoi. With each death it was Suarez' duty to prepare a lengthy report for his superiors, describing how the incident occurred, and fixing blame elsewhere than on himself. The sergeant-major questioned everything and seemed intent on blaming Suarez for any losses his squad might sustain, so Suarez took particular pains to insure that he did not contradict himself or say anything that could be contradicted by others.

Civilians traveling inland from St. Augustine were sometimes accosted by Indians who were more criminal than hostile. Other than being robbed, stripped of their clothing and made to run for their lives, they seldom suffered any lasting injury other than to their dignity.

Only the Franciscans seem to be free to travel without interference.

As it was his duty, Sergeant Suarez reported to the office of the sergeant-major upon his arrival at the Presidio. It was a fine office on the second floor of the government building, with an excellent view of the harbor. An open air porch faced toward the north, affording a view of the grand church at the Mission Nombre de Dios, as well as the Indian village that surrounded the mission.

It was this porch where the governor joined the sergeant-major each day when weather permitted, and the two men sipped sangria and discussed matters of state. Sergeant Suarez coveted this office and all the honor and privilege it carried.

"You will find that these requisitions have been increased since last season," the sergeant-major said, as Suarez thumbed through the packet of forms that had been handed to him.

"It is the governor's belief that the villages to the northwest, particularly, are run by slackards who need more motivation."

Sergeant Suarez rebound the papers and shuffled his feet as if to stand, but though better of it and sat back to address his superior.

"You may inform the governor that I am in full agreement that many of the chiefs are less industrious than others, and I know who they are. I visit every village in the territory three or four times a year and I keep my eyes open," he said.

"And what have you learned?"

"As you know, the soil is not uniformly suitable throughout the territory for corn. In Guale, for instance, the inland villages were, for the most part, located on rivers that flood from time to time, and the soil is rich enough to support two crops a year, but Guale is no longer available to us.

"The villages of the Utina, except for those directly on the River San Juan are also blessed with good soil, and should be as productive as the fields at Guale, and yet the chiefs cry and moan that the land is poor, or that the men are too sick, and that the quotas are unfair and unattainable. I know this to be a lie."

"And the truth is . . .?" Gonsalves asked.

"The truth is that among the Timucua the most productive fields are held by members of the White Deer Clan. Each chief has his own plot, and so do members of his family. These people do not even work their own fields. Their subjects do the cultivation and it is expected as tribute.

"The chiefs, even down to the village level, feel that their personal lands are exempt from our levy. They would not say this to our face, but I have heard that some of the common people have complained that they have picked hundreds of arrobas of maize that is never counted at their granaries."

"You have proof of this?" the sergeant-major asked.

"Last fall my men and I accidentally stumbled across a corn crib, where none should have been. I associated it with the village of Toassi in Mocama. There was a dim, indistinct trail that led toward the village.

"It had rained recently, and yet there were fresh footprints leading away. The crib was empty, except for fifty or sixty ears of fresh corn that they missed in their rush to hide the rest," Suarez said.

"And what action did you take?"

Suarez leaned forward in his chair, his chin only inches above the mahogany desk. "I took exactly the action you have authorized me to take in such matters," he said, "nothing more and nothing less."

"Which was?"

"I asked about, politely, and the Chief lied to my face. He denied any knowledge of the corn crib, and I stood there with my hands full of ears of corn as proof. Then I did as you have ordered me to do. I addressed the Franciscan Priest and showed him my proof, and asked his consent to beat the truth out of the chief," Suarez said, spittle flying off his lips.

"Pareja, I assume, refused to grant his permission," Gonsalves said.

The sergeant was on his feet now, looking down at the sergeant-major. "You give me all of the responsibility, and none of the authority. You threaten me if the assessments are unfilled, and you forbid me even the right to threaten those who steal the government blind," he said.

"I will speak to the governor of your concerns, but I suggest you try to get along with the priest," Gonsalves said, standing to indicate the conversation was ended.

"You give a cowardly half-man of a priest authority over me, and he laughs in my face."

"You have said quite enough, Suarez. I'll ask you to leave now before I have you thrown out," Gonsalves said, reaching for his desk bell to summons an aide.

Suarez left the office hurriedly, bolted down the stairs and out into the warm sunlight of the plaza. He sat for a time on a bench under a tree, his face red. He was shaking.

When he calmed himself, Suarez reached into his satchel and withdrew a packet of personal items. He pulled out his captain's insignia and affixed it to his tunic and went to the office housing the archives where he was admitted without question.

The room, which was really a shed extending outward from one wall of the Presidio, was crowded with dusty boxes and crates stacked from floor to ceiling. Even the one window which would have afforded light was covered. Two walls of records, higher than a man's head, separated only by a narrow walkway between them, with a tiny desk just inside the door.

The clerk on duty had guarded the trove of official materials for twenty years, since he was disabled from further military duty by an Indian arrow near the San Juan River. His duties were to keep the documents safe from fire or pilferage, and on the request of a superior to produce what was required.

The clerk studied the list Suarez handed him:

> *Investigative files and materials pertaining to Juanillo Revolt, Guale, 1597, including Tolomato, Tupiqui, Ospo, Asao. Investigative files and materials pertaining to Santa Lucia tragedy, 1566. Investigative files and materials pertaining to Potano incursion, 1567. Investigative files on Drake's raid on San Augustin, 1586. Investigative*

files on all hostile encounters between His Majesty's Army and Indians.

The Guale records were of recent vintage, the clerk explained, and could be found quickly since he was the man who had filed them and because they were occasionally reviewed by the governor and his adjutant. Likewise, the reports generated by Drake's attack could be located.

Because the Presidio was burned by Drake, some of the records prior to 1586 had been destroyed. Some things had been saved, but they had never been cataloged and it was clear that the clerk had no intention of spending time looking for a needle in a haystack.

For two days Suarez read the detailed and exhaustive reports from Guale, some of them inscribed in the tiny, neat penmanship of Vincente Gonsalves. Depositions of Indian witnesses, testimony given before a scribe under oath, along with inventories of the deceased Friars' personal effects and even a list of their recovered body parts.

The actual cache of physical evidence was preserved in a single leather trunk and sealed, thus not available to Suarez.

It was during the third day of his search, while he was reviewing an inventory report from the investigation at Santa Lucia, that an item piqued the sergeant's interest. The writing was faint, faded and indistinct. Suarez picked up the ledger and walked outside into the sunlight and read the material again.

Returning to the clerk's desk he set the Santa Lucia document aside and ordered the clerk to bring him the material he had reviewed two days before, the records from the investigation at Ospo and Asao.

Before noon, Suarez believed he was on the right track. When the clerk found a charred, thirty-five year old investigative folder concerning the Potano incident, and brought it to Suarez, he soon knew he had made an important discovery.

At 2 o'clock the clerk said that he would be closing the repository for a siesta, and that Suarez could return in two hours. Sergeant Suarez said that he was very nearly done, and would like to be on his way back to San Juan within the hour.

They agreed that Suarez could remain inside and work by candlelight, and let himself out and lock the door when he was done.

When he was alone, Suarez located the sealed trunk with the artifacts from Guale, Santa Lucia and Potano. He heated the blade of his stiletto with the candle, until the thin blade glowed orange. Then he went to work.

CHAPTER 11

"Crying Bird was much younger than me. My eighth summer was his first. Of course I loved him, he was my brother and we had both lost our mother, but with that much difference in age we could not play well together.

I am ashamed to say that he made me nervous to be around him. I was always anxious to get out of our house early in the morning before Niho thought of some task I could do to help her with Crying Bird. If she told me to help, I could not refuse or argue, but it was better not to be there to be told in the first place.

Sometimes I felt guilty about not helping, but it was better than having to stay with him half a day while Niho worked or went visiting her friends. He had stopped his crying during the day, but each night he would cry. It always made me crazy.

Now I remember how sad it made Niho, and how angry it made Apoholo. To go without sleep is a bad thing. After a long time, the baby did not cry so loud that he disturbed the whole village.

In his third year it was time to teach him to swim, and to run and hunt as the rest of the children do. We had a game the children played in the forest. We called it Spot the Deer. You may have played the game in your own village. Everyone I have ever talked to, and every tribe I ever visited knew of this game.

We played at night. One of us would be the deer, and would move about in the woods or maybe stay still behind a tree. The others would go looking for the deer. Someone would shout 'I spot the deer!', and if it was the deer he would give himself up, and the other person would become the deer and the game would begin again. If the person spotted was not the deer, he must shout 'Hunter!' and the game would continue.

Like all the games we played, this game taught us to stay perfectly still and to hide well in the trees. It also taught us to move swiftly to get away, and to move without stepping on leaves or breaking branches.

One night the game was being played. Ten of us were there. I was the oldest and Crying Bird one of the youngest. Because of my age and size, I insisted on being the deer in the first game. I had a head start, but circled around the others and climbed into the crook of a sweet gum tree that was full of leaves.

I watched as the others waited awhile, then scattered in different directions looking for me. Crying Bird had played the game before, so I was surprised that he did not run into the woods. He looked around and then sat down. I thought that maybe he knew I was nearby and was waiting for me to make a sound.

I could hear the others running around and shouting that they had spotted the deer, only to discover that they had just spotted each other. Soon they were deeper in the woods, and I could no longer hear them.

There were no bears in these woods, and no wolves or panthers. The only sounds were the songs of the forest at night: the 'whoo-whoo' of an owl, a chorus of frogs, the lovely call of the whip-poor-will, and the sound of mourning doves coo-ing to each other.

Then another sound, the call of the crying bird, echoed through the forest. He sat on a log in the middle of a clearing. 'Yeoouing! Yeoouing!' he bawled. He was frightened and lost and alone, and he cried until I came out of the tree and took him by the hand. I shouted to the others that the game was over and took Crying Bird home.

Between my twelfth and thirteenth summers I grew very tall. I was almost as high as I am now, although not nearly as muscular and strong as I became later. I was good at sports and could swim and run as fast as anyone in the village.

In my fifteenth year I ran the tribal races at Acuera, representing our village. I won the longest race, the one that takes all day to run. I was as swift as any of the others, but I was also smarter and stronger. At the start I was in last place, but soon I began to pass the others. I ran steadily all day. I carried a deerskin of water so there was no need to stop along the way.

You may have noticed the tattoo on my right arm. That was my reward for winning. I was tattooed by Acuera's own tattoo man. You may notice these marks further down the arm. I won five years in a row, and each time I got a new stripe.

I raced against the best of other tribes, when we were not fighting with them. I was never beaten after the tribal race. I am now an old crippled man. Would you like to race me?"

De Coya smiled. "In my fifteenth year I will race with you" he said.

"And I will be in my seventieth year. That will make it a fair contest." Marehootie said.

"Was Crying Bird a fast runner?"

"No, he was not a runner. He was not a wrestler, or a hunter or an archer. He could swim a little, but only because I threw him out of a canoe into the river and told him I would not save him. 'Swim or drown' I hollered.

This was more frightening than the day I thought the young boy had drowned on the Wekiva. Crying Bird struggled in the water, went down and came back up. He must have thought I was serious, that I would not save him. He began to paddle the way a dog does, then he stretched out and used his arms and legs and swam to the shore down steam.

When he crawled onto the bank he was crying, as usual, and saying that he would tell Niho what I had done. I said that if he told I would throw him in every time he came near the water.

That evening I told Niho and Apoholo that Crying Bird had become a good swimmer. They were both proud of him. This was the first thing he had ever done to make them proud. Crying Bird looked at me and smiled, but said nothing,

Because of my nature I was not expected to become a warrior and might never be considered as chief of the village, but I had trained to assist the *isucu* which is an honored position in the tribe.

The war chief of our village was an old man before I was born. In all his life our village had never been to war. Whenever there was talk of attacking the Mayaca he would recommend war, but that was his job. He was always too old to fight a war or lead warriors, and probably did not know how. He did know when it was his time to speak to council and recommend war, and he did so even if we were not threatened and were angry at no one. He was good at his job.

He died peacefully in his hut at the age of ninety years. I was seventeen at the time.

After he was buried with all the honors due a *paracusi* the village council met to choose a new war chief. There were no threats at that time. The Mayacans were not contesting any territory and the Spanish had not been seen for many years. Nor were there any suitable men in the entire village who were willing to become Ibitibi's war chief.

Chief Ibitibi spoke to Acuera and told him that the village elders did not see any reason to appoint a village war chief. He said that Acuera's tribal war chief was a good man, and the braves in our village would be under his command. Chief Acuera became upset and told Ibitibi that we must have a *paracusi* because every village always had a war chief, and we were no exception.

That presented a very difficult problem for the village council. My Uncle Apoholo would have made a fine war chief, but he was of the White Deer Clan, and it would be below his dignity.

My father still lived in the village but said that a leg injury he suffered while killing an alligator had made him lame and unsuitable to lead men in battle. He had received such an injury years ago but had recovered. No one ever saw him limp.

The war chief was responsible for posting the guard each night, and for making sure no one shirked his duty by sleeping on the job. Our village had always been very safe, and the dead war chief sometimes forgot to assign guards at all for long periods of time. When there was a threat from the Mayacans or from someone else a guard would be posted, but most of the time no one at all was awake at night.

The new war chief would be expected to post guards and would not be popular, especially if he insisted the guards remain awake. He also would have to train the men to be sure they were strong and able to defend the village if we were attacked.

I decided to have some fun. I told my uncle Ibitibi that I would be *paracusi*.

Maybe you can imagine what would happen next. I had grown as tall as anyone in the village, and could outrun everyone. Everybody liked me. I was full of jokes and loved to play pranks, but I was a hard worker although most of my jobs were the ones usually done by women.

Everyone was talking about it for days before the council met to decide. Some people wanted me to be war chief, but many wondered about a war chief who was as much woman as man.

Those who were polite would say that a prankster should not be war chief. 'How could you tell if when he raises an alarm he is not just looking for a laugh?' they would say.

Secretly, I did not want to be *paracusi*. I wished to continue to work with *Isucu*, an honorable position in the tribe. I had a plan.

I went to Alobo and asked him to support me at council and to speak to Chief Ibitibi in my behalf. I knew that Alobo did not like me. He believed a person of my nature would be too meek to be war chief.

I had no ill will against Alobo. I was sorry for the shame he suffered when he got an arrow in the butt at the camp on the Wekiva. I told him that if he would agree to be *paracusi* I would change my mind and speak for him. He was reluctant, but I reminded him that as *paracusi* he would have a seat at council and receive many honors.

He still said no, but I could tell he was thinking about it. Then I reminded him that *paracusi* always wore a beautiful tattoo on his right biceps.

When I was allowed to speak to council in Alobo's behalf, I knew some people believed he was a coward. I said that I had

seen him bending over to pick up one of his arrows that had
fallen to the ground that night at Wekiva, and it was only when
he was struck in the butt that he fell to his knees. It was a new
way to look at an old story.

A lobo became *paracusi.* He never thanked me for lying to
council. Perhaps he thought I had spoken the truth.

* * *

By his fifteenth summer, Crying Bird had shown no manly
talents. He had no interest in the ball game the young men
played. He did not have the nature of a woman, but he was too
weak and slow afoot to become a warrior. His only interest was
our Uncle Ibitibi's work with wood.

As Crying Bird grew out of childhood he did not cry all
night as he had. By that time the rest of us had accepted the
crying as background chanting and we were able to sleep most
of the night, but the crying was replaced by something even
more upsetting After sleeping soundly and quietly for most of
the night, Crying Bird would suddenly scream so loud that we
were quickly awake with our chests pounding in fear.

The crying that had almost soothed us was gone, and the
screams awakened half the village just as the loud crying did
during the first years of his life.

Blind Jarva took Crying Bird away from the village and
talked to him for a day. When they returned Blind Jarva said
that Crying Bird was haunted by evil spirits that came to life in
his sleep. Crying Bird had told Blind Jarva of dreams that were
so frightening even he refused to retell them, for fear they
would become his own. Blind Jarva and Isucu talked to each
other, and studied the matter.

The only hope was a curing ceremony that the *jarva* of
Acuera was trained to perform, with the help of our own *isucu*
and his spirit potions. We feared that the council would order
Crying Bird out of the village if the cure was not the right one
but we all were sure that the powers of a *jarva* and an *isucu*
combined could not fail.

I was part of the cure ceremony, since I was the brother
and my blood would be needed. I can not tell you of the cure as

such matters are sacred to our people. Crying Bird was so thin, and his skin as pale as a cloud, and he was frightened. The cure went all night. The smell of the burning herbs and tobacco made me sick, and I had to crawl out of the hut to vomit.

When dawn broke the rest of us sat around a fire. We prayed and had words of encouragement for each other. Isucu said his medicines were strong, and that *Jarva* of Acuera spoke clearly to the Spirits in Crying Bird's behalf. Father Sun lifted his sleepy eyes above the horizon and it was a new day.

From inside the hut where Crying Bird lay sleeping we heard the 'Yeoouing! Yeoouing.'

The *jarva* of Acuera was saddened by his failure and left for his own village.

* * *

The village council house was full. The ceremonial black drink was passed among the elders, but the mood was somber and the men were quiet. Torches lit the inside, flickering and casting strange and fearsome shadows on the faces of the people with whom I had lived all my life. Chief Ibitibi, as was the custom in our village, received the cup last. He sipped slowly, and then he called my name.

'Marehootie, approach the council.'

I stood by the door, uncertain what to do. Ibitibi asked me again to come forward. My uncle Apoholo pushed me roughly from behind, and I was propelled forward toward our chief. Ibitibi reached out his hands, offering me the cup. Men of my age had been admitted to council years before, but I, perhaps because of my nature, had never been invited.

My hands trembled as I took the cup. The taste was bitter and sharp to the tongue. The cassina did not taste much different from other teas I had drunk my entire life. I smacked my lips and took a larger swallow, as I had seen others do. A murmur passed through the room, and I handed the cup back to my uncle, the chief of Ibitibi.

'The Spirit has blessed the children of Ibitibi with Marehootie, who has the gentle nature of a woman and the strength and swiftness of a panther. Because he also knows the many secrets of nature and of the swamp and glade and forest, he joins council today and will bear the title and responsibility of *Isucu* of Ibitibi.'

My head was swimming from the effects of the drink, and my whole body was wet with sweat. I was invited to sit on the bench to the right of the chief. I had not noticed that the seat of *isucu* was empty.

I saw the first *isucu*, the man who had taught me everything I knew, many times later. He left our village and became a trader up and down the river. He dealt in roots, and leaves, and flowers and lichens and berries and other magical things.

The subject of the council that evening was my brother, Crying Bird. It would be pointless and painful to tell you all that was said. We all loved him, and he was one of us. But one thing important was said. The *jarva* of Acuera was there. He said that Crying Bird was possessed by an evil spirit that had killed his mother and no amount of conjuring would change that fact. Only Crying Bird and the Great Spirit could cast out the evil one, if he were to be defeated at all.

He also warned that the whole village was in danger, and the evil spirit would pass to the rest of us when it tired of torturing Crying Bird.

The council pronounced that Crying Bird should be banished from the village.

The next morning, at the age of fifteen summers, weak from loss of blood, pale from lack of sun and thin as a reed, my brother was ordered from the village.

He carried with him only enough water and meal cakes for two days. He had no weapons with which to defend himself. *Jarva* danced and chanted, chasing the evil spirit away. He wiped out my brother's footprints with a pine straw broom so that the spirit would not be able to find its way back to our village.

It was the same as my mother's death, but even more painful if that is possible. Niho grieved for a season, crying quietly on her cot, trying not to disturb the others. Amita also missed Crying Bird who she loved as a brother.

Crying Bird would be dead, and I would be *Isucu.* I wept openly, as a woman would. Ibitibi, chief of the village, mourned with the rest of us.

I could not sleep at all. Oh! How I longed to hear the "Yeoouing, Yeoouing" that I thought I hated. That night, and for many nights I slipped out of the village in the direction Crying Bird had gone, and climbed the tallest tree I could find and listened for him.

When winter came and the trees dropped their leaves I could see much further into the forest.

Have you noticed that you can see and hear more clearly in the winter? If you are alone and quiet and patient, I believe you can watch your own birth. It is said that a *jarva* can see his death approach at that time of year.

I fell out of the trees two times. The last time I broke my leg. Niho made me promise not to go out at night again, and I never did. I decided that Crying Bird was dead.

When you see me run, you will notice that I limp. My right leg is shorter than the other, but I am still fast enough to beat you."

CHAPTER 12

"The summer after my mother died our men returned to the camp on the Wekiva. I was too young to go. No women or children were allowed. *Isucu* made the journey and returned with many interesting plants that made effective potions. The fish were still plentiful and the canoes returned loaded with many arrobas of food.

In my thirteenth summer I was allowed to return to the camp. There had been no further threats from the Mayaca. *Isucu* was ill that year and I went in his place. Many of the men complained 'If *Isucu* can not cure himself, what hope is there for the rest of us?'

Isucu had drawn maps of the forest and swamp on deer hide, and showed me where to look for all the herbs and plants the village could use or trade. It was a very good summer for our village and for all Acuerans.

We were forty strong that summer. We had six men from Acuera, and five each from Piliuco and Mocoso. The village that the Spanish now call Santa Lucia sent three men. The rest of us were from Ibitibi. What a great celebration it was when we returned at the end of the summer!

And so it was in the summers that followed. Sometimes *Isucu* and I would hunt together, sometimes alone, but we never found any more Mayacan arrows. We discovered more medicine plants, and each summer we found more good quality yaupon. You have to pick it at just the right time, and you must roast it just so. I may show you all these things some day.

It was in my twenty- third summer when we went to the camp and discovered that the Mayaca had not been there. We had to clear out our own burned huts from the summer before, and not theirs. When we broke camp we didn't bother to burn our huts or destroy the weirs and fish traps.

When we returned the Mayaca again had not been there in the winter. We just moved back into our huts and went to work. We had reason to celebrate. The cowardly Mayaca feared us now that we were warriors and not women and children.

The council decided that it would be safe for some women and children to return with the men the following summer. I had hoped that Crying Bird would be allowed to go. He would enjoy returning to the place of his birth, and I could teach him about the plants.

Of course he was dead by that time and I was *Isucu.*

It is the custom among my people, and yours, that the chief bear the same name as the village he rules. Ibitibi, as I have said, was the brother of Acuera who was the *holata aco,* or chief of all the Acuerans.

Our village was a poor one in terms of those things that usually signify wealth. We had no vast storehouses filled with maize for the winter and no slaves to do the hard work. Each family lived in one house, and did not have a second house constructed to keep out the winter wind as the Mocamans and Yamassee do. As you shall see, however, there was a time when Ibitibi prospered and was respected up and down the river.

Uncle Ibitibi was chief, but scarcely more than a headman. He was not the kind of leader that braves will willingly follow into battle, but he was smart as a raccoon and very cunning in some ways. He was also a dreamer. He dreamed of ruling a village where all the people were warmly dressed in the winter, and well fed all year long, and he dreamed up ways to make it happen.

When Chief Acuera came to the village, Ibitibi was always envious of his regal bearing, his tattoos and the beauty of his deerskin matchcoat. Other chiefs would stop at our village on their way upstream or down and Ibitibi would be jealous of their wealth. He would not be impolite to our guests, but he asked questions on how they acquired their walking staff inlaid with metal or their gorget inlaid with precious stones.

After such a visit, Ibitibi would speak to the elders of the village about the need to produce tradable goods. Only if we had things of value to trade, he would say, could we ever hope to acquire beautiful and useful things to make our lives easier and more enjoyable.

The war chief sometimes said it would be easy to raid a Mayacan or Utina village, and take slaves at the same time. He could not name any wealthy neighboring villages that were smaller or weaker than ourselves, however, so we continued to listen to Chief Ibitibi's dreams.

I have already told you that the yaupon and medicinal plants were traded to our advantage, and *Isucu* and I got much credit. Before she died, my mother's pottery was valued by the traders for its strength and beauty. She mixed animal hair and moss with the clay before it was fired. I made it known that I would follow in her steps, but my pottery was a poor substitute. Maybe I was too impatient, or had forgotten something she had said about the process. My pottery was pretty, but it was brittle. The traders said that it sometimes broke in their canoes and that no one would barter for such inferior work.

Our chief was a skilled worker of wood. He felled an old cypress tree while I was still a child and made two war canoes from it, by burning it with hot coals and chipping out the burned wood. He fashioned cutting tools and awls from shark teeth, bone and shell and the same chert we used for arrowheads and spear points.

He worked slowly, always thinking ahead to where he would make the next cut. He made mistakes, of course, but learned from his mistakes. After he had worked all winter on the first canoe, and when he was almost finished, he found a small crack in the bottom.

Many canoe builders would fill the crack with pine tar and go on. Not Ibitibi. He put the canoe aside and started on the next one, taking more care and studying the grain carefully to insure there would be no cracks.

When the second canoe was completed he tested it to assure it was buoyant enough to carry ten braves and stable enough not to swamp in bad water on the big lake. It had to be light enough to be carried over land, and strong enough to withstand snags in the river and alligator attacks. When he was satisfied that he had done his best, Ibitibi placed his mark on the bow.

Traders who visited our village watched the canoe being built. They all said it was the finest war canoe anywhere on the river. The chief of Tacoy heard the stories of the traders and came to see it.

He made a generous offer to Ibitibi, who surprised everyone by saying it was not to be sold. Tacoy is a powerful chief who could have returned with enough men to take the canoe without trading anything, and said he might do that if Ibitibi remained stubborn. Our chief still refused and Tacoy left very angry.

The council questioned the chief that night about his refusal to deal with Tacoy. We were a small village, and not strong or war-like. We had no need for a war canoe, and we could certainly use the goods offered for it. Chief Ibitibi said he knew what he was doing.

Within a few days the story had been spread up and down the river by the traders. Imagine, a war canoe so valuable Tacoy would go to war to have it, and Ibitibi would die before giving it up!

We soon had visitors from Emola and Malica, and as far away as Potano. More than twenty offers were made, each exceeding the last. Finally, when the offers would go no higher, Ibitibi traded the canoe to the village of Satureiwa. The goods offered filled three canoes, and consisted of deerskins, fine matchcoats, jewelry, maize, metals we had never seen before, and many things I can not recall.

Chief Ibitibi told a trader that Satureiwa wanted a second canoe, and that Ibitibi would be happy to make canoes for anyone who could match the price. He even offered handsome commissions to traders who found buyers. The traders are very sharp dealers. They would tell each chief that the chief's worst enemy had ordered a war canoe from the famous canoe builder, Ibitibi.

Soon, after Satureiwa had taken his canoe, a raiding party tried to steal it from him. Luckily, a guard had been posted at the water and raised the alarm. When the thieves were discovered they tried to destroy the canoe by shooting it with arrows. The wood was so hard most of the arrows just bounced off. Those that stuck did no damage.

Satureiwa said that the arrows were the kind made by Tacoy's people.

Seven more canoes were built that year, and five the next, and a few each year after that. Even Tacoy sent his *inija* to negotiate for a canoe. He was too proud to come, himself.

The whole village worked on the canoes under Ibitibi's critical eye, but no one was allowed to work if he did not take pride in what he was doing.

I have never heard of an Ibitibi canoe sinking from a leak, or breaking on a snag in the river. There were some that were sunk in battle, but always by braves in another Ibitibi canoe.

There were only a few large chiefdoms in this land. Utina was the largest, with about forty villages. The Potano people were always the enemy of Utina and were great in number. Many of Satureiwa's villages, up and down the coast and at the end of the river, were small. The Acuera have never been plentiful, powerful or war-like, compared to the others. Neither were the Surruque or the Ais.

Chief Ibitibi always said that some day there would be no more buyers of the war canoes. When each large village had one or two they would be satisfied. He built a few two-man canoes, but no one would buy them. The war canoes used the grandfather cypress which we had growing at the very edge of our village, but the smaller canoes used young cypress and pine which were plentiful everywhere. Why should they trade with us when they can do as well for themselves?

For awhile there were no more canoes to be built, and we had little to trade other than the yaupon. We were spoiled and had no way to provide ourselves with the tools and body ornaments we were accustomed to. We had grown fat on maize cakes, but couldn't grow our own because of the poor soil, and had to do without.

Ibitibi spent his time in the shade of an oak tree near the river bank, looking up river and down river hoping that a trader would come with news of a village needing a war canoe. He busied himself carving pieces of cypress left over from the first canoe built.

Chief Ibitibi knew that when he died there would be no one with his love of canoe building. When he was three years old Crying Bird could be found sitting at Ibitibi's feet whittling and carving scrap pieces of wood.

This haunted child who grew slowly and could not outrun a rabbit, and who could not shoot an arrow straight, could look at a piece of wood and see the figure it would become under his blade.

Crying Bird listened carefully when Ibitibi spoke to him, and learned from him the lessons of woodwork and of life. He spent every day with his uncle and loved him dearly. He might have become the next canoe builder had he not died in his fifteenth year.

It was a wonderful thing to watch those two, the old man and my pitiful brother. Ibitibi would bring a cypress stump and ask Crying Bird what it was. He would turn it around, looking at it from every side. Perhaps he saw nothing at all. Sometimes he said 'There's an owl in this tree,' or 'a bear with his mouth open, growling.'

Uncle Ibitibi would look to see if he had the same vision as Crying Bird, and if he did he would begin to carve. Sometimes he would hand the piece to Crying Bird if he was uncertain of the next cut, or if he was tired.

Our uncle was no longer a young man, and a lifetime of working with his hands had left them gnarled and swollen and painful. I prepared a potion to ease his pain, using the bark of the willow tree. It helped a little, but the work was still difficult.

Crying Bird became an excellent carver, the knife flew in his hands. Before the first shaving hit the ground, another was loosed from the wood to join the first.

Soon the working area was littered with wooden owls, rabbits, bears, deer heads and alligators, each carefully crafted with fine detail. Some were stained blue and brown and yellow and red. The alligators were in shades of green and black and were very lifelike.

Here, even my help was needed. I had knowledge of stains and paints that could be rendered from the plants. For the blue colors I used the indigo plant, and it worked as well on the woodwork as it did on tattoos. All the other colors were available in nature. All it took was knowledge, imagination and patience.

A trader came one day and bargained for a wooden bear and for the head of a fox. At first Ibitibi said that he would not trade something as useless as a wooden animal, but when the trader offered two arrobas of maize, he agreed.

Before long the traders were back, asking if certain animals, fish and birds could be carved. On their return to our village the finished pieces would be ready to be delivered. Then the haggling would begin. Our chief soon learned to get the trader to agree to the trade before he or Crying Bird would begin the work.

It always surprised Ibitibi that people would give up so much to decorate their village or their council house. Soon he realized that many of the requests were for clan symbols, such as the alligator, the bear, the panther, the fish, the buzzard and the quail.

Since these clans were present in most of the villages everywhere, there were many possible buyers. If the Fish Clan in Enecape, for instance, had their symbol displayed in the village, members of the Buzzard Clan would be jealous until they had their own wooden buzzard.

A *niaholata,* or woman chief, in a village even further north than the end of the river asked for an eagle with its wings stretched as far as a man could reach his arms. She had heard of Ibitibi and had seen his work, and told the trader to make the trade and deliver the goods in advance.

At first Ibitibi said no. He had no idea how such a thing could be accomplished. Crying Bird said he could do it if he could attach feathers made of pine or hickory or some other wood other than the cypress. He also said that only a new cypress tree would be used, since the old growth wood was too hard for delicate carving.

The trade was made, but Ibitibi was not happy. He thought the trade of pieces of copper and high quality freshwater pearls was sufficient, but he did not see how Crying Bird could make an acceptable eagle. He refused to distribute the copper and pearls among the villagers until the work was complete and accepted when the trader returned two moons later.

Crying Bird found a hickory tree that had been struck by lightning and split asunder and shattered. He gathered enough pieces in one morning to carve the eagle feathers. A young cypress had also been split down the middle by lightning, and from half of its trunk an eagle begged Crying Bird to release it.

He worked day and night. Ibitibi watched his every move but made no suggestions. The work on the wing feathers was so delicate no one had ever seen anything like it.

When the trader returned Crying Bird showed him how the wing feathers were to fit into the holes he had bored along the edge of each wing. He told the trader that when he delivered the eagle to the *niaholata,* he should tell her to use pine tar on the quill of each feather so it would not fall out. The difference between the colors of the cypress and hickory was truly beautiful.

The trader left very happy on his long journey to the north. He packed the eagle and its feathers separately in different places in his canoe, for fear a thief might discover the precious cargo.

The pearls were soon traded for maize, and the copper fashioned into ear ornaments and bells. Nothing quite as beautiful as the eagle had ever been made in our village, and nothing ever would again. It was Crying Bird's fifteenth summer."

* * *

The old man was silent for a while. He massaged his forehead as if the memories brought physical pain

De Coya spoke. "You seem tired. It might be well that you rest for a time. I have not mentioned it to you earlier because I did not want you to worry, but Father Pareja wants to visit with you in the afternoon to talk about his work."

The Acueran looked up. "You say he is coming here? Today?"

"He told me that he is anxious to start. He also said that he feels badly for keeping you here so long. His duties, you know..."

"But he wants to talk to me here, in my cage, and not in the convento?" the old man asked.

"He said that you might feel more comfortable in familiar surroundings. His apartment is much too small for the three of us, and the classroom for the students, which is much larger, will be used for studies. Father Pareja asked me to help him carry his desk and a chair across the church yard."

Marehootie stood and walked to the window and looked out "Hmmph" he grunted. The boy let himself out, promising to return soon.

* * *

Father Pareja arrived when the sun was three fingers beyond its highest point. De Coya entered first, dragging a chair over the threshold. He was followed by Father Pareja and a military guard, each puffing greatly under the weight of a small desk.

The boy left again, and soon returned with several books, a stack of thin parchment pages and a quill and inkwell. Father Pareja thanked the guard who left immediately and returned to his post. The three who remained could clearly hear the metal door latch as it was slid into place.

"I am Father Francisco Pareja, as I'm sure you know by now. By what name shall I call you?" he asked slowly in Spanish. Juan De Coya translated as well as he could into the Utinan tongue, as he had been instructed to do.

"You may call me Marehootie. Many people do." De Coya translated the answer into Spanish.

"'Marehootie'. That is an interesting name. I don't believe I have ever met an Indian by that name. What does it mean?" Pareja asked, smiling broadly.

The old man listened intently to the question. He paused, then he said "It is me. It is what I call myself."

"Marehootie," the priest said.

"Marehootie," de Coya repeated.

"Marehootie," the old Indian agreed.

Silence followed. Father Pareja studied the list of questions he had prepared. Before he could speak, Marehootie asked a question.

De Coya laughed out loud. Even the old Acueran allowed himself a quiet chuckle at his own joke.

"What did he say?" Pareja asked.

When he regained his composure, de Coya answered. "He says 'Pareja' has a strange sound. He wants to know what it means."

Father Pareja smiled at the old Indian. Then he laughed. "That's good! That's very funny," he said slapping his knee.

The priest re-focused his attention on the papers he had prepared.

"I have heard that you are gifted with languages, and that you speak many of the dialects of the tongue we sometimes call Timucua," he said. "It may be that you can be of help to me with some of my writings."

Pareja spoke slowly, one phrase at a time, allowing the boy to translate his Spanish into the Utinan dialect. The boy was quite good, and it took only a short time for Pareja to explain that his first task was to prepare a dictionary of common words that would be understood by as many Indians as possible, and to make note of variations in language between the different dialects.

"How would an Acueran say the number '1'?" he would ask. Then, when he had heard the word pronounced several times by the Indian, Pareja would spell it phonetically, and write the word on his parchment. When he was satisfied, he would ask how an Utinan would say the word, then a Yuferan, then a Satureiwan until he had asked about each of the dialects.

To his delight, Pareja discovered that almost all of the dialects were identical with numbers, except for slight differences in pronunciation. One exception was the Tawasan dialect which used distinctly non-Timucua sounding words for the numbers 6, 7, and 8. Perhaps the Tawasans, being far to the west, had borrowed from another tongue, Pareja surmised.

He asked Marehootie why the Tawasan numbers were different.

"Tawasans try to impress people by speaking like the Apalachee," he said. "They may not speak the same numbers we do sometimes, but they understand what we say."

Before it became too dark to work Father Pareja had exhausted a list of fifty common nouns, making note of only a few variations between the dialects. Marehootie made the task easier. Before long he would say "We all use the same word." Pareja would listen carefully, spell it out using the Spanish alphabet, then go on to the next word on the list.

When it was time to go, Father Pareja thanked Marehootie and promised to return in two days, unless his duties interfered. The Priest offered a prayer that God bless their work together to the benefit of all Timucuans, and that God preserve them until they meet again.

Despite the fact that his head was bowed and his eyes closed, de Coya peeked from the corner of his eye. Marehootie's eyes were wide open and he was looking directly at the young Indian.

CHAPTER 13

"**D**uring my childhood I heard many disturbing stories that worried the elders. The year of my birth an army of bearded people landed on our shore to the west, and made its way to the north, killing innocent people and robbing them and burning their villages.

An Acueran village furthest to the west had been robbed of all its maize. I have already told you the story of how the Spanish were frightened and fled from our land. The army was led by a man called de Soto.

I have not told you the whole story. The murderer de Soto spoke to the village chief of Piliuco words he called 'Requirementos.' The same words he spoke to Piliuco he also spoke to Chief Ocale, Chief Potano and many others. Later, they all agreed about what he had said to them. Every Acueran child can recite the words. This is what de Soto said:

> 'We ask and require you to acknowledge the Church as the ruler and superior of the whole world, and the high priest called the Pope and in his name the King as lords of this land.
>
> If you submit we shall receive you in all love and charity, and shall leave you, your wives and children, and your lands, free from servitude.
>
> 'But if you do not submit we shall powerfully enter into your country, and shall make war against you. We shall take you, and your wives,

110

and your children,and shall make slaves of
them, and we shall take away your goods and
shall do you all the harm and damage we can.'

I'm sure Fr. Pareja knows these words, and would not deny that they were said. You might ask him. Perhaps he can explain to you what right the Spanish had to make these demands.

There was a message sent by Chief Acuera to de Soto. It was spoken many times by Acuera to the slave from Pahoy who took the words to his master. This, too, is well remembered by the children of Acuera. Chief Acuera answered, saying:

'I am king in my land, and it is unnecessary for
me to become the subject of a person who has
no more vassals than I.

I regard those men as vile and contemptible
who subject themselves to the yoke of someone
else when they can live as free men.

Accordingly, I and all my people have vowed to
die a hundred deaths to maintain the freedom of
our land ,both for the present and forever more.'

This oath was made by our chief in the year of my birth. It has been part of me every day of my life. It will be on my lips when I die."

The old Acueran stood up from his stool. He walked to the window and put his hands on the back of his hips and stretched his back and looked out into the church yard. He took a sip of water then sat down again and resumed his story.

"Acuera sent scouts to follow the Spanish as they fled. The army moved slowly, and did not travel far in a day. It was easy to keep up. The Spanish were so blind they could march through a forest and never see the people watching them. It was almost a game as the Acueran scouts would get dangerously close to the Spanish without being seen.

The Spanish went through many small villages in search of food. They stopped for a few days at Aguacaleycuen, and our scouts were so brave that they walked right into the village as if they belonged.

When they witnessed people being killed and women being mistreated they left the village and camped nearby with a party of Potanan scouts who were also watching the Spanish.

Another party of Utinan scouts was there also, so you can see that your people were not always the friends of the Spanish.

It was said that the daughter of Chief Aguacaleycuen had been taken hostage, and that the chief was captured the next day.

Another army of Spanish had marched from Ocale to Aguacaleycuen to join up with de Soto's army. Our scouts became frightened when they discovered an army approaching from their rear, with another to the front. Our men disappeared into the forest and returned to Acuera.

The Potanan and Utinan scouts continued to follow the Spanish toward Apalachee. Near the village of Napituca an ambush had been laid by the brave Yustagans. It was a terrible battle. The Spanish had weapons that blow holes in people from a great distance.

A hundred warriors swam into a lake to escape the arquebus. They swam around all night. Those who came out were shot. The rest swallowed water and drowned.

Many Yustagans died that day and the next, and some of the Spanish. When the battle ended the Spanish tied nine chiefs to trees and ordered their Tocobagan slaves to shoot them with arrows. Chief Aguacaleycuen was one of those murdered. His daughter was never seen again. All of this was witnessed by the Potanans and Utinans who were following the Spanish.

I have been told that one of the Utinans was a very brave warrior. When the battle was over, and after it became dark he climbed to the top of a tall pine tree that looked down on the Spanish soldiers where they were sleeping. This tree was sparse and provided little cover. He tied himself to the tree. He had no plan for escape.

When morning came he shot all of his arrows at the Spanish soldiers as they awakened and began to move about.

He shot six arrows and killed six soldiers, yet they still did not see him in the tree. When he had no more arrows he cursed them loudly, and it was only then the Spanish looked up and saw him.

They shot him with muskets and he died, but his body did not fall from the tree. They kept shooting, using his body for target practice until their leader told them to stop wasting gun powder.

The Spanish commanded their slaves from Tocobago and Pahoy to practice shooting the dead Utinan with their arrows. Of course they refused. To shoot an arrow into the corpse of a brave man is against their beliefs. The Spanish killed two slaves for their disobedience, but good slaves are hard to find so they stopped killing them.

* * *

"Have you heard this story in your youth?" Marehootie asked.

"I may have heard that story when I was a baby. When you said the warrior tied himself in a tree, I knew what was coming next. Yes, I believe I have heard it before. Is it a true story?" de Coya asked.

"I was told the story by your own uncle, the Chief of Coya. He said that the dead Utinan was your grandfather, your mother's father."

The boy sat quietly. Finally he spoke. "I have had a strange dream that comes to me sometimes. I have seen the man in the tree."

The Acueran and the young Utinan each studied in their minds what the other had said. From outside the sounds of military commands echoed through the village, as the sergeant trained his men with their marching. Finally, Marehootie spoke.

"I don't know whatever happened to the devil de Soto. There are many stories of the crimes he committed.

For many years the huge boats in which the Spanish sailed had been seen in the waters to the east. Many of these boats sunk in the storms or ran aground on sandbars and reefs. Even

113

to the south and the west the Calusa saw many boats wrecked and took slaves and killed some who showed no respect.

Many of these ships were full of gold and silver and pearls and precious jewelry that these people valued greatly. Calusa gave much of this metal to his friends. If you remember, the French asked Satureiwa where he found a bar of silver. You know the story, how the French misunderstood what Satureiwa said. I will not repeat it.

Members of the council were convinced that since the Spanish had come seeking these shiny metals, and we had none in this land, they would take their evil ways elsewhere. You and I both know how wrong they were.

When Alobo became *paracusi* he said the threat of the Spanish returning made it necessary to post a guard all night. Everyone agreed that we should be alert for their return, but since they came in great armies and made much noise when they moved we would know of their presence days before they reached the village. But Alobo said he was *paracusi,* and in matters of defense he must be obeyed. The council supported him.

I was assigned to guard duty with the rest. It was too late to change my story about what happened at Wekiva. Guard duty was not that great a hardship on me, since I had lived with Crying Bird and could get by with very little sleep."

* * *

When the story was done, the Acueran asked that the boy leave him so he could rest.

"Nariba, you say that you know my uncle. He left the village before I was born. He returned once or twice, and then left again. It always made the women cry. It was his brother who became headman of the village, and who delivered me to the Franciscans when I was five summers old," he said.

"What you have said is true. I am pleased that you are finally remembering who you are," Marehootie said softly.

"But how is it that you know the Chief of Coya?"

"I can tell you nothing more now. Perhaps some day I can say more. For now I will only say that, next to my brother, the Chief of Coya was the bravest man I have ever known."

CHAPTER 14

"Juan de Coya, today I am going to surprise you with my story. I will tell you of a miracle that happened many years ago. Do you know what that means?"

"Father Pareja speaks of miracles every day. Jesus walked on water. He turned water to wine at a wedding feast, and later he fed a multitude on just a few fish and small loaves of bread," the boy answered.

"But did he tell you about Lazarus, the dead man who came back to life? That was a real miracle, don't you think?"

The boy frowned. "You have seen such a thing?"

"You may listen and judge for yourself," the old man said.

Marehootie lowered his head, his chin on his chest. His lips moved silently in an ancient prayer. When he was done he looked up, directly into the eyes of the boy.

* * *

"What I shall tell you now I have seen with my own eyes. Do not ask me how this happened, as you would not ask Father Pareja how Lazarus came back.

It was a day in the early springtime. I remember that clearly as we were preparing for the Festival of the Sun that was to be celebrated the next morning. Because the *jarva* of Ibitibi was blind, it was my responsibility as *isucu* to prepare for the ceremony.

Utinans have a ceremony that is very much like our own. It is observed on the same day of the year. It is the day Father Sun shows his face as long as he sleeps. It is a sign that he will

116

bless us more each day. You Utinans had a little different idea, that it is a day to celebrate fertility within the tribe, but the Utinans always said they did their best work in the privacy of their huts."

The old man chuckled softly. The boy did not seem to understand his joke, so the Acueran went on.

"I was away from the village a short distance where I could work without being seen, preparing a stag head for the next morning. My uncle Apoholo had put on a deerskin cloak in the early morning and had crawled on his hands and knees into the middle of a small herd that always fed in a meadow near the spring. His arrow was true, and he felled an old buck with large antlers.

We said our prayers of thanksgiving and respect for the Deer God. Apoholo butchered the deer and carried it to the village, leaving me with only the head.

I mounted it in the fork of the tree we used each year for the ceremony. I decorated it with a garland of springtime flowers and plants. Dried fruits and nuts and berries were sewn onto the small twigs and branches surrounding the deer head.

I had been working intently, but had that strange feeling I sometimes get that I was being watched. I stopped working once or twice and looked around but saw no one. I wanted to call out 'Who's there?' but my eyes told me I was alone so I continued to work.

When I was done, I stepped to the edge of the clearing to admire my work. It was beautiful! The best I had ever seen. The children would be amazed the next morning when the procession from the village reached the tree just as the sun shined his face on the tribute I had prepared.

'Good work, Marehootie,' a voice called from the thicket of sweet-gum behind me.

I jumped a little, but was not really startled since I suspected someone might be sneaking up on me for a prank. I was looking toward the sun and could make out only the silhouette of the tall man who emerged from the trees.

He was tall, as I have said, as tall as anyone in our village, and powerfully built.

He was dressed only in a simple loincloth of deerskin, and his feet were without moccasins and he showed no weapons of any kind.

I did not recognize him and yet he had called me by name.

'Do I know you?' I asked, moving toward him but circling slightly so the sun was no longer in my eyes.

This man wore tattoos, all in blacks and blues and reds, as fine as those worn by Acuera, himself. Both arms, from the back of his shoulders down to his hands, and the outside of the calves of his legs were adorned. But this was not Chief Acuera, this man was younger and stronger.

'Your eyes must be failing from old age if you do not know your own brother,' he said.

I was suddenly angered at what he said. 'You are not my brother. He is dead and you are a cruel imposter.'

'Then walk with me to the village. Niho will know me and my sister Amita will welcome me home, even if you will not,' he said.

I remember very little about our return to the village. My head was spinning. How could this man be Crying Bird? He was twice the size of my brother and in no way resembled him.

The reaction of the villagers was the same as my own. It might be possible that Crying Bird had lived, had he found shelter in another village, and it was possible he might have grown to a man in just two years. What none could believe was that this grown man with chiefly bearing was the same thin, ill child who had been sent away to defeat his demons or die.

He was surrounded by our people. Some of the children reached out to touch the tattoos. The women covered their mouths and held back. A young man stepped forward aggressively to challenge him, and then thought better of it when he saw the muscular arms and shoulders.

Niho cried for joy. No one could tell her this was not her son. The rest were unsure. Apoholo held Niho back and looked threateningly at the stranger, as if he would fight.

Chief Ibitibi approached and the others separated to allow him to draw near.

'Who are you?' he asked directly, after having looked him over carefully from head to foot.

'It is I, Crying Bird. Do you not recognize your own nephew, my chief?'

Alobo stepped between them, and with his knife drawn commanded the man who claimed to be a boy to sit in the dirt. He smiled broadly and did as he was told. He was held under guard while the chief and his principal men met in the council house to discuss this startling thing that had occurred.

Very few believed it was Crying Bird, sitting outside in the sunlight. I felt in my heart that this might be my brother, and said so when I was called upon. That made two of us, Niho and I, who believed. None of the others did.

Alobo thought it might be a diversionary tactic to disguise an attack. He sent braves in different directions to see if there were threats to the village.

'Where are you going?' our prisoner shouted as he saw the braves scattering into the woods and launching their canoes to move up-steam and down, and he laughed out loud.

The laughter struck me in the heart. It was Crying Bird's laugh, although now deeper and throatier than before.

Ibitibi devised a test. With the villagers standing around, Ibitibi approached Crying Bird and told him to stand. He handed him a block of wood, not much larger than the palm of his hand.

'What do you see?' he asked.

Crying Bird looked into the eyes of Ibitibi, and then he lifted the lump of wood into the air turning it around in the sunlight until he had seen it from every angle.

Then a startling thing occurred. Instead of answering the Chief, Crying Bird opened his mouth to the heavens. 'Whoo-whoo, whoo who whooogggh.' You will pardon me for such a poor imitation. I am no good at such things, but that day in the village Crying Bird did a perfect cry of the barred owl. It was so convincing that an owl was awakened from its slumber in the swamps across the river, and answered his call.

As everyone knows, one call of a barred owl is an evil omen, and some of us were frightened. Crying Bird raised his hand signaling us to be silent. In a moment there was another call from further into the swamp, and the people laughed in relief.

Ibitibi still was not convinced. 'Show me!' he commanded, handing Crying Bird a cutting tool.

'This may take awhile. I have not done this in two years' he said.

Crying Bird sat down in the dirt and began working slowly with the knife. Soon he was working faster, cutting, and then studying the next cut, then holding the wood up to the sun to see the grain more clearly. Once or twice he spit on it, then wiped off the spit and dust on his loincloth.

When he was done, he stood and handed a wooden owl effigy to Ibitibi, who looked at it through wet eyes. When he saw it was perfect Chief Ibitibi wept unashamedly, and embraced Crying Bird. The owl fell from his fingers into the dirt. I picked it up.

Crying Bird kissed Niho and Apoholo and the others of the White Deer Clan. Amita, now grown to womanhood from the gangling girl of two summers before, stood back, biting her fingers. Crying Bird picked her up and swung her around.

'Amita, I wouldn't have recognized you!' he said. I will never forget what Crying Bird said to Amita. He himself was so changed that it is a wonder that he was recognized at all. Alobo would have killed him immediately as an enemy or as a spy if he had been encountered outside the village. It was fortunate Crying Bird made himself known to me, his only brother.

Crying Bird slept that night on his own bed. He did not cry. He did not scream in fear in the middle of the night. He snored like an angry bear.

At daybreak we welcomed Father Sun, together. Blind Jarva led the way. The first rays of the sun lighted the deer head, the garland of flowers and the shiny antlers. We all prayed it would be a fruitful year."

* * *

"Juan, I have now told you the story of the return of Crying Bird. Can you accept on faith that which you have not seen?"

"I'm sure it seemed a miracle to the people of your village, but since I was not there I would need some proof," he said.

The old Acueran grunted as he stood up from his stool. He moved to his pallet and got down on his knees, rummaging through his deerskin pouch. He stood again and approached Juan de Coya who was standing near the door.

Marehootie reached out his hand and Juan opened his own palm to accept what was being offered. He saw in his hand a finely crafted wooden likeness of a small barred owl.

* * *

"The village council met again that night. Alobo had asked for the council to examine the man who claimed to be Crying Bird and to ask him questions about his journey of the last two years, and by what right he wore the tattoos that now covered his body.

It was clear to everyone that Alobo did not believe Crying Bird's claim. When Alobo first approached Ibitibi to request the council meeting it was denied.

'How does the Buzzard Clan question the White Deer Clan?' Ibitibi asked, and sent him away. The White Deer Clan is the clan of chiefs. The Buzzard Clan does not produce chiefs, but only common people and warriors. Alobo was only *paracusi* because there was no one from a higher clan that would take the job.

Later, Alobo spoke again to his chief. 'We hold White Deer in great respect and could not challenge them. Some of us, however, perhaps some White Deer themselves question whether this man is Crying Bird or some imposter.'

You can see that Alobo had put Chief Ibitibi in an uncomfortable position. If Alobo named a member of the White Deer Clan who did not believe the identity of Crying Bird it would cause a loss of face within the clan. However the council decided, it might cause a division within the clan that might effect not just the village leadership, but the entire Acueran tribe since Crying Bird was also a nephew of Chief Acuera and might be considered as his successor.

Chief Ibitibi made a very wise decision. He granted Alobo's petition for a council meeting, without asking him to identify a member of White Deer who doubted Crying Bird's story. Perhaps Chief Ibitibi had his own questions of Crying Bird concerning the tattoos he now wore without approval of any chief.

On cool evenings when the air is light the smoke from the council fire rises and escapes through the hole in the roof of the council house. It is said that on these nights the council sees clearly. When smoke gathers and will not leave it is said the council can not see clearly and may make misjudgments.

This night the air outside was cool. Smoke from the council fire and from the torches did not linger, but escaped to allow the elders to make good judgments. Crying Bird stood before the council, his arms crossed over his chest and a pleasant look on his face.

With each question he would turn his head to face the questioner. He did not make his voice loud like the thunder to impress anyone, but he answered directly and in a manner everyone could hear.

He said he did not know where he had wandered because he met no man on his journey. He said he was fed by the spirits that visited with him each night, and the devil that had tortured him was slain. He said he had many visions of great importance that he was commanded by the spirit to tell. Some of them he did not understand.

Crying Bird was examined closely by the elders. They looked at the blues and reds and blacks of the markings that adorned his body.

Chief Ibitibi asked Crying Bird about the tattoos, the one on his right shoulder and arm that was appropriate to a warrior chief of high standing, and the one on the left shoulder and arm that might be worn by a *jarva* who could speak directly with the spirits in the other world.

Before he could answer, Blind Jarva rattled his attention stick and rose to his feet. 'I should answer that for Crying Bird, for I am sure he does not know how,' he said.

A murmur passed through the room. Crying Bird looked relieved that he would not need to answer.

Blind Jarva shook his stick again and continued to shake it until there was silence throughout the council house. 'Crying Bird has always had the markings. He was born with them. I could see them all his life. Only now are your eyes opened,' he said.

Chief Ibitibi spoke after the tumult of words that followed. 'What are we to make of all this, *Jarva*?'

'The markings of a great war chief with the markings of a shaman can mean only one thing. Crying Bird is *Atichicolo-Iri*, the Spirit Warrior, come to save the Acuera."

CHAPTER 15

"**B**y morning Crying Bird was not on his bed. I went looking for him, and asking among the early risers if they had seen him. An old man pointed across the river. Crying Bird was on the other side, sitting on a log in a small clearing. Blind Jarva sat on a stump in front of him, and they were talking.

Blind Jarva's stick was standing upright in the river bank. He did not wish to be interrupted while they talked.

When Father Sun looked directly down on them they continued to talk quietly between themselves. No one on this side of the river could hear what they said. It would show disrespect to cross the river or call out to them to ask what it was they discussed so privately. Into the night they talked. Crying Bird built a fire to warm them. The fire went out, and they still talked.

When I awoke the second day Crying Bird was on his bed and was asleep.

Across the river Blind Jarva remained, praying to the Spirit and wailing in a loud voice. He flailed with his stick and beat on the bushes and the ground.

When it was almost dark Crying Bird took a canoe and went to the old man who was by now lying on his back. He bathed him in the river, then carried him to the canoe and brought him to the village. My brother put the old man to bed in his house.

The next day Blind Jarva went to where Chief Ibitibi was doing his woodworking. After they spoke, three messengers were sent out of the village, each in the direction of an Acueran village. When they returned the next day none of the messengers would speak to anyone but Chief Ibitibi. We all knew something important was about to happen but we did not know what it was.

Ibitibi ordered that the council house be prepared for a meeting. Several of the men had been using the house to dress their arrows and string their bows. Artisans had been using the house for their carving of children's dolls, and the potters for the shaping of their pottery. They all removed their materials and tools and soon the council house was clean, and the benches arranged as Ibitibi directed.

Seven village chiefs arrived, each accompanied by his *jarva*, if he had one, and with his *paracusi* and his most trusted advisor. Acuera was the last to arrive, and like the rest traveled without the usual *anacotimas* and lesser officials. His *inija* was with him. He also had the tribal *jarva* and *paracusi* but no one of lesser standing.

The black drink had been prepared and was shared among the chiefs first, then among the others according to their rank. Though I had been asked to attend by Ibitibi, I was clearly outranked by everyone else and drank the cassina last. Crying Bird was there, but because he was not admitted to the council he did not drink.

Chief Ibitibi, as host, spoke first. His voice cracked with his feelings, so strong they were. He told of the amazing events of the last few days and of the return to the village of Crying Bird. All in attendance knew of the banishment two years before as it was a well-known story throughout Acuera that a nephew of the White Deer Clan had been sent away.

He described the joy we all felt that one who had been lost and for whom we had all grieved was restored in such a miraculous form. He spoke of his own doubts that this was truly the lost son of Acuchara, so changed and matured he was.

He told of the test he had put to Crying Bird, and asked me to show the rest the owl effigy. Many of the men had seen the artistry of Crying Bird, and agreed that this was indeed his work.

Finally, Chief Ibitibi told of what Blind Jarva had said about the tattoos.

'From his birth you say?' Acuera asked, looking at Blind Jarva, who did not answer.

'From his birth,' Acuera said again, but this time not as a question but as a statement of belief.

Crying Bird stood before them all, naked but for his loin cloth, turning this way and that as they asked. The *paracusi* looked carefully at the tattoo on the right arm, all in red against the copper skin, tracing their fingers along its path. Many of them had similar designs, but none nearly so grand and fearsome.

When they were finished the Jarva of Acuera and the other *jarva* inspected the resplendent tattoos on the left arm and shoulder, all in brilliant blue and black designs. Each of them wore a tattoo on his left arm, but none to compare with the dramatic ones worn by Crying Bird, depicting all the Spirits of the other world.

One of the village *jarva* was so overcome by his feelings he would not look at the tattoo or touch it, but hid his face in his hands.

When they were done, the *jarva* of Acuera asked that he be heard. Chief Acuera bid him speak, and the foremost shaman in the land stood before the leaders of Acuera with the light of seven torches flickering across his wise face.

'There is a legend, as old and honored as Spirit himself, so much a part of who we are and what we are that we, the Acuera nation, would not exist but for it. Through each generation from the beginning of the world, from the time the seed was dropped on this land by an eagle sent by the Sun God, we have all known that if and when we ever lost our way and Acuera were to be destroyed because of it, one would be sent among us, one so wise and strong and pure of spirit that we might yet be saved.

'We are a strong nation, and yet we are not nearly as numerous as the Potanans, the Calusa or the Appalachee. The Utinans are as many as the stars in the heavens, and have many times been our enemies and would covet our lands and take us as slaves and destroy us as they would an ant hill in the middle of their camp.

'But they would not, and they could not. We are not Gods, we are men who would live in peace if we can and fight if we must. As men we are as cunning as the fox. We are as strong as a mighty bear, as wise as the owl, and as resourceful as the raccoon. And we are as brave as a mother panther who would attack a pack of wolves to save her whelp and yet we could be destroyed by those more cunning, more strong, more wise, more resourceful and more brave. Spoken another way, we could be destroyed simply by those who are more numerous and willing to die. That is, we could be destroyed if it were not for the promise that we would be saved by the one we know as *Atichicolo-Iri.*

'Blind Jarva of Ibitibi has said that our brother Crying Bird is *Atichicolo-Iri,* and perhaps always was, but we did not know him. This could be. I know the spiritual history of this mighty nation. I keep in my heart the stories told by our people from the beginning of time. I believe that no one has ever said he was this God in human form.

'I can also be mistaken. I see the wisdom of the ages in the faces of all of you, the mighty leaders of Acuera. Do any of you know of any Acueran, even an imposter, who has claimed the name we hold sacred?'

Some said 'No', others just shook their heads. No one in the world had ever made such a claim.

Chief Acuera spoke quietly to his *inija*, covering his mouth so that no one else would hear what he said. This was not unusual since the chief rarely speaks out on contentious issues, but having heard all sides will only then announce his decision which becomes the decision of us all.

When they had talked, *Inija* stepped down from his lofty bench and spoke to them all.

'Jarva is well-informed. No one has ever been called *Atichicolo-Iri*, and Crying Bird might be he, and yet Crying Bird has made no such claim.

'Blind Jarva is the most ancient of all the living *jarva* of the Acuera, and he is well respected. I call upon Blind Jarva to tell us what he knows, that we might be able to agree with him, or seek other proofs.'

All eyes moved to Blind Jarva who was seated next to me. He did not stir, or make any effort to answer. The torch light glinted on the whiteness of his sightless eyes. Time went by. Some began to clear their throats in the way people do when they are nervous or ill at ease.

Finally, Blind Jarva began to speak. His voice was old, and his words so rounded and worn down by time that he could barely be heard. He had spoken many words before some of the others knew he was trying to speak. I was close, and I heard every word.

'The Spirits have beckoned me to join them, but there is left for me one last task to be undertaken before I may rest,' he said. None of this was heard by the others.

'I have lived one hundred years, and each day I have prayed to the Spirit for guidance, as I do tonight,' he said.

'Halfway through my life I was blinded by Father Sun when I looked into his face seeking his wisdom. Few of you were alive at that time, maybe none of you here.

'Those who were there cried 'Poor Jarva, he has been struck blind by the Spirit,' and later said 'What good is a blind *jarva,* for he must see into both the world of life and the world of death. He must see our joys and see our miseries that he might pray the prayer of thanksgiving and beseech the Spirit for relief of our pain.

'I tell you now that Father Sun blessed me that day, the day he took my sight, for he gave me vision. My heart shows me things your puny eyes can not imagine. The Spirits of those who have gone before are here with us. Can you see them?'

Blind Jarva gestured with his hand toward the council fire, which was now just glowing embers of red and yellow. Every eye looked into the fire.

'Let us welcome Shomani, the paramount chief of Acuera who died before I was born, and his granduncle, Salamani, who is with him, and all the others. Only the *jarvas* here have ever met them, but all of you remember Acuchara who is here also to honor her son.'

Each *jarva* grunted and nodded his head in recognition."

Marehootie paused for a time and wiped his moist eyes.

"I can tell you that before Blind Jarva said her name I knew she was with us. I smelled the sweetness of her skin and of her breath when she kissed my cheek. Crying Bird told me later that he too had felt a presence. He said his whole body sensed a gentle drum beat, as a baby in the womb would feel his mother's heart."

Marehootie blew his nose on a rag before he went on with his story.

"The old *jarva* had gained his strength now, and his voice was heard by everyone. He said that he was there at the birth of Crying Bird. Only the *jarva* and the midwives are allowed in the birthing hut with the mother, and he is present only to accept the child from the Spirit and to bestow his blessings.

Blind Jarva said that when he held the child and gave it his prayers of protection he sensed the presence of a powerful Spirit, although he did not know which spirit it was. He said the child bore the markings on his shoulders and arms, and he asked the women to wash the child clean of the birthing materials and when they were finished the markings were clearer than before.

He asked the women again to wash the child, and the women refused to do it because the child had been washed twice and was clean. The women saw no blemish on the child.

Blind Jarva said he was stirred in his heart, and it was made known to him by the spirit that he must not remark further on what he saw, and that this child was marked for greatness later in his life.

'That time of greatness has dawned,' he said.

Jarva told of the pain that was borne by Crying Bird, and of the tears that issued from his eyes while he was a child. He told of the frights the child suffered each night that made him cry out in the darkness, and despite the tender nurturing of Niho the child was inconsolable.

'Many in the village would say 'Poor child has lost his mother and misses her,' and would secretly blame Niho for failing to comfort the child. That was foolish. Niho was a loving mother and is not to be blamed. Neither is it true that the child suffered from the loss of Acuchara. She was with him in spirit and comforted him when she could, although he never knew her.

'What then is the reason for Crying Bird's suffering? Some of you already know the answer. Some of you will never understand if I talk forever. Let me say this: Growth only comes through pain, and Crying Bird had to grow, and thus suffer more than any man.

'And what of his fears, his crying out? We are, each of us, the host of many spirits, both good and evil. It is what we are. The sweetest among us is capable of the most terrible crimes. Brother kills brother, and we say it is because the one lay with the other's wife, or the killer's crops were ruined and he was angry with the world and struck down his brother, or that he was suffering a fever and was out of his head.

'But this is false reasoning. Some will share their wife freely. Crops fail all the time. Men become fevered and sometimes die, but these men do not usually kill their brother or someone else. It is an evil spirit dwelling within that sometimes takes control and does terrible things.

'Crying Bird was born with evil spirits, as we all are, and Crying Bird was visited by other evil beings during his lifetime but many more than the rest of us. It is Crying Bird's destiny to be pure of spirit, as we all should seek to be. The truth is that we live with evil impulses, sometimes give in to them, but deny that they exist.

'But the child could not live with evil if his destiny was to be fulfilled. These evil ones do not leave willingly, as anyone knows who has tried to give up a bad habit such as eating the wrong thing or overcoming a lust for another man's wife.

'As the Great Spirit tore at these evil spirits to cast them out they hung on tenaciously, ripping the very flesh of the child before letting go, and threatening unspeakable horrors if they were dispossessed of their comfortable place within the young child.

'I did not say these things when he was banished from the tribe two summers past. Perhaps at that time I, the *jarva*, did not fully understand. Did I know that he was to be *Atichicolo-Iri*? No, I confess it, but I did know even then that for this child to defeat his own devils, he must meet them alone.'

Blind Jarva asked for a drink of water and it was given to him. When he finished, he apologized for talking so long and saying so little. He said he had talked with Crying Bird for two days upon his return and had been told of many amazing and disturbing visions.

Crying Bird spoke to him of his wandering through land he did not recognize, and of his hunger and thirst. He told *Jarva* he did not know how to find food, other than the berries that grew wild. He was too slow to catch even a rabbit. He soon became ill from eating a poisonous fruit, and no amount of water could slack his thirst.

He found himself between a great river and a swamp, in a hammock of hickory and sweet-gum. It became dark, and he lay his head down on moss. He had not been able to eat anything since he was poisoned, and he knew his death was near.

He was awakened by the call of a limpkin, or what we call crying bird. It seemed strange to Crying Bird that he should be greeted thus by one who bore his own name, and he gave an answering cry. The bird spoke to him in a tongue that he could understand.

Another bird flew to the tree and sat on a branch above the first. Then another, then another, until the entire tree and every limb strong enough, bore a crying bird, so many they could not be counted, each looking down at the child.

Then a nearby tree was filled and another until the entire forest was alive with the brown-speckled birds, each with a message for Crying Bird, all speaking at the same time and yet all clearly understood.

Then another miraculous thing occurred. The first bird was a sobbing woman, her wings now hands covering her tears. Then the second bird was changed to a crying woman, then each in turn throughout the forest. Hundreds of women crying for their lost husbands and children and babes yet to be born.

Thus it went, all through the night.

When Crying Bird awoke, the sun was high in the heavens. The trees were empty, but for the first bird that remained.

The bird spoke to Crying Bird in the strange tongue he understood, and told the boy what he must do. Crying Bird did as he was told. He reached up and took the bird off its perch. He broke its neck. He plucked its feathers and cooked it over a fire and he ate the bird.

He took the bird's breast bone and used it to pin up his hair, and he removed the bird's beak and kept it also. He washed the bird's blood in the river and, thus nourished, went on with his journey.

Each day thereafter, as he was told, he would find a limpkin sitting on a low branch waiting. He found apple snails upon which the limpkin survives, and picked out the meat with the beak he carried with him.

'This may be hard for you to believe. We all know that limpkins are the most skittish of all birds and will immediately flee if any of us comes near,' Blind Jarva said.

'Perhaps that is because we are of unclean spirit,' Chief Acuera suggested.

Blind Jarva was tiring, and drained of energy by all the talk, and asked if he could rest. Chief Acuera said the council meeting would start again soon, and many of the men walked around the village relieving themselves and speaking quietly of the things they had heard.

Blind Jarva said a prayer, then lay down on his bench and napped until the men returned.

* * *

'Last summer this village had a very bad storm that started late in the day and lasted half the night,' Jarva said when they had all returned.

'It was such a large storm I believe that most of the villages of Acuera would remember.

'There was not the kind of winds we see in *Huque*, but the thunder and the lightning can not be forgotten, and the rain washed away half the village.'

Several chiefs said they did remember the storm, and each had a story to tell of how his wise leadership saved his village from destruction and death. Blind Jarva waited patiently for the bragging to run its course. He knew such stories were necessary to keep the listeners involved in the business, and it was interesting that each story was better than the one before.

When it was time, he went on.

'Crying Bird tells of such a storm. He has no remembrance of time, but from his description I believe it was the storm we all remember. If we are talking about the same storm, I believe he was in the land of the Acuera at the time.

'He tells me of the lightning that never stopped, and that in the night the heavens were as light as day, with banks of clouds as high as the moon. He built a lean-to of palmetto fronds and saplings as we all learn to do as children and as we all know he got wet anyway.'

Laughter interrupted him, as everyone wanted to share his own experiences of trying to stay dry in a storm. When quiet was restored he went on to tell Crying Bird's story of the storm.

'He described the changing shape of the clouds. They were at first canoes of such size they couldn't even be imagined, casting about on seas so violent the canoes would be rent by lightning and sunk to the bottom.

'One after another, they came, each larger than the one before, sometimes colliding together with horrible cracking sounds and flashes of white light that hurt his eyes to see.

'Then they were gone. As suddenly as they appeared, they were gone and replaced by great rolling banks of clouds moving through the night directly toward Crying Bird as he huddled in the dark, their front edges alit with lightning going first one way then another, but never stopping.

'Then the clouds themselves separated into individual creatures of sound and light, each with two heads and many legs, followed by more of their same kind, Men with bearded faces and hats of metal and arms that crackled flame.'

Suddenly, Blind Jarva was interrupted in a rude manner before he could tell the vision. The *paracusi* of Acuera spoke out.

'We have all heard these stories before. Not twenty years ago the Spanish were to our west, and we have all heard the stories of our elders and the traders and the Potanans of how they kidnapped and enslaved peoples, killing them with their guns and robbing them of their foods and burning their villages.

'We tell these stories to our children because they are true, and because we would have our children avoid these vicious animals if they would dare to return. Who here has not known of a child who had bad terrible dreams after hearing these stories?

'I believe Crying Bird may have imagined or dreamed in the storm, and his story is not a vision from the Spirit at all.'

Every eye turned toward Crying Bird, who looked on and said nothing.

Blind Jarva began again to tell the story of the storm, but it was clear that few could believe it. One by one the chiefs and other officials crossed their arms over their chests, signifying they were not convinced, and insulting the *jarva*.

'What other stories do you have that you believe are visions?' the *inija* of Chief Acuera asked.

Blind Jarva was quiet, his head bowed. When he finally began to speak his voice was again old and worn.

'Crying Bird tells of his last vision, not more than a moon past. The spirit showed him the villages of Acuera in another time. There is no laughter of children and no games being played in Mocosco and no music or dancing. The crops are wasted by animals and there is no one to chase them away in Ibitibi. There is nothing to eat in Piliuco. The mothers have no milk for the babes in Acuera.

'There are no chiefs, and no braves in our villages. There is sickness throughout Acuera. People walk bent over, with sores on their faces. Their skin is peeling back.

'Then, the most horrible of all. All the charnel houses are full. The dead lay among the ill in the center of the village. Holes are dug in the burial mounds by wild animals, and the dead arise to bury the dead.'

There was nothing but silence that followed the *jarva*'s speech. There were no questions. He slowly rose to his feet and with his stick walked to the door. He was already so bent over with age that he did not need to stoop as others do to walk out.

The Chief of Acuera finally raised his voice to thank the

Blind Jarva, who was by then gone and did not hear. Crying Bird said he could add nothing to what Blind Jarva had said, and with Acuera's permission he followed *Jarva* out of the council house.

It was late, and many were exhausted and disturbed by what they had heard. Chief Acuera, however, required everyone stay until the business had been done.

The *jarva* of Acuera spoke first. He complimented Blind Jarva on his spirituality and his knowledge of Acueran beliefs. He held Blind Jarva in high esteem among all *jarva*, he said, for his ability to conjure up the spirits of Shomani and Salamani, and even Acuchara who had been with them.

He said many good things about Crying Bird and said all of Acuera should rejoice at his safe return. He went so far as to say that my brother might be considered as the next *jarva* of Ibitibi when the Blind Jarva passed to his home in the Spirit world.

He invited others to speak. Some did, some did not. Finally, Chief Acuera rose to his feet.

'We are told that *Atichicolo-Iri* will come to save Acuera in the final days, when we are threatened and divided and starving. I believe that, as all of you do.'

A murmur of agreement passed through the room.

'Acuera is not now threatened by our enemies. Even the Mayaca leave us in peace and do not invade our land. There is not much illness now. Our mother's have a lot of milk, unless my eyesight is failing.'

Laughter was heard throughout the house.

'We are prosperous, thanks to Chief Ibitibi and the trade he has generated from the handiwork and sweat of the people of this village. Our storehouses are full, although we don't want that to be known for fear the Utinans would steal from us. It is our belief that the time is not right for the appearance of *Atichicolo-Iri*.

'He will be here when he is needed. Now we are doing very well by ourselves'."

CHAPTER 16

Father Pareja was pleased with the progress he had made with the old Indian. In four sessions over a two week period he had compiled a list of over two hundred nouns and fifty verbs and had made some progress with common phrases.

To his surprise he had found fewer than twenty variations among the dialects. The tongue heard in the villages to the northwest, which he now called "Timuqua", varied most from the others, and it might be necessary to incorporate alternative words in his writings. Differences in accent and rhythm of speech were present, but it was clear that the words they used were substantially the same.

Other duties, however, loomed on the horizon. Holy Week was six days away, and there was much to be accomplished and little time to spare. Father Marron had sent a letter saying that he would be at San Juan del Puerto for Holy Thursday and Good Friday, and that he hoped to be at San Pedro de Mocama for Easter Sunday.

There would be three hundred Indians in attendance for the Holy Days, and much to be done in preparation for the masses that would be celebrated, the Sunrise Service and the Holy Thursday Procession of the Cross. As with every special occasion there would be great demand for the priest to be available to hear the confessions of those who had traveled the farthest.

"I would like you to help me today, if you will, with the questions I will ask when I hear the people's confessions this coming week," he said. "Fortunately, we will only be entertaining those who speak the Mocaman dialect and those who speak Utinan or 'freshwater' as I prefer to call them."

"Those tongues are very similar. Sometimes the Utinans speak more quickly, and you must listen harder when they speak," the old Acueran answered after de Coya interpreted the Priest's remarks.

Father Pareja sat at the desk that had remained in the Acueran's cell since the first time they met. He had prepared in Spanish a dozen questions that he sometimes used at Confession to determine if the Indians still clung to the old ways or if they had progressed spiritually with their Christian beliefs. Many of the priests, particularly those new to the field, spoke little of the language and understood even less.

When he was ready and had the inked quill poised over the page, he began. "Please speak slowly, so that I might write down your answer," he instructed.

"How would I ask a Mocaman 'Have you said that no one should open the storehouse until a shaman has prayed'?" he asked.

The boy translated the question and the Acueran answered, pausing after each word so that the priest could record what was said accurately. Pareja asked the question a second time and listened carefully, comparing what he heard with what was now written on the page.

Father Pareja then spoke the words in the Mocaman tongue. Marehootie smiled, nodded and said something in his own dialect.

"What was that?" Pareja asked, looking up from his work.

"He said that you hurt his ears, but that he will make an Indian of you yet," the boy said, smiling.

The Priest chuckled and went back to his work.

"How would I ask an Utinan 'Have you believed that a Shaman's prayers and superstitions will cure a person who is dying'?"

Marehootie repeated the question in Utinan. Then he spoke again.

"I have seen Christians pray over their food and over those who are sick, also."

The priest looked up again. He placed the quill into the ink well and removed his glasses. He pulled a kerchief from his pocket, rubbed his eyes and replaced his glasses, looking at the Indian.

"Ah! but there is an important difference," Pareja answered. "Christians invoke the names of The Father and The Son in their blessings. Heathens speak the words the devil puts in their mouths."

"We never knew that devils existed until you Spanish came to our land," Marehootie said.

Father Pareja paused before answering. "Without the word of God to enlighten you, it is not surprising you were blind to Satan's influence."

The priest went on to ask about common superstitions, such as the belief that the call of an owl was an omen of danger, that the first fish caught in a new trap should be released or no others would come, and that whistling in a canoe would calm bad waters.

Pareja asked the words that should be put to a chief to determine whether he was serving as a good Christian influence on his subjects. "How would you say to a Mocaman chief 'Have you taken the daily wages of those who work for you?', and 'Have you arranged for someone to be married in the traditional way without first notifying the Friar'?"

"How would I say, 'Do you believe it is a sin to kill?', and 'Do you believe it is a sin to lay with another man's wife?' and 'Would it be a sin to steal another man's coat'?"

As time went on, the Acueran answered before the question has been interpreted into Utinan by the boy. The priest sometimes used Mocaman words and phrases in asking his questions. By the end of the day, their fifth day together, the Indian and the priest, both adept at languages, communicated well with little help from de Coya.

* * *

After Pareja had gone to the convento to rest before evening vespers, the boy remained. Marehootie prepared to sleep.

"Can you tell me why the priest thinks it strange that we do not kill all the fish, but allow some to live?" Marehootie asked.

"I do not know," de Coya answered.

"Or why we whistle when we are in rough water, or whenever we might be nervous or afraid?"

The boy shook his head.

"The priest tells us not to kill, or steal, or lie, which we don't do very often, yet the Spanish do all of these things. These Ten Commandments he speaks of, they only apply to us," the Acueran said.

"The soldiers, being Catholic, can go to Father Pareja and confess their sins," the boy explained.

"The next time I have to kill someone, perhaps Father Pareja can listen to me and forgive me of my sin," the old man said, pulling the thin blanket up to his neck, and rolling onto his side.

CHAPTER 17

"On the morning after we learned that my brother was not *Atichicolo-Iri,* the Chief of Acuera did not leave early as was his habit when he visited Ibitibi. He met with the village chiefs and with his *inija* and tribal *jarva* in the council house.

They had not been meeting long when I was summoned to join them. You can imagine how my knees shook standing before all these chiefs, not knowing if I had done something wrong. *Inija* must have sensed my fears and he assured me that I was not in trouble. In fact, he said, my help was needed.

He said that Crying Bird's return and reformation was such a wondrous event it should be celebrated. He said that the chiefs had discussed what had been said the night before, and feared they had shown disrespect toward Blind Jarva. They wanted to publicly honor him along with my brother."

* * *

Marehootie paused in the story and stretched out his leg and massaged the calf.

"It will rain soon, and I fear it will be a bad storm. This broken leg of mine always tells me. Perhaps it wants to make sure I find cover and not get wet," he said.

"Juan de Coya, do you know the word *Tacachale*?" he asked.

"I have heard it before. I believe Utina has that word but I do not know what it means."

140

"'*Taca*' is fire, or flame. '*Chale*' is to purify. So it is the Acueran word that means the flame that cleanses or purifies. Now that you understand, we can go on.

Inija of Acuera asked me if I knew of the *Tacachale* ceremony, of the chants and prayers, the potions and herbs to be thrown in the fire, and of the order of the ceremony. I confessed that I did not, and that of all the lessons I had learned from the first *isucu* there was no mention of this observance or any other.

Inija said that the ranking jarva usually was in charge of *Tacachale*, but since this one would honor Blind Jarva it was not proper that he do all the work.

The *jarva* of Acuera assured me that he would train me in the ceremony. I was to visit him in Acuera and he would provide me with what I would need. He said there is no more sacred ceremony among the Acuera which is why it is so seldom observed.

But, he said, the elders of the tribe had attended *Tacachale* in years past, and if mistakes were made they would speak up and I and my family would be shamed. My knees began to shake even more violently than before."

* * *

"The council house in Acuera is much larger than the one in Ibitibi. There was room for five hundred people or more for dances.

It is arranged in the usual way, with a raised platform for chiefly people and slightly lower enclosed benches, or cabins, to each side for village leaders. Around the inside wall are benches for the common people, and even a second half circle of benches inside that circle, closer to the fire. For dances the inside benches are removed to make more room.

I was at Acuera for three days meeting with the *jarva*. I thought it was a great honor that he housed me in the council house. On the second night when I returned to my bed there was a trader lying asleep on my pallet and I had to find another bench and rest my head on my arm.

141

These river traders are a rough people. I don't know why Acuera allows them to sleep in the council house along with honored guests such as myself.

The lessons given to me were very hard. On the second day I kept forgetting my answers as *Jarva* went over what I needed to know. The chants were simple ones but there were three different chants. I sometimes forgot the words. *Jarva* was very patient with me, but he must have thought I was stupid."

De Coya interrupted. "I feel the same way, some times. Father Pareja wants us to learn the catechism. Before we can remember it all he wants us to recite the 'Our Fathers,' then the Ten Commandments. It never stops. Sometimes I want to give up when I really feel dumb, and maybe go back home."

Marehootie looked at de Coya before he answered. "I believe you are a very smart boy. You will know what you need to do and say when it is time."

"The third day he taught me the dance steps to teach the women. That was easy and I understood the first time and did not forget. He repeated the order of the ceremony and we went through it step by step until I knew it like I know my own name.

He gave me the potions to throw into the fire, and we practiced at the council house. I was amazed and delighted how the flames would jump and change color, reds, blues, yellows depending on which potion I used. He gave me his costume to wear, the mask with hawk feathers and the vest with copper adornments. For the first time, I really became excited.

Then, just before I was to go back to Ibitibi he asked me to sing the chants. I was the same stupid Marehootie. I still could not get it right. *Jarva* said he would be at the ceremony but that he could not do my job for me. When I got home I thought maybe I might die and not have to embarrass my family.

There was no time to worry, so I just gave up worrying and went to work. Chief Ibitibi ordered the entire village to cooperate with me. By the time I got to Ibitibi I already knew who I wanted for the ceremony. I needed five people for the ceremony and twelve women to dance. We also needed help in decorating the council house, and arranging the benches so there would be room.

Niho had women working with her to make the costumes.

I was very busy, and we had only a few days to get ready. Some people complained that I was not polite to them in telling them what to do. Crying Bird was no help. He laughed at me and called me 'Boss man' and 'Nervous Old Woman.' I thought he was ungrateful because I was doing this all for him.

I did not sleep the night before *Tacachale*, although everything was in readiness. Everyone knew his part and when he would be expected to perform. The dancers all knew their steps. I was less sure of the chanter. I had elders advising me, people who had seen the ceremony before. I hoped that they would feel responsible for any mistakes I made, and might not criticize me.

Some of the chiefs from the farthest villages came the day before. Acuera arrived in the middle of the day, with all of the tribal leaders. I have never seen so many beautiful match coats and tattoos. Each tribal leader had his hair pinned on top and decorated with animal skins and ocean shells and flowers. Seeing them all I realized how important *Tacachale* was to the Acuera.

The men worked hard to prepare a proper feast. Four arrobas of maize had been secured from the storehouse at Acuera. Our chief gave his consent because he believed this ceremony was a celebration for all of Acuera, and not just the village of Ibitibi. Bread was cooked and gaucha baked for the chiefs.

My Uncle Apoholo took a party down river and killed a manatee in the early morning. Before it was time to eat, the pleasant smell of the roasting meat made everyone hungry. The men took their meal at the council house. The women and children, of course, ate at home. I carried some of the manatee and porridge to Niho and Amita. Other men took food to their families and no one complained.

The *jarva* of Acuera did not talk to me or come near me. Perhaps he did not want to be blamed for my failure. The ceremony began as the sun set and did not finish until the sun reappeared.

It was like a dream to me. Every one knew his part. Even the chanter made no mistakes. At the end I threw much more

143

fire potion than was necessary. The 'whoosh' from the fire almost knocked me down. It was a wonderful *Tacachale*, better than anyone could remember. Crying Bird and Blind Jarva received much praise and recognition during the ceremony.

* * *

Blind Jarva was also greatly honored at his burial. He died five days after *Tacachale*. It was as if *Tacachale* had satisfied him with his life and had cleansed him for his journey into the world of spirit.

He was of the Fish Clan, and he rested in their charnel house for thirty days and nights. The women of his clan mourned every day and night. Their cries and shrieks were painful to hear. The men of all clans had long faces, but they did not cry for to do so would be un-manly and an insult to Blind Jarva. The men of Fish Clan cut themselves with shells and sharp sticks and bled. Those who loved him the most cut off their hair.

When his body was wasted his bones were cleaned and dried and put in a satchel, which was carried on the backs of his relatives for seven more days. He was buried in the clan mound a short distance from Ibitibi, along with his drinking cup and other property known only to members of his clan. His attention stick would be given as a badge of office to the next *jarva* of Ibitibi.

In the days that followed there was talk among the elders of who would become the next *jarva* of Ibitibi. Acuera himself had said that Crying Bird might be considered. Some elders said that it was not the place of the Chief of Acuera to be telling Ibitibi who it should choose for such an important position. Some thought he was just being polite to Crying Bird because the council did not believe that he was *Atichicolo-Iri*, as Blind Jarva had said.

I heard Alobo tell some of the old men that because some of Crying Bird's visions were not to be believed, he would be a poor *jarva*.

I did not care if my brother became *jarva*. It would be an honor if both of us sat at council, but Crying Bird did not seem

144

to be interested. No one else mentioned it, but I wondered what kind of sorcerer he would be when the tattoos on his right arm indicated he was a warrior chief.

Because there was no agreement among the elders on who would be village *jarva,* or whether we even needed one, Chief Ibitibi did not call for a council. He did not enjoy disagreement, as Chief Acuera did, and avoided it whenever he could. If Chief Acuera insisted we have a *jarva*, Chief Ibitibi would deal with the problem then. Perhaps he wanted to save Crying Bird the embarrassment of being rejected once more.

For awhile things were quiet in the village. Since Crying Bird returned we had had tribal council, a *Tacachale* ceremony, the death of our beloved *jarva* and controversy on who would replace him. It was a relief for me to get back to being an herbalist.

Crying Bird worked again with Chief Ibitibi at his woodworking. Traders would come with exotic woods from far away, such as elm and cedar and bay, and Ibitibi was always a willing buyer. In turn, he would trade the clan effigies he and Crying Bird had fashioned.

Using heart of pine, Crying Bird carved clan symbols taller than a man stood. These made excellent support poles for charnel houses. Trade was brisk and profitable. Before he could finish a set of four poles, a trader would be there waiting for delivery.

Sometimes Crying Bird would have visions and strange dreams, and would talk about what he had seen. He was not embarrassed that many people did not believe him. Some rude people would call him '*yaba*', or what you might say 'wizard' behind his back.

Because he was bigger and stronger than the rest, they would not call him '*yaba*' to his face, but he had a gentle nature. I was more sensitive and told one young man that he should be kinder to my brother.

* * *

Things changed the day Crying Bird walked into an ordinary council meeting and asked Chief Ibitibi for permission to speak.

He told of a vision he had that day while sitting near the river carving on an effigy. He said he looked down river toward the land of the Utinans, and saw a large canoe of bearded men that stopped in village after village where the men were peacefully greeted by the people.

At each village one of the bearded men would give gifts to the villagers, and in turn they would allow him to paint pictures of them. He would continue with his painting until he had the likeness of everyone in the village, and the people were happy to receive his gifts of beads and bells of copper. Then the bearded men would waive good-bye and move on to the next village.

It was a curious story, and everyone listened. Some were amused.

Then Crying Bird said that when the bearded ones left, those who had their likenesses painted no longer had faces. The people could not recognize even their own child, or parent or wife. When they looked into the river there was no reflection. It was as if they had never been, or that they were already dead and in the Spirit world.

Some of the council members were disturbed by the vision, while others said that Crying Bird had an active imagination and should not be taken seriously. Alobo told Crying Bird to leave the council house, but Crying Bird stayed where he was.

When Alobo took him by the arm to remove him, Crying Bird said 'Take your hand off of me.'

When Alobo tried to use his strength, Crying Bird shoved him roughly with his right arm, knocking Alobo onto his butt. It was the first time anyone had seen Crying Bird's strength. I was very proud of my brother.

Chief Ibitibi ordered Alobo to keep his hands off of Crying Bird. He thanked my brother for sharing his vision, and told him that it would be discussed by the council. Crying Bird left the house, and spent the night on the other side of the river where he had once communed with Blind Jarva.

146

The village council could not reach agreement on what to make of Crying Bird's story, and soon ended the meeting.

Crying Bird did not return to Ibitibi the next day, but we could see him when he stood and walked around. He appeared to be praying and talking to the Spirits. That night I prepared food for him, and would have taken it to him. My uncle Apoholo said that Crying Bird needed to remain alone.

After it became dark everyone in the village could hear the calls of many crying birds across the river, and we talked among ourselves about what this might mean.

Soon after the sun came up many of us were gathered at the river watching Crying Bird. He was not in a hurry to come home.

A trader's canoe was seen coming from the north, piled high with arrobas of trade goods. The children were excited. The traders always brought treats for the children, berries or nuts from far away.

I was walking back to the village when the trader called out my name. It was my friend, the first *isucu*. I hurried back to greet him. He was always a good customer for our yaupon leaves, and he usually had an assortment of medicinal plants that did not grow near Ibitibi.

His usual smile was not to be found when he stepped out of the canoe. He ignored the children and took me by the arm and walked quickly toward the village. He was tired and upset. 'I have traveled two days and nights without stopping. I must speak to Chief Ibitibi immediately,' he said.

Our Chief was at his woodworking, and still had a cutting tool in his hand and a broad smile to greet *Isucu*. The children had followed along begging, and many of the men and women had gathered to hear the news.

After they embraced, *Isucu* spoke. 'I have come from the land of the Utina and did not stop for two days. The Utinans have invited the enemy into their villages. I saw men with metal hats and beards on their faces.' He stopped to catch his breath.

'Another trader told me that these people are called the French. They came from the ocean, but now they are among us. They are welcomed by the Utinans as friends.'

'Why would Chief Outina allow these people to live? They endanger us all,' Ibitibi said.

'I am told the French do Outina's bidding and have attacked his enemy, Potano.'

'But to welcome them into their village . . .'

'They flatter Outina, and bear trinkets and small gifts for the people,' *Isucu* said. 'They have with them an artisan who paints pictures of the people.'

Chief Ibitibi ordered me to cross the river and fetch my brother."

* * *

"Do you understand the importance of what I just said, that my brother's vision had been proved true by the news *Isucu* brought from up-river?" Marehootie asked his young listener.

The boy paused before answering. "Was it that Crying Bird had great powers, that he was a Shaman?"

"You are partly right, but I want you to think about your answer until tomorrow. There is more you should understand by now. I don't want to go on with my story until you have had time to reflect on what has been said."

De Coya stood and prepared to return to the convento. "I will not be here tomorrow, or the next. I will come with fresh water every day but my duties with Father Pareja will keep me busy until after Easter."

De Coya looked down at his feet. "Did I tell you that Father Pareja has chosen me to carry the cross during the Holy Thursday procession?"

"That must be a great burden for one so small."

"It is a small cross to bear, and made of light wood. We will be rehearsing tomorrow and the next day. There will be singers and musicians. There will be dancers, also. Father Pareja says that there will be three hundred people watching. It all depends on me. There are fourteen different places I will need to stop along the way, and at each the priest will read scripture."

"And if you do not stop where you are supposed to, the musicians can not play, the singers sing, the dancers dance or the holy man speak. As I said before, it will be a large burden for one so small," Marehootie said.

"Like you and *Tacachale*."

"Like me and *Tacachale*," Marehootie agreed. "I would like to be there and see you in your time of glory," he added.

CHAPTER 18

"What is your name?" the sergeant demanded.

An oil lamp burned dimly, emitting a thin black plume of smoke and casting ugly shadows over the bearded face of the interrogator.

The Acueran had been shaken awake in the middle of the night and dragged from his prison to Suarez' apartment. His hands were trussed behind him and two military guards stood behind him, to either side.

An Indian interpreter stood next to him and repeated the question in the Mocaman dialect.

"I have many names. The first one was given to me by my mother on the day of my birth. When I was twelve summers, my *holata* gave me my adult name by which I am known in my village. I am called *isucu*, just as you are called sergeant. Those are not really names, but are more like titles, wouldn't you say? You may call me Marehootie, if it pleases you."

The interpreter struggled to keep up, paused and started over again. Suarez wrote as quickly as he could on the parchment before him, scratched out the first words, then placed the quill back into its holder and listened to the last words of the interpreter.

"It pleases me to call you 'Insolent Indian.' It seems to fit you," he said.

"'Insolent Indian.' I like it. It has a good sound. Then I shall call you 'Spanish puerco.' It fits, also," Marehootie answered, smiling.

The interpreter had not finished when the sergeant nodded to the guard. The blow was unexpected, and caught the

Acueran in the temple. His knees buckled, and he was on the floor. Before he could rise, a soldier's boot kicked him in the low back.

"Do not bruise him," Suarez instructed. "You may teach him good manners, but try not to get his blood on my desk."

The Acueran was dragged to his feet, and then struck in the stomach by a club. When he straightened up, a soldier stepped in front and lifted his knee into the old man's crotch.

He was standing again, held erect by the guards.

"As you can see, we know how to deal with insolent Indians. We will speak again, perhaps at a more convenient time when you will be happy to answer my questions," Suarez said.

The Indian, who was to interpret, held back and said nothing. "Tell him what I said," Suarez commanded.

When the words were spoken in Mocaman, Marehootie spoke. "And we know how to deal with Spanish pigs," he said.

Suarez listened to the interpreter's words. The old man hawked deeply into his throat. The sergeant glanced back at the Acueran just as the wad of spittle struck him on the forehead.

* * *

Much later Marehootie awoke in his cell. His ribs and back ached from the beating he had taken. He had no memory of what occurred after he spit on Suarez. He smiled as he remembered the look of surprise on the sergeant's face, his eyes crossed as the phlegm dripped down his nose.

The boy had been there while he slept and had left fresh spring water. The old man felt with his hand under his pallet and withdrew his medicine bag. The rest of the day he moved slowly about his cell, preparing and administering cures for his aches and pains.

The effects of the medicines were such that his pains left him. He felt warm and comforted. He had pleasant visions and he was visited from time to time by the spirits of his ancestors.

As evening came he could hear the chorus rehearsing in the council house. The familiar Catholic music wafted from the village and through the mission grounds.

As it was his habit before sleeping, his fingers felt for the necklace of freshwater pearls that was his rosary. The pearls were gone.

* * *

Thursday morning broke clear and cold. A northeast breeze excited the seabirds. Terns and gulls dived for forage, then swept away upward from the water. Sandpipers chased receding waves, searching for treasure, and then scampered to safety before the next surge engulfed them. Single file formations of twenty or more stately pelicans flew to the south, passing others of their kind headed northbound.

From the mainland villages of Molo and San Mateo, Potaya and Chinysca the freshly scrubbed but poorly dressed faithful moved to the east where canoes awaited to carry them to the island Mission of San Juan del Puerto.

Clan members moved as a group to the tune of laughter and singing. The island villages of Alicamany and Hicachirico played host to relatives, and some of the travelers who came early stayed the night in the council house at Carabay.

Father Pareja was worried that there was not enough food laid by to feed the multitude at the evening meal and went in search of the head cook. Perhaps she could convince the chief to contribute ten arrobas of maize from the granary.

"There will be three hundred mouths to feed," he shouted over the laughter and chanting of the cooks, helpers and children in the busy church yard. Already three large pots of corn chowder, fish and venison stew bubbled on the fires, scenting the air and teasing the noses of anyone nearby. Breads and cakes of corn and hickory baked in the oven and in the coals of the fires.

"Loaves and fishes, Father," she said expansively, waving her arms about, "Loaves and fishes! And when that's all gone, God will pour down manna from Heaven," she exclaimed.

Chastised by one with more faith than he, Father Pareja laughed and wandered off to inspect the staging ground for the procession which would begin at mid-day.

Juan de Coya had been in his place near the end of the procession line for a full hour when Pareja approached. The boy had the arm of the wooden cross strapped to his right shoulder, and had practiced dragging it about. He wore a crown of thorns, with the points carefully removed the night before.

Once again the priest talked to the boy about the route of the procession, from the church yard into the village of Carabay, around the north side of the council house, and then into the village square. He reminded him of each spot where he should pause for the singing, dancing and scripture reading that would take place.

"And you must display the dignity of our beloved Savior. This is a very solemn event," he said.

The procession began slowly. A line of singers and musicians led the way, followed by a troop of dancers. Twelve men, the Disciples, were dressed only in loin cloths and flagellated themselves with whips of palmetto fiber, drawing blood. They were followed by Jesus. The priest, barefooted and bareheaded, dressed in his simple brown robe and carrying his breviary, walked behind. At his side Father Marron walked solemnly, his head bowed.

The crowd lining the route was boisterous, with cat-calls and funny insults to hurl at their friends, the musicians and dancers. Only low murmurs greeted the disciples. When the boy came into view the crowd became quiet except for an occasional sob or cry from the women.

At each station of the cross, the boy paused and stood quietly while Pareja spoke. When the priest nodded, the procession moved on.

A small barking dog followed de Coya, attracted to the cross dragging in the dirt kicking up dust. When the boy stopped in the square, the dog approached and would have urinated on the cross if de Coya had not suddenly kicked out, sending the dog home with a yelp.

Laughter echoed through the square with shouts of approval from the young men. Juan smiled and acknowledged them with a wave of his free arm, then made his face solemn once again.

Father Pareja took his place. He gave the boy an approving look, and then faced the crowd to read the final scripture and deliver his message. Father Marron intoned the benediction.

Juan cut his eyes about, looking for familiar faces in the crowd. Two tall men stood under a hickory tree talking. One was thin, with his hair worn around his shoulders. He leaned against the tree for support. The boy did not recognize the other man, whose hair was pinned up, and decorated with sea shells in the manner of a Mocaman chief.

CHAPTER 19

"You asked me if I understood the importance of Crying Bird's vision of the French coming up the river. I said that he must be a great Shaman, but you said there was more to it," de Coya said.

"So I did. There is more to it, as you say, but I have been thinking that if my own people were blind to the truth I should not expect more from a young boy who was not even there," the Acueran answered. "Perhaps it will come to you when you learn more. Listen carefully to the rest of the story."

The old man moved slowly to his pallet, and lay down. "My back complains to me if I sit too long. I have much to tell you today, but I need to rest at the same time. Where did I stop? Ah, yes, it was about the journey to Mayaca."

* * *

"There are many ways to enter the land of Mayaca. If you are in a hurry you can reach the villages of Mayacoya or Mayaguaca by way of the river and then travel a short distance over land to either village. The *paracusi* of Acuera had another route. He suggested we travel over land and enter the great swamp, traveling east. That approach would have the element of surprise. Mayaca would not expect that strangers would approach from the swamp.

We were not in a hurry to reach Mayaca, and we certainly did not want to sneak up and startle them. Ours was a peaceful mission. We chose the well-traveled trails beyond our camp on the Wekiva, the same trails where *Isucu* and I discovered the Mayacan arrows years before.

Chief Acuera was clear in his instructions. Crying Bird and I would visit Mayaca, Potano, Yustaga and other tribes to the west, north and east of the River of the Sun. We were to warn of the coming of the French, and of their murderous alliance with Chief Outina.

We were to form alliances and to resolve minor disputes that divided us from neighboring tribes. Our message was that the French must be expelled from all of Cautio, that everyone must fight them, and that Outina should be punished along with the French.

The Acueran council had argued for a day on how this might be accomplished, and whether Crying Bird should be given the power to bind the people with treaties. Chief Acuera resolved the issue when he named Crying Bird his special *inija*. Crying Bird was the chief's nephew and in the line of succession, and it was quite proper under Acueran customs, he said.

There were older cousins who were closer to Acuera in the line of succession, but they remained quiet. They knew that these were serious times. They were also cowered by Crying Bird's powers. The council was not called upon to reconsider whether he was *Atichicolo-Iri*.

To signify his authority, Acuera ordered that Crying Bird be tattooed on his right hand with the chiefly design of red and black. The tattoo took three days to complete. On the first day the skin was punctured and the ashes rubbed into the wound. I applied a poultice and after the swelling went down the skin was again cut and juice of the berry was applied. The resulting marking was very beautiful to see.

I was to accompany Crying Bird. I have always been good at languages, as you know. All my life I have talked to traders in their native tongues. Just as Crying Bird was blessed with his visions, I was blessed with an ear for words.

Chief Acuera also said that I was to bear the burdens of our travel. It would not be seemly for the chief's *inija* to be seen carrying burdens. I had a strong back, and because of my nature it was expected that I do hard work.

156

Later I told my brother it would be an honor to carry the dung of such a distinguished and powerful person. He laughed and punched me in the ribs knocking the wind out of me. I did not laugh when I hoisted the burden on my back. Chief Acuera had many gifts of great value and even greater weight for the chiefs we would meet on our journey.

We were at the Wekiva in two days. The Mayaca were not there and had not been there in the winter. Our people would be there soon, as it was in the springtime.

I especially wanted to take this route. Crying Bird had not returned to the Wekiva since his birth, and I wanted him to experience its peace and serenity before the difficulties that lay ahead. It was as changeless and beautiful as always. After we had our meal of corn cakes and drank the spring water there was time for a walk before sleeping.

We had not gone far from camp. I was showing Crying Bird red and pink wildflowers that grow in that season, and explaining their uses. I was proud of my knowledge. It would make our travels less painful and would even save our lives. Crying Bird asked me to follow him, and he moved off through a glade that gave way to a hammock of hickory and sweet-gum.

He stood in one place for a long time, looking about, and then he turned and faced me.

'This is where the crying bird came to me,' he said.

* * *

We lay awake and talked of many things. My thoughts raced from one doubt, one fear, to another, and back again to something else. I had no idea how we could walk into the enemy's camp and walk out again with our scalps. What if my mind froze over like a creek in winter, and I was unable to understand another tongue, let alone a different language? I recalled the difficulty I had remembering the *tacachale* chants and how that haunted me.

'You will know what you need to do and say when it is time,' my brother said as he drifted away into sleep.

We found the well-marked Mayacan trail and set out on our first long walk. The canoe journey, even against the current, was easier than walking with my burdens. Most of the time the trail was flat and level. Some places, particularly near creeks or ravines , or where we had to duck under low hanging limbs or cross streams it was more difficult.

Crying Bird walked fast, as I usually do when my leg is not hurting. At times I had to hurry just to keep him in sight.

When the sun was straight up we stopped beside a stream. I went to relieve myself and when I returned Crying Bird had divided my burden and had placed part on his own shoulders. I reminded him about what Acuera had said. 'We won't see anyone we want to impress today,' he said.

We camped in a hickory grove and did not build a fire.

In the morning we set off again. We had attached to our clothing shells and dried bones that rattled and announced our coming. We talked loudly and sang songs and chants we could remember from the time we were children.

After we had traveled a long distance we rested under a hickory tree. Crying Bird put the entire burden on my back and we set off again. I could tell that the trail was rising. The hickory and sweet-gum gave way to live oak trees and stands of long-needle pine, and the ground was sandy instead of mucky.

I was telling Crying Bird a funny story, when he raised his hand for silence.

'Keep walking and talking. We are being watched,' he said.

I was about to say something about his active imagination when I was struck in the back by an arrow shot at close range. The ground came up to kiss my face.

The Mayacan who had shot me was nervous. He danced around with another arrow at the ready, not sure whether he should shoot Crying Bird, also.

My brother kneeled beside me and pulled the arrow out of my pack. It was stuck in the effigy of a bear, and had split it from top to bottom. Crying Bird looked at the Mayacan and said firmly 'This was a gift from my chief to Mayaca, and now you have ruined it.'

The young brave continued to dance around, telling us in Mayacan that we were his prisoners and we had better watch what we do if we want to live.

Crying Bird asked me to tell the boy about the chief's gift.

I spit Mayacan sand out of my mouth and repeated Crying Bird's complaint. It did not occur to me that I was speaking Mayacan, but the warrior understood my words. He dropped his bow and took the wooden bear from my brother's hands, as if he could fix it.

Before long we were on our way again. The Mayacan had dislodged the arrow and was studying the bear. Crying Bird walked ahead, carrying the boy's bow. Before we got to the village I told the boy that we could find a more suitable gift for his chief, and placed the bear back in the pack.

Crying Bird handed him his bow, and motioned that he walk behind.

'Now we will be your prisoners,' he said. I translated perfectly.

Mayacoya was a pitiful village. It was no larger than Ibitibi, and not nearly as clean. The people's waste area where they dumped their *asrupa* was close to the hut in which we were held. The smell was unpleasant. Perhaps they intended that we not be comfortable. The hut was also full of fleas as if animals had been kept there.

We met no one important for two days and were kept in the hut. I could hear our guards talking among themselves and was able to understand much of what they said. I learned that Chief Mayaca was away at another village, and that a messenger had been sent to find him, reporting the capture of two Acueran spies.

We were fed a rancid stew of shellfish and root vegetables. The meat was not fresh and it was difficult not to vomit. The water tasted strange and had a bad odor.

On the second day we were taken out of the hut one at a time to walk around the village. The young boy who had captured us was now a hero, and showed off by pushing me around, roughly. Crying Bird told me that he had not been treated badly, and he took this as a sign that he was viewed as a chief or at least a principal man.

The *paracusi* of Acuera had asked that we report back to him what we saw in the villages of Mayaca. There were no more than two hundred people in Mayacoya, and many of them were women, children and old men. Unless the men were away hunting or fishing, I doubted that there were more than forty braves capable of fighting.

The village was built on a small hill and there was good visibility all around. A stream runs past to the south at the bottom of the hill, and beyond there is a marsh of reeds and cattails. I do not know if the marsh is fed by a river or large lake, since our approach to the village was from the opposite direction. There was no swamp. Perhaps the *paracusi* had been referring to Mayaguaca or one of the other Mayacan villages.

'Come out, immediately,' it was the voice of our captor. I crawled out of the low opening and was greeted by a blow to the side of my head. I remained on my knees, my ear ringing. Crying Bird followed me, but crouched as he went through the door and immediately stood. The young guard did not offer to strike him.

The guard was unarmed, as if he could handle both of us with his bare hands. There were other guards nearby with their arrows ready.

We were taken to the center of the village. There was a council house, much like the one in Ibitibi but without the decorations we Acuerans hang on the walls and from the ceiling. Crying Bird was allowed to enter on his own. I was shoved roughly.

I whispered to the guard 'If you push me again, I will show Chief Mayaca his bear.' From that time I was treated more gently.

Chief Mayaca was seated in the chiefly seat. He wore a tall head-dress of osprey feathers, without which he would be a man of ordinary height. He did not choose to speak to us directly, but spoke through his *inija* who stood beside him.

'Two spies of the Acuera, come to claim this village as their own, I believe, as they do all other lands of the Mayaca,' the *inija* said, speaking to the other officials. Crying Bird stepped forward and spoke directly to the *inija*.

160

'I am Chulufi-Yuchi of your brothers to the north, the people of Acuera. I am of the village of Ibitibi, and my mother's clan is White Deer. I am a prince, and in the line of succession of Chief Acuera.'

At this point, Crying Bird waited until I translated into Mayacan what he had said. *Inija* nodded, acknowledging he had understood my meaning.

'I come with greetings from my chief and with gifts and with good will. My mission is of great importance to the chiefdom of Mayaca, and to all chiefdoms throughout Cautio. My chief has ordered that of all the chiefs, great and small, that I speak first to his brother the great Chief of Mayaca.'

I continued to translate.

Crying Bird gave Chief Mayaca an eagle effigy that he had carved. It was one of his most beautiful. It had eyes of green carved from a shell. Mayaca inspected the gift and grunted his approval. Having received tribute, it was no longer important to be polite.

'How should we know that you are who you say?' *Inija* said.

'I bear the royal mark cut into my own flesh by the great Acuera,' Crying Bird said, holding out his right hand.

Crying Bird was gestured forward, where the *inija* and Mayaca studied the tattoo. When they were satisfied, he stepped back to stand beside me.

'I come with my brother, Marehootie, our chief's *isucu* and speaker of many tongues, whose talent is essential to the success of my mission.'

The Mayaca were well known for taking hostages to insure their own safety. Many were killed, and some kept as slaves. Crying Bird worried that they not consider me a gift between chiefs, and was protecting me with what he said. I worked hard in my translating to make his meaning clear and that they understand my importance.

Inija and Chief Mayaca spoke among themselves and I could hear every word. I asked myself if they might be so stupid that they did not know I understood what they were saying. Did they think that I could only speak Mayacan, and could not understand it when it was spoken? These people might be even dumber than we had thought. Then it occurred to me that maybe they did not care if I understood them. If we were not to leave the village alive, what did it matter what we heard?

Inija finally spoke. 'We welcome your gifts and good will. We would welcome a treaty that Acuera give back to Mayaca what is rightfully ours. The camp that we call Clear Creek, and which you mistakenly call Wekiva, has belonged to Mayaca from the first days. The fish and wildlife there have been destroyed by you greedy people, and there is little left of value for us to take for ourselves.'

'I have authority to discuss the use of the camp, once the main business is solved. Acuera respects Mayaca and would not keep that which in truth belongs to Mayaca,' Crying Bird replied.

'And even Ibitibi? Has your chief told you to give back the ancient Mayacan holy place?' the *inija* asked.

Crying Bird faced the *inija* directly. He was slow to speak. When he had calmed his own anger, he answered.

'I do not know all the history between our peoples. I can not speak for what others know or believe they know. For myself, until this day I never knew that Mayaca made any claim on Ibitibi. We are an ancient people, as you are. Which of us occupied land beyond memory and legend can not be known. I would say that there is no argument between friends that can not be settled through good will.'

Inija spoke. 'Beyond the short memory of the Acuera, perhaps, but we of Mayaca have not forgotten. Our homeland stretches from the big lake. It was bequeathed to us by the Spirit. Most of what you claim as your own is ours, and we will have it back.'

The *inija* of Mayaca spat on the ground. There were guards around us now, and they shoved and pushed us from the council house. Outside, in the bright sunlight of a spring day, the people of Mayaca gathered. Men scowled and women made high-pitched derisive calls. Small children threw sticks. We were taken to our hut.

When it was dark I told Crying Bird that we should try to escape. If we could reach the marsh we might be able to elude them. I told Crying Bird that I thought they intended to kill us in the morning.

'Don't be an old woman!' my brother said, and rolled over on his flee-bitten mat. In a short time he was asleep. I lay awake saying my prayers. I heard their whispers when they came for us.

The village was asleep all around us. We were taken again to the council house. Chief Mayaca was there, and his *inija*, and no one else. Our guards were told by the *inija* to stay outside the door and not listen.

Mayaca spoke directly to us. 'We know why you have come to Mayaca. It is not to make gifts, and it is not to heal old wounds.'

I interpreted what he had said, and waited for Crying Bird's reply.

'The Chief of Mayaca is wise,' is all he said.

'You must know that the same traders who sell you their worthless goods visit Mayaca. They deal in more information than deer hides. Some of their words are worthless, some are true. You have come to Mayaca because you believe the stories of the coming of the people called the French,' Chief Mayaca said.

'We do believe it is true. We have heard that the Utinans used the French to attack Potano, and that the French have the same terrible weapons the Spanish used to murder Acuerans, Potanans and Yuferans years ago,' my brother said.

Inija whispered in Mayaca's ear. 'What do you ask of your new friends, the Mayaca?' the chief asked.

'To join with us and the other tribes in ridding Cautio of the French curse, and in punishing Outina,' Crying Bird said.

'What other tribes are with you?'

'None yet, but we believe there will be many when my journey is done.'

'Let me ask one more question. Are you the *Yaba of Acuera* who had visions of the French even before they appeared?'

'I am,' my brother said.

'Ah, perhaps the traders are reliable people, after all,' he said, smiling. Then he became more serious. The only torch flickered across his dark eyes.

'You may tell your chief that when the time comes, Mayaca will stand with Acuera against the French and Olate Quai Outina. When it is time to redeem our land, we will fight whoever occupies it."

* * *

Marehootie asked for water, and the boy dipped the drinking gourd into the bucket. The old man struggled to rise, but could only prop himself up on an elbow. De Coya supported the back of the Acuerans head so that he could drink.

"You are hurt. I have watched the way you move today, and you are in pain," he said after he had helped the Acueran lay down once more.

"It is only because I am old. You will be old too, some day," he said. "Perhaps I should rest now. Come back when you can."

CHAPTER 20

"Chief Mayaca and his *inija* made suggestions for our journey. Long before sun-up we put Mayacoya behind us, with the young man who had captured us as our guide. We traveled to the west until we came to the River of the Sun. We had never seen this part of the river since it was south of the land of Acuera. The river was narrower here, and more shallow.

A canoe had been hidden under palmetto branches, and we were soon paddling against the gentle current. We were on the river for a short distance. Our guide pointed us to the southeast, and left us on the river bank as he returned to Mayacoya.

Chief Mayaca had insisted that we spread the news of the coming of the French to his allies, the Ais. He said that he had sent a messenger to Chief Oathaqua to expect us, to listen to what we said and to treat us as guests. I wondered if the Ais would be as gracious as the Mayaca.

The Ais occupy the land between the headwaters of the river and the ocean to the east. The trail was well-worn and easy to follow. The sun was high overhead when we reached the first small village, and we were met there by another man who by his gestures indicated that we should follow.

I tried to talk to him, to learn the language. He spoke differently than the Mayaca, and the tongue was hard for me to understand.

We walked a great distance and then canoed across another river. We soon came to a much larger village, one set high on a mound of sand and shell. There were no crops at all growing outside the village, and no forests or swamps. We did see large areas of marsh along the river.

Inside the village long fish nets woven of palmetto fiber hung on posts, drying in the sun. We had used similar nets, but much smaller, at the Wekiva. We also saw spears with points fashioned of fish bones, and long fiber ropes at the other end. It seemed that these people existed on what the river and ocean provided them.

In the center of the village an old man was tied to a post and was being whipped. Many of the old men and women bore whip marks on their backs and on their legs.

We were taken to a large council house, better than the one in Mayacoya. Inside, the chief and his principal men were waiting for us. The chief's headdress was of shell and the feathers of sea-birds.

Oathaqua was a young man, even younger than Crying Bird. This is not unusual. Many chiefs are young men or women. What surprised us was that the council members were all young men of fighting age. I looked around the house and saw no one who was as old as me.

The chief spoke first, without conveying his thoughts to his *inija*, which is the custom in many tribes.

'My brother, the great chief of Mayaca, has sent word of your coming. You are welcome in the land of Ais,' he said.

'I bring you greetings of the great Chief of Acuera. He sends his best wishes to you and your people. I also bear gifts for you and for the other great chiefs of Cautio, for I am on a long journey of great importance to us all,' Crying Bird said.

He spoke slowly, pausing after each thought that I might translate. My skills with the Ais language were poor. I sometimes used Mayacan words if I did not know how the Ais would speak. The council members laughed among themselves at my poor efforts. I believe they understood my meaning and they were just being mean and impolite.

Crying Bird explained the reason for our visit. He spoke of the French and their alliance with Outina. He told of the battle in which many Potanans had been slaughtered. He talked of our new friends, the Mayacans, and how they had promised to join us in expelling the French and punishing Outina.

166

Oathaqua listened, but he was distracted when members of his council would speak out of turn and laugh out loud. They were not criticized or punished for their behavior.

At one time the chief spoke to his *inija* who hurried out of the council house. When he returned he had with him a small, bearded man who had his hands tied together and appeared to be a slave.

'Do you believe this man is the French?' Oathaqua asked.

'I do not know,' my brother answered.

'His name is Perchuco. He says that he is Spanish. His boat was sunk and he washed up on the shore. We let him live because he is entertaining. Would you like to hear him sing?'

Without waiting for an answer, Oathaqua made a command to the slave who began to sing and dance. He was quite funny, and we all laughed at him. Oathaqua clapped his hands and the slave stopped immediately and sat on the dirt floor with his head down.

'Perchuco tells us the French are devils, even worse than his own people. He says that they should all die for invading our peaceful land without being invited,' Oathaqua said.

Oathaqua was speaking more slowly now and this made it easier for me to interpret what he said.

'I would agree with what the slave Perchuco has said, but I do not believe he means to say that his own people should be killed,' Crying Bird answered.

Oathaqua felt what my brother had said was funny, and he laughed out loud, along with the others. 'I don't care what he means. He is my slave and he will say what is expected of him.'

'Would you like to have the slave for your journey? He has a strong back and he is very obedient. He is afraid to run away. When you are done with him you can trade him or kill him.'

'The gift of a slave is more than we could re-pay. We have only a small token gift of a wood carving, which comes with the best wishes of the chief of the Acuera,' Crying Bird said, handing the effigy to the *inija* who handed it to the chief.

'Fine work. Very beautiful,' Oathaqua said. 'Who carved this?'

167

'It is my work, done under the guidance of my uncle, the chief of Ibitibi.'

Oathaqua fixed my brother with a hard gaze, as if he had been lied to. His look was returned with a pleasant one from Crying Bird.

'Then the trade is made. We have many slaves. I have two more right now, and they are always crashing their boats. The Surruque have slaves. So do the Tequesta. The Calusa have so many they can afford to eat some and still have slaves for work and entertainment,' he said.

All of his council laughed again. These people certainly have a good humor about them.

'The women are the best. They make willing and enthusiastic concubines,' Oathaqua said.

'You may tell my brother, Mayaca, that we will join in the fight against the Utinans. They are a murderous people. As for the French, we have never seen them. Apparently their ships do not come our way. If they do, we will kill them here, or take them as slaves.'

The chief ordered the slave whipped to remind him to be obedient.

* * *

We set out the next morning. Our guide took us as far as the River of the Sun. The slave was quite strong, and could carry our burdens. His legs were short, however, and he had to trot beside us to keep up. I asked him to speak with me in the language of the Ais, and he talked a lot.

I asked him about what we had seen in the village, about the whipping of the old people. He said that they were no better than slaves and that the Ais respected only those who were young and strong. This was very strange. I had never known a people that did not respect and honor those made wise by age.

He told me he had been a slave to the Surruque before being traded to Oathaqua. 'The Surruque are much nicer people, he said. 'They only beat me when I deserved it, or when I was thinking about running away.'

* * *

In the days that followed we passed through many small villages, stopping only for food and rest. At Urriparacoxi, where our father had been born, the village was almost deserted. We spoke to two old men guarding a field of crops against crows and rabbits.

There were no young children in sight, and we asked them where the children were. They said that there had been so much illness since the Spanish invaded years before, and so many deaths among the young and old alike, there were few children born now. They spoke of other villages that no longer existed, where the people had all died or had simply moved away to live with relatives in more healthy places.

As we were walking away one of the men called to us, and motioned for us to hold up. He was crippled with age and hobbled as he walked. He wanted us to draw near and held his finger to his lips to show he wanted to speak quietly and not be overheard.

'Are you Acuerans?' he asked in a whisper.

When we said we were, he told us that several men who had the accent of the Utina had been looking for us the day before.

'How many were there?' Crying Bird asked.

The old man said he saw only two, but that one of them glanced into the woods from which they had come, as if there were more waiting out of sight.

'Which way did they go?' my brother asked.

'That is an interesting question. They made a big show of going south, but that is the direction from which they came. I kept my eyes open, and saw them circle around us down toward the river. They were going toward Ocale to the north.'

* * *

Crying Bird said we should slow our pace and be more cautious. Utinans are good stalkers and move quietly in the forests. They also know how to lie beside the trail to ambush the enemy.

169

Perchuco was delighted that we would move slower, and began to sing in his own tongue, and to whistle. My brother scolded him and told him to stay quiet if he did not want an Utinan arrow in his back.

The country was beautiful with rolling hills and open forests without small bushes to provide places for hiding. There were many tall pine trees and live oaks, whose lower branches swept out and sometimes touched the ground.

Crying Bird said that we should start sleeping in the oak trees, since they are so easy to climb. I told Crying Bird that I had broken my leg falling out of a tree. I did not say it had been his fault, and that I was looking for him when it happened. He would have felt responsible.

I could still climb a tree easily. Finding a comfortable limb to sleep on was difficult. I did not sleep well the first night, although the moss made a comfortable pillow for my head.

My brother chose the wrong tree. He had climbed quite high and had settled himself onto a wide limb, when he suddenly scampered down to the ground. He whispered that the tree was already occupied by a raccoon and her babies. He climbed the next tree which was unoccupied and settled in for the night.

Perchuco refused to climb a tree. We told him to make his bed away from our resting places, so that he would not attract the Utinans to us when they came to cut his throat. He said he would rather fight the Utinans than break his neck.

The second night we found other oak trees, but the forest was not clean. There were palmettos and other shrubs everywhere. Again, Perchuco chose to sleep on the ground a short distance away. I lay awake listening to wolves calling to each other, and to the pleasant sound of whip-poor-wills.

During the night I was awakened by the sound of an owl. There was only one call, which is a very bad omen. I could see Crying Bird in his tree. He was alert and looking down at the ground.

When I looked down from my perch I was startled so badly I almost cried out. A man was crouched on the ground, hiding behind the trunk of my tree! Without even thinking I

170

jumped on his back and it broke my fall. Before he could get to his feet I had sliced his neck with my shell knife.

It was terrible. There was blood everywhere, but none of it was my own. It was the first man I ever killed, and I knew I would need a curing ceremony. I satisfied myself with knowing he must have heard the same owl I did. This time it was a bad omen for him, and a good one for me.

I ran to Crying Bird's tree. He was on the ground standing over two men who were both dead. His knife was stuck in the back of one of them. He said that he had broken the neck of the other Utinan.

It was dark and there was no moonlight. I did not see the gaping wound in my brother's side until he lay down and asked me to do what I could to stop the bleeding.

Perchuco had been awakened. The Utinans had not seen him at all where he had slept under a blanket of moss. He told us that there was a fourth man who had run down the hill toward a wooded creek bed.

Crying Bird told me to follow the man and kill him. I refused to do it. My brother was bleeding to death, and he wanted me to continue the fight.

I did the best I could for my brother. I burned the edges of his wound and made a poultice with comfrey leaves and spider webs I had brought from Ibitibi. His wounds were bound with palmetto fiber and moss. By morning the bleeding had stopped.

We ordered Perchuco to bury the dead Utinans. He did a good job.

Four days and nights we made camp near the creek. The water was clean and we had enough food to eat. Crying Bird disapproved of the camp, saying that the man who had survived might return with others. We had no choice, I said. The second night my brother was hot and sweating. By the next morning he was saying strange things and making no sense.

It is dangerous to listen to someone who is crazy. It can make the listener crazy, too. I heard him talking to someone who was not there. I put my fingers in my ears and hummed to myself so I couldn't hear."

* * *

Marehootie rested for awhile and was quiet. "I am tired now and need to take some cure medicine for my pain. Then I will sleep, but I want you to return in the morning. There is much more you need to know."

"Father Pareja is hearing the Confessions of the people. He will be busy with that until dark, and again tomorrow morning. There is nothing he needs me to do and I would like to hear more of the story, so I will come back then."

The boy had opened the door to leave, but turned back.

"I saw you in the village," he said.

Marehootie looked at him, but closed his eyes and did not answer.

"Who was that Chief with you under the tree?"

The old man motioned with his hand for the boy to leave.

* * *

"Nariba! Old man, wake up," the boy pleaded, shaking him gently. It was early evening and the sun had not set.

The Acueran lay on his side, a pleasant look on his face, but he did not awaken.

"Forget him. We do not need him awake for this business." Sergeant Suarez stepped back to the doorway. "Bring the chief in here," he ordered.

A moment later a soldier stepped through the door holding a man by the arm. He was a tall man, and had a stern look and a chiefly dignity about him.

"This is the man I told you about, Chief Tacatacura, the Acueran," Suarez said, gesturing toward the old man asleep on his bed.

De Coya stepped away from the bed and translated what Suarez had said into Mocaman.

"I would like you to look carefully at his face. I want you to tell me if you recognize this man from Guale. Have you ever seen him on your travels to Tupiqui or Tolomato? Perhaps you have seen him with the Indian called Juanillo. I believe they were friends."

Tacatacura stepped toward the cot and stooped to get a good look. The sun was still above the horizon and shone through the window lighting the face of the sleeping man. The chief reached out, grasped the man's chin and gently turned the head to see the face fully.

"Why is he sleeping this time of day? Has he been hurt?" he asked.

"Do you need him awake? Do you want to hear him speak?" Suarez stepped to the water pail, filled the gourd and sloshed it in the face of the Acueran who sat upright in his bed.

Marehootie spoke a few words in a language Suarez did not understand and immediately fell back into his sleeping position.

Suarez turned to de Coya. "What was it he said?"

"They were only words. He made no sense," the boy answered.

"Would you like him awake so he can stand? That might help you identify him," Suarez offered. Tacatacura did not answer until the boy spoke the words in Mocaman.

"I don't know this man," he said.

Suarez frowned, but said nothing when the boy gave him the answer.

The sleeping man began a raspy snore, and the chief of Tacatacura stepped toward the door as if to leave.

"Wait, stop," the sergeant commanded. "There is something more I need to know."

Suarez had a small deerskin bag with him. He loosened the drawstring and shook the contents into the palm of his hand. Luminous pearls, each the size of an acorn, shown with hues of blue and green and pink in the fading sunlight from the window.

"Extraordinary, wouldn't you say? Have you ever seen anything like them?"

"Beautiful," the chief said, "and valuable. Where did you get them?"

"Have you seen such pearls before, perhaps in Guale?" Suarez asked.

"Where did you get them?" Tacatacura asked impatiently.

"I took them from the old man. As evidence," the sergeant replied.

"These are common trade pearls, but they are valuable to people who do not have them. Some of the rivers and creeks to the northwest, around the land of Cofahiqui have them in abundance. I do not believe you would find any in Guale, unless they traded for them." The chief had spoken slowly, allowing de Coya to interpret his answer.

Then he said "I have one such pearl, myself." The chief opened his shirt, exposing a single fresh-water pearl suspended by a fiber string around his neck.

Suarez cupped his hand over the open bag, and in the process dropped two pearls on the dirt floor. A soldier quickly went to the floor, collected the pearls and handed them to his superior.

"Since they belong to this innocent man, you should return them to him," Tacatacura said as he turned and stepped out of the door.

CHAPTER 21

I t was full dark when the old man awakened. The boy had stayed with him when the others left. The Acueran's deep slumber was worrisome to him.

Marehootie was refreshed by his sleep. After he relieved himself he drank some water and ate a soft piece of corn cake that was left from the religious feast. He walked around, stretching his back. "Sleep is the secret cure of all *isucu*," he said, "both for themselves and for their patients."

De Coya told the old man about what had happened while he slept, about the visit of the sergeant, about the pearls and what Chief Tacatacura had said.

"The chief said he did not know you, yet I saw him speaking with you on Holy Thursday."

Marehootie was seated again on his stool, in the dark. De Coya sat on the floor, his back to the wall, awaiting an answer.

"Are you sure it was me you saw?"

"It was you. You even smiled at me."

"Perhaps I was laughing at the dog."

The boy laughed out loud and pointed his finger at the dark shadow across the room. "I knew it was you!"

"Are you certain it was Chief Tacatacura with me?"

"He looked like the man who was here today," the boy answered.

"Then you are not sure," the Acueran said.

The old man uttered an Acueran prayer. When he was finished, he continued his story.

* * *

175

"My brother did not die at that place, in those woods. My magic cured his fever and his good sense returned. He was very sore and I gave him things to eat and smoke that made the pain go away for awhile. When he was able to travel we set out again, moving as fast and far as he could tolerate.

We passed the small villages of Luca, Vicela and Tocaste. Our intent was to rest for a few days at Ocale where we had friends we had traded with in the past. Because Ocale was to the east of the river called Withlacoochee, and the smaller villages to the west, we did not visit them. We saw only one campfire, and no one at all fishing on the other side of the river.

The friends we hoped to see were away from their village on trading journeys. We were welcomed by Chief Ocale, who was a very old man. He did not use the council house much, except for ceremonies and official business. We sat with him and two of his principal men on a hill overlooking the river where there was shade and a pleasant breeze.

Hollowed gourds hung suspended from the trees, providing nesting places for the purple martin. These birds love to eat mosquitoes, and they are good to have around the village.

The Ocale tongue is so much like our own I did not need to interpret. Within a short time we were all comfortable with the other's way of speaking. Chief Ocale knew of our journey through traders who visited his village. Word of our coming was moving faster than we could travel.

The chief no longer had his teeth, yet he still chewed tobacco and would frequently spit. He told us many stories of his life and what he had seen. Some of his stories were familiar to us, but some things we did not know.

He was already a chief when the Spaniard de Soto came through the country, robbing the people and stealing the food they had stored for winter. Ocale had hidden one storehouse of corn. If he had not, the Spanish would have eaten or taken with them even the last ear, leaving nothing for planting.

He spoke of old friends who were taken by the Spanish to carry their burdens, who were murdered when they tried to escape to their own families. Some had been killed because they stumbled or were unable to carry such great weight. The

Spanish had dogs, he said, and they enjoyed watching the dogs tear people apart.

There were more than five hundred soldiers at Ocale, and they had horses and weapons. Some wore armor that made the arrows bounce off.

Chief Ocale asked if we had heard of the massacre at Napitucka. We said we had not heard the story. I soon recognized the tale, but let him tell it because he was an old man and wanted to talk.

He told of the Spanish taking hostage the young daughter of Chief Aguacalequen to insure that they were not attacked, and how they lured the chief into their camp to get his daughter, then took him captive also.

At Napituca the Spanish were attacked by many warriors, including the brave Yustaga and their brothers to the south, the Potano.

'Do you know how that battle ended?' he asked.

I knew, but said I did not.

'When the fighting was done, the Spanish killed those they captured. More than 150 braves were butchered. Some were chopped in the neck with a sword. Others had large holes blown in them by guns that sounded like lightning hitting a tree. They even tied some to stakes and burned them to death.'

The old chief paused and wiped his eyes with the back of his weathered hand.

'There were many chiefs who were captured. I believe there were nine if you count Aguacalecuen who they already held as their hostage. They were tied to trees. Men of Uzita and Mocoso who were their slaves were told to shoot the chiefs with arrows. It saved the Spanish much gun powder that day.'

While he was telling his story, our slave Perchuco was kicking a ball with two young children. He also sang and danced for them.

'No one knows what happened to the daughter of Chief Aguacalequen. She never returned to her village,' Ocale said.

A woman walked up the hill to where we were and gave the old chief water to drink from a gourd. We each drank after the chief. He introduced us to the woman who was his grand-

177

daughter. When she was gone away he continued with his stories.

'There was another one, you know, another Spaniard who came before de Soto. I never saw this man, but my uncle told me about him. He was called Narvaez, and he was a fool.

'He was not a large man, although he was taller than most of the Spanish. The hair on his head and his beard were the color of maple leaves before they fall from the trees. He had only one eye. He had an evil look.'

The shriek of children playing was heard. Perchuco had a blindfold over his eyes and was staggering around as if to grab the children who were running about. I knew he could see, but the children did not.

'Because he was such a fool he failed to kill as many as he wanted. He came ashore at the same place as de Soto did twelve summers later, but stayed near the water as he moved his men to the north. There are very few villages there, and he did not find even one. There are not even trails to follow to get where he was going.

'There was a chief whose name was Dulchanchellin who left his village to greet the Spanish. His people we now call Yustaga. The chief was carried on the shoulders of his people, and he had flute players with him to serenade his new friend, Narvaez. He invited him to his village which was two days away. The Spanish were surprised to find a village with so many people.

'The Spanish were fed maize and they rested. Dulchachellin told Narvaez that the Appalachee were his enemies, and asked if the Spanish would help him attack them. The Spanish refused to go to war, but took some of the villagers hostage to guide them to Appalachee. Narvaez believed he would find gold there.

'Narvaez was a brutal man. He bound the men with vines made of metal so that they could not run away. If they refused to work he fed them to the dogs. They were brave men. They led the Spanish through the worst places. They waded through swamps and crossed rivers at the most dangerous places. They struggled through thickets that would not let a rabbit through.

They led the Spanish into ambushes so some of them got arrows in their backs.

'When the soldiers finally reached the land of the Appalachee they were all injured or ill with the fever. A few Appalachee were taken hostage. Just as the men from Dulchanchellin had done, they led the Spanish through terrible places.

'The Spanish walked all the way through Appalachee without seeing any large villages. They never visited Ivitahuco. They never saw the council house in Inihica that is so large that three thousand people can meet to dance and sing, and conduct their business.

'They thought Apalachee had no people. They did not know where to look and which way to turn. They were blind fools.

'They ended at the small village of Aute. They made rafts to float away, tying to escape Appalachee. Some say they all drowned.'

Chief Ocale closed his eyes and leaned his head back against a tree. 'I hate the Spanish. I am an old man, but I would kill any I can find with my bare hands.'

It was time for the chief to rest. We would talk more later.

When we were alone Crying Bird spoke to Perchuco and told him of Chief Ocale's strong words against the Spanish. He was told not to talk to anyone, even the children, for fear someone might recognize his manner of speaking. Perchuco said he would remain outside the village until we were ready to resume our journey.

Crying Bird said to Perchuco that in the days to come we would meet many people who would gladly kill him for being Spanish. He told Perchuco to leave Ocale and to find refuge where he could. He gave Perchuco the bear effigy that had been split by the arrow.

'If you steal anything from us we will find you and take your skin,' Crying Bird said.

By evening there was no wind and the mosquitoes came out to feast. We had more to discuss with Chief Ocale, and we went to his house. A fire of dried maize was under each seat and the smoke kept the mosquitoes away, although it made my eyes water and burn.

Chief Ocale said he had been thinking about the slave we had with us, and he asked if he was Spanish. We said that he might be French or he might be Spanish, that they all looked alike to us. Crying Bird said that Perchuco had wandered off while the chief was resting, and we did not know where he was.

The chief sent some of his men to find Perchuco while we talked.

We told Chief Ocale what we knew of the French, of their alliance with Outina and their war with Potano. Chief Ocale said that Potano had been attacked twice and not just one time as we believed. We said we would be in the village of Potano within a few days, and would learn the truth.

Chief Ocale said we should tell Chief Potano that Ocale would send forty warriors if Potano planned to strike at Outina. Crying Bird and I looked at each other. If Chief Ocale had forty warriors, they must be invisible. Perhaps they still lived in his memory.

We thanked the old chief. We did not tell Ocale about the Utinans we had killed. He was a good old man, but he loved to talk.

I was concerned we had not had a curing ceremony to rid ourselves of evil spirits that are everywhere death is found. I asked if there was a *jarva* who could perform cures. Ocale said their *jarva* had died of a rattlesnake bite. I said that if he could not cure a snake bite, he must not have been a very good *jarva.*

I should not have said that to Chief Ocale. The *jarva* had been his sister's son, and Ocale was upset. Crying Bird said I should learn to listen more and talk less. He may be right about that.

In the morning we said good-bye. Chief Ocale gave us a strong man to carry our burdens as far as Potano. His men had searched all night but did not find Perchuco

'You should take better care of a slave, than to let him wander about,' he said in parting.

* * *

The trails between Ocale and Potano were well marked and there were no rivers to cross. I had nothing to carry other than drinking water, and my leg did not hurt me. Crying Bird was still bothered by the pain in his side but did not complain. We moved faster than the man from Ocale. He knew the trail and would catch us later when it was time to eat and sleep.

It took only two days to reach Potano. Of course, we were expected. The Potanans were at war now, and the tribal council was meeting.

It was a large village, and much like some others we had seen. There was one difference. Potano had a tall fence of tree trunks that surrounded the village in a great circle. The wall was twice as high as a man, and the end of the fence circled past the other end, so that no one could enter the village without passing through a narrow opening with the wall on each side.

There were two guard houses, one at a distance from the village and another at the entrance. Each had holes so that the guards could shoot out, but not even the finest archer could shoot in. Whoever planned it must be very smart.

Even while the council met, the warriors used the council house fire to heat chert for arrow heads.

After we were welcomed and gifts exchanged, we got right to the purpose of the meeting. Chief Potano was a tall man, even compared to others we had seen. His face was dark, as if he spent every day in the sun, and lined so that he looked older than he was. He had tattoos all over his body, with some on his face.

Crying Bird told of the help offered by Chief Acuera, Chief Mayaca and Chief Ocale. Chief Potano said that he was not surprised that Oathaqua of the Ais had made no promise of help.

'I can not abide a people who treat their own fathers as slaves,' he said. 'and they are greedy people. They might kill the French on their own, but if you ask them to do it they will want to be paid.'

Chief Potano told of two battles with the French. The first time Chief Outina had crossed the river, and Potano sent a scouting party to stop him or to determine his intentions. The Utinan camp was found and scouts watched it all night. There were one hundred Utinan warriors and fifty foreign people.

In the morning the *jarva* of Utina told the chief that the stars said it was a bad time for an attack, and that the Potanans were alert and strong. The scouts heard Olate Quai Outina tell the others that they would not fight, but go home to fight another day.

The scouts slipped away to deliver the news to Chief Potano. They were in no hurry and were overtaken by the French. Two of the scouts were caught and butchered. The other scout arrived at the village to the east of Potano, where many warriors were waiting for word. The French attacked and killed many with their weapons. They burned the village and took women with them.

Five days later another village was attacked. This time the French had the Utinans with them. Chief Potano knew of their approach, and some people had left the village to go to Potano or to hide in the woods.

'Many who stayed behind died,' Chief Potano said.

A war party of Potanans slipped behind the Utinans and French and ambushed them when they tried to return home. 'Many Frenchmen felt the sting of chert that day,' Potano said.

Chief Potano had ordered the construction of the wall around the main village after the first attack. Every tree near the village was felled, so there were no trees attackers could hide behind to launch their arrows.

* * *

Later, Crying Bird and I met privately with the chief and his war chief, the *paracusi*. The warriors working on their arrows left the council house and a guard was posted outside the door.

Chief Potano did not want me there. He considered me nothing more than a bearer of burdens and of no importance. Crying Bird said I was his brother, and that I needed to know the plan in case he was killed or captured. Chief Potano looked at me strongly and promised me an interesting death if I betrayed him.

Paracusi told his plan for an attack on the French who had a camp they called Fort Caroline near where the river meets the ocean. He said we might be helped by Chief Satureiwa who had sway over thirty villages.

Satureiwa had welcomed the French when they arrived, the *paracusi* said, and offered his help to them, feeding them maize for the first winter. In the spring the French made a treaty with Satureiwa's worst enemy, the Utinans, and Satureiwa did not trust the French any longer and wished them dead.

Chief Potano said he did not completely trust Satureiwa or his nephew Athore who controlled many villages. 'If Sarureiwa will swear his allegiance to me I will trust him. If he hesitates in any way, you are not to tell him of our plans,' he said to Crying Bird.

Crying Bird told Chief Potano that we would visit Yustaga to ask for their help and then travel to Satureiwa. We had by now been traveling more than sixty days, and believed we would be home in Acuera in another fourteen days.

Chief Potano wondered if Yustaga would help. They were even further to the west than Potano, and a great distance from the River of the Sun where the battles would take place. The Yustagans had proved themselves valiant warriors against the Spanish, just as the Acuera had, he said, and perhaps they might help in some way.

Crying Bird thanked Chief Potano for his praise of Acuera.

Potano had a very good *jarva*, and he performed a cure for us to rid us of the bad spirits who followed us since we killed the Utinans. I had been feeling worse each day, and the cure surely saved our lives.

Chief Potano enjoyed the story of how we killed the Utinans. He did not believe that I had killed one, and said so. My brother insisted it was true, and the chief began to respect me more.

* * *

We left Potano the next morning, after only one day. Chief Potano provided a bearer for us who knew the way to the land of the Yustaga.

Again, the trails were wide and well marked and we moved easily to the north and west. There was a deep river to be crossed and the current was swift. The bearer from Potano said there was usually a man with a canoe there to carry travelers across, but he was nowhere to be found.

To make matters worse, the bearer was a poor swimmer and refused to swim across even after Crying Bird offered to carry the burdens. We camped at the river, hoping the man with the canoe would return in the morning. Crying Bird shot a turkey with an arrow and we had a good meal.

After dark the sky lit up with lightning. There were no palmetto bushes that we could use to build a lean-too. When the rain started we had no place to hide and stay dry. It was a miserable night. Only what was packed in animal skins stayed dry. Everything else was soaked.

When the sun came up Crying Bird was in a cheerful mood despite the fact that we were all wet and the man with the canoe had not returned. He said that we would swim the river. Everything we had already was wet, so it could do no harm.

Crying Bird waded into the river with a large bundle. He swam on his side holding the bundle in the air. He was a strong swimmer. When he came back we divided the rest of the bundle and swam across together. The man from Potano refused even to get his feet wet, and stood by the river shaking his head. He waved to us and then he turned back toward Potano.

We arrived at Aguacalequen the second day after crossing the river. This is the village I told you about earlier, where the devil de Soto kidnapped the chief and his daughter, and later murdered the chief along with all the others at Napituca.

An old man provided us shelter to sleep, and shared his food with us. He said there had been so much illness, and so many deaths there was no one left of the White Deer Clan. Less than forty villagers were still alive and they helped each other so freely they felt no need for a chief.

The man was caring for his sick granddaughter, a child of about ten years. The parents had both died when the child was an infant. He said that since the time of the Spanish, illnesses would come and go, killing many people.

I asked to see the child, telling the old man that I was *Isucu*. I had no magic for the Spanish sickness and should not have offered my help. The girl was fevered and sweating. Her eyes were dulled, but she smiled at me and thanked me for my cures. She had red blotches all over her face and body, and they were bright red around her belly.

I had no idea what herbs to use, other than those to relieve a fever. They did not work on her. I was with her through the night, washing her with cool water and saying all the right prayers.

In the morning the old man thanked me, saying she looked much better. He offered to pay me with breads made of hickory nut meal. To refuse the offer would be an insult and he might think that we thought he was so poor he had nothing of value to give. I accepted the cakes, and we were on our way.

* * *

If Aguacalequen was a disappointment to us, we should have known that Napituca would be no better. This is where the brave Yustaga and Potanans had fought de Soto and died, where so many chiefs were tied to trees and shot to death. Only a few people still lived there.

The spirits of the dead so troubled Crying Bird that he fell into a spell, and did not recognize me or talk to me. He walked in circles slowly, with his head down. He began to call the names of long-dead chiefs. He fell to the ground and prayed. He cut his flesh with a shell until he bled. I took the shell from him, and he did not resist. It was as if I were not there.

I led him back onto the trail. When we were away from Napituca we stopped to rest. Crying Bird slept for a long time although it was in the middle of the day. When he awoke he was himself again. He never spoke to me of what happened at Napituca.

* * *

Uzachile was a prosperous place where Houstaqua was chief. Before we reached the village we followed a trail which led between fields of maize being tended by the people. Other crops were planted in the same fields. I believe there were beans and squash and pumpkins.

The center of the village was busy. There was a large grain storage that looked full. The village was laid out in an orderly fashion, and the houses were neat and clean. The people were well fed, and there were many children at play.

The same gourds we saw in Ocale were hung from the trees here, and the birds were almost tame, fluttering about chasing mosquitoes and other birds.

Uzachile had survived and prospered because it had been abandoned and burned by the people when de Soto's army passed through. When the Spanish were gone the people came out of hiding and rebuilt Uzachile even better than before. Aguacalequen and Napituca were destroyed by the Spanish and many people were taken as slaves or killed.

Uzachili had also been visited by the army of Narvaez, the Spaniard described by the Chief of Ocale as having red hair and an evil eye. The Yustagan chief was Dulchanchellin, the uncle of the present chief called Houstaqua. Dulchanchellin had foolishly tried to befriend the Spaniard, even entertain him with his flute players. The Spanish stole all the maize and killed anyone who did not submit.

My brother brought the greetings of Chief Acuera, and of Chief Potano. He praised the valor of the Yustaga people for their resistance to the Spanish years before and told of having spoken to spirits at Napituca. He said the spirits did not rest well and would rise to defend Yustaga if the Spanish ever returned.

Chief Houstaqua nodded pleasantly, and recalled that the brave Acuerans were the first to kill the Spanish. He was an impressive man and his face was painted black. He asked if our Chief of Acuera was the same chief we had twenty years before. This came as a surprise to us that he would not know. Crying Bird said that this was, indeed, the brave Acuera who

186

killed Spanish and that he was still strong and in good health.

Crying Bird presented the chief with a splendid wood carving. Houstaqua was pleased, and marveled at the fine workmanship. For all their wealth, the Yustaga had no woodcarvers, he said. Houstaqua apologized that he had no return gift, and said he did not know we were coming. He promised that before we left he would give us a fine match coat of painted deerskin for our chief.

Crying Bird and I spoke among ourselves. How was it that the chief of the Yustaga did not know that Chief Acuera was still alive, and that we would be visiting his land? Both of these things were well known every other place we had journeyed.

We were overheard by the *inija* who spoke our tongue. He explained that the traders who brought news to Yustaga were from the north and west, and that they seldom got information on happenings from the east or from the River of the Sun.

The Chief was pleasant, and a gracious host. He would not promise men for battle, however, until he spoke to his brother, the Chief of the Potano. He said he would send his *paracusi* to visit Chief Potano. My feeling was that we had not impressed Houstaqua with the urgency of our mission or of the danger from the French.

Chief Houstaqua invited us to watch a ball game between the men of Uzachili and those of a neighboring village. It is a similar game to the one sometimes played at Acuera, where the men kick a ball trying to hit a goal on top of a tall pole.

The game was very rough and some of the players suffered broken bones. There was much gambling going on with people betting on the outcome. The players from Uzachili all had similar tattoos and the other team all had their faces painted blue and yellow. Chief Houstaqua told us that the best players were very popular with the unmarried women of Uzachili.

It was the tradition among many of the villages that disputes be decided on the playing field, instead of going to war with each other. This game was being played to determine disputed fishing rights between the villages.

The sun had not yet risen when we thanked Houstaqua for his hospitality and for the beautiful match coat, and set off to the east for the land of Satureiwa."

* * *

It was the middle of the night. The Acueran was still strong and his thoughts were clear because he was well rested. The boy, however, was tired from the stress of the Holy Days. He fell asleep for a long time, and the Acueran waited patiently for him to awaken.

The boy stirred. He was awake and uncomfortable for having slept sitting up. "I'm sorry, Nariba. Did I fall asleep while you were talking? *Paqe, Paqe*" he said.

"Our time is short," the old man said, "and if you are awake now there is more to say that you need to hear."

The boy stood and stretched his limbs. Then he relieved himself and drank more water.

"Before you begin there is something I must tell you. While you slept the sergeant showed Chief Tacatacura your pearls that he now carries in a leather pouch. Did he steal them from you? If he did, I will tell Father Pareja and he will make the sergeant return them to you."

"They are mine. They will be returned to me without help from the priest. You should listen now. You may hear more about pearls if you keep your ears open," the old man said.

CHAPTER 22

“The journey to Satureiwa was at least ten days, and Houstaqua did not offer to provide us with a bearer. Perhaps he did not believe our story, or the journey was just too far for him to order someone to accompany us. It may be that his men were soft from eating gaucha and the work would be too hard.

The trail from Uzachili to Satureiwa took us back through Napituca and Oritina, where it turned to the east. We would not need to go back through Aguacalequen where the little girl was dying.

My mood was not good. For the first time since leaving Mayaca I had to carry the burden. Now there was a heavy deerskin match coat, besides. Sometimes when it appeared we would not encounter villages, Crying Bird would shoulder part of the load.

He said that I was too old for this kind of work. I accepted the insult to get his help.

My head had been hurting while we were in Uzachili. I carried willow bark potion but it did not help. My back was aching and also my shoulders. Before we reached Oritina I felt dizzy and had trouble keeping my balance. I told my brother I needed to rest for a day, but not in a village where I might spread my illness to others.

We made camp on a hill outside Oritina, where there was a breeze. I tried to eat to keep up my strength, but my stomach would hold neither food nor water. Crying Bird said it was a pleasant night, but I was chilled and shaking.

I asked Crying Bird to look at my body for red blotches. He found red marks around my waist, but nowhere else. By morning I felt worse. He looked at the marks in the daylight and said they looked like red bug bites. He did not recognize the Spanish sickness.

The next day Crying Bird took my loin cloth and long pants and smoked them over a fire. I was able to eat a little broth, and the red marks did not look as bright and they had not spread. I applied a poultice and the marks went away.

The next day my brother told me to get up. He said that two days was enough to get over what he called 'Spanish red bug sickness.' I love my brother, but he would make a poor *isucu*. He had no idea how close to death I had been.

* * *

We saw many trails going north and south that crossed our own, but few people other than traders. On the fourth day we came to a small village where trails crossed. We were told that we could rest in the village and that two widow-women prepared tasty meals for travelers.

The women welcomed us. It was not yet dark, and our hut looked over a small pond where we could bathe. We ate our meal of maize cakes and meat stew, sitting around a fire with other travelers. Crying Bird and I had a story to tell strangers who might be curious and want to know our business. We listened to the others and heard some amazing news.

A trader from the east said the French were being fought by the Spanish. He said both sides were forcing the chiefs of different villages to provide warriors, but no one wanted to help the Spanish because of what de Soto had done. He said Satureiwa was so angry with the French he refused to help them.

To make matters worse for the French, the Utinans who had used the French to fight Potano were too far away to help.

Crying Bird and I went to our hut and talked about what this might mean. We could continue to Satureiwa or return to Ibitibi and report these events to Chief Acuera. What the traders know here, it was sure that Chief Acuera would know soon, my brother said. We wanted Satureiwa to join us in attacking the French, but the Spanish might kill them before we have a chance.

'If the devils do not succeed in killing each other, we can kill whoever survives and be rid of them both,' Crying Bird said with a smile on his travel-weary face.

'Then we can re-pay the treachery of Olate Quai Outina,' I said.

The moon was bright. We could see the shadows it cast through the doorway of our hut. One shadow moved and we could hear someone breathing. Crying Bird moved so fast he was a blur. When I followed him outside, my brother was on top of a man and holding a knife to his throat.

'Do not kill me, Chulufi-Yuchi,' the man shouted.

If the man had not used my brother's Acueran name, his throat would have been cut at that moment.'

'You do not know me. How do you call my name?' Crying Bird demanded. By now the commotion had attracted others to see what was happening.

My brother and I dragged the man into our hut. I held the knife to his throat while he told his story. It was the second time I had been so close to killing a man. It was not the last time. I did not know how sharp the blade was, or how tightly it should be held against the skin. His neck bled a little.

'I am Nihoto, my village is Cofahiqui and I am of the Clan of the Panther. I have come to find you and take you to the leader of my people,' he said.

He said a trader from the south, a dealer in medicinal herbs, told of the mighty Acuerans and their resistance to the foreign armies. The trader told of the treachery of Outina, and the murderous attack of the French on the peaceable Potanans.

The trader described my brother as a great *Yaba* who had visions of the French before they were seen in Cautio, and told of our journey to join the people together to expel the invaders from our land.

'It was from this trader that I learned your tongue. I believe he was once the *isucu* of your village and that you are Marehootie and you are now *isucu*," he said, cutting his eyes so he could see me.

Finally, he said his people had suffered greatly at the hands of the Spaniard de Soto, and the leaders of his people wanted to know how they could help.

The name Cofahiqui was vaguely familiar, as if I had heard it once long ago and never again. The man calling himself Nihoto said his village was to the north, and he had traveled a long way to find us.

It was disturbing that our journey was so well known. We did not trust this man. He could be an Utinan sent to kill us, and one who was a fast talker, weaving a believable story to save his own skin.

Yet, his story made sense. If he was a liar, he was the best I had ever seen. The way he described the old *isucu* made me believe him. My brother held a small torch in front of the man's face. His eyes were wide with fear but they looked steadily into Crying Bird's face. He did not sweat.

'How are we to know you are not lying? We have important business to do here, as you have said. We have no time to go north. Our business is to the east and to the south' Crying Bird said.

The man reached into the waist of his britches. My grasp of the knife tightened, and blood trickled down his chest. His hand held not a weapon, but a leather sack. Using one hand and his teeth he loosened the drawstring and spilled the contents on the floor.

There were pearls and they glistened under the torch light; seven of the finest quality I had seen.

'These are a gift for your war against the French. If you will go with me and meet the leaders of my tribe we can be of great help to you against both the French and the Spanish,' he said.

I relaxed the pressure of the knife and cleaned the wound on his neck. He became even more talkative, trying to convince Crying Bird to go with him. Crying Bird could think of many reasons not to go to Cofahiqui, and the two of them argued through the night.

I sat outside the hut watching for Utinan spies who might be listening. Nihoto promised to carry the burdens. He said it was a long walk, but that we would be given canoes and oarsmen for our journey to Satureiwa, which was completely by water.

* * *

Crying Bird shook me awake. Nihoto was gone and the women were already up, tending the fire. We thanked them. They accepted a small carving in payment, on which they could make a great profit with the traders. They offered maize and hickory nut cakes for our journey, which we accepted.

They did not say that we should come back. We were not traders, and they knew they would never see us again. As the sun rose it was in our eyes as we took the trail toward Satureiwa.

We had not gone far when we came upon Nihoto, sitting on a log. He took my burden on his back and we followed him to where another trail crossed our own. We turned to the north. It was more comfortable walking without my burden, and with the sun no longer in my face.

When the first day was over the scenery had changed. The trees were mostly tall pine and there were no more palmetto bushes. As *isucu* I always look for medicinal plants, but there were few I recognized now. The ground was different. There was no sand. The dirt was copper colored, almost red, and it stuck to our feet where it was wet.

On the second and third day we passed to the east of a large swamp. Nihoto told us what it was called, but I do not remember.

We walked so long I lost count of the days. I am sure it was further than Nihoto had promised. He was an entertaining host and told many stories to pass the time. We stopped in a few villages. Nihoto knew all the *holatas*, but did not tell them who we were or our business. He simply said that we were the guests of Cofahiqui.

The chiefs and the other people looked at us curiously. The women marveled at Crying Bird's tattoos. They had no tattoos, and they dressed differently than our people. They were polite and they did not laugh at our differences or ask us any questions.

The land was very hilly. Even without a burden to carry it was tiring going up and down and up again.

Near many of the villages there were fields of crops. The maize grew taller than we had seen before, coming almost to our shoulders. There were beans and squash, as we expected, and melons that grew on the ground. An old man tending a field broke open a melon for us. The meat was yellow, and very sweet. I had never tasted anything as good.

He gave me seeds, and with Nihoto interpreting, told me how the seeds should be planted. The melons would grow in sandy soil, he said.

Crying Bird stood to the side with an unpleasant look on his face. He was anxious to go. I thanked the old man and we were on our way.

* * *

Our arrival at Cofahiqui was a surprise to us. Nihoto had not warned us that we were coming near. A runner had come to us early in the morning and spoken to Nihoto in their tongue which I did not yet understand. For the rest of the morning I walked with Nihoto and he told me much about the language of the people of his village.

We heard the music of flutes and bells and of drums before we could see the musicians. We walked around the side of a steep hill and saw a river and on the other side a beautiful village. People were there in fancy clothing, dancing and chanting and singing. When they saw us a loud cheer arose.

A large canoe moved toward us from the other side. I told you before how we attached two canoes together to move our dying mother from the Wekiva to Ibitibi. This was like that one, but it also had a thatched roof over the platform to keep out the sun.

Under the canopy, waving her hand slowly in salute was a *niaholata*, or chieftess. We were surprised, since Nihoto had not mentioned that a woman was their chief. Perhaps he believed we would not travel so far to see a woman.

She was beautiful, with fair skin and hair that hung to her waist. She was not young, nor was she old. She may have been a few years older than me but it was hard to say. She was not fat, and she was tall and stood erect with a regal bearing.

I was struck by her beauty. Were it not for my nature I would have wanted her for a wife. Crying Bird was as moved as I was, I am sure, but he does not show his feelings in his face. It is sometimes hard to tell what he is thinking and feeling. Anyone can see my face and guess what I will say before I say it.

She was *niaholata* over Cofahiqui and six other villages. She greeted us warmly. Her voice was smooth and clear as spring water and as sweet. She smelled of honeysuckle.

At her request we joined her in the canoe and sat with her in the shade. When we got to the other shore, we were met by her principal men and women who all showed their excitement and pleasure at our company. By now I could understand some of what they said, but Nihoto translated since he was fluent in both tongues.

She said we must be tired from our long journey, and we should bathe and rest and then put on new clothing. A celebration would be held later, with good food and entertainment. There would be time to talk of serious matters tomorrow.

We were taken to a council house that was unlike ours here. There were walls within for privacy, and water for bathing. Nihoto showed us spices to be rubbed on our skin after bathing, along with balms and poultices for blisters and scratches and fleas.

Fine clothing was there, made of the bark of a tree that was soft and spun so delicately that it felt good against the skin. When I asked Nihoto about it he said the inner bark of the slippery elm and the mulberry tree were used for clothing. The weavers of Cofahiqui are superior to those in Acuera. Our people used the same tree bark, but the clothing is rough against the skin.

Nihoto offered women to help us bathe and dress if we wished. My brother said we could wash and dress ourselves. I thanked Nihoto and he left to visit with his family. He would return in time for the ceremony.

After we were clean, we rested. There were shades and when they were in place it was dark and cool inside. The only sound was of children playing on a ball field nearby. Women scolded them for making noise while we slept. That quieted them for awhile, but I lay awake listening for their laughter. I was at home again, and I dreamed of Ibitibi and its chief, and of the dead Acuchara and of the dead *jarva* and his wisdom.

* * *

When I awoke my bother was sitting on the edge of his cot watching me.

'How well did you sleep?' I asked.

'Only wild animals and old men sleep during the daylight,' he said.

We moved a shade aside and saw that evening was approaching. Activity was beginning in the council house, though the people were trying to be quiet.

I dressed in the beautiful clothing and put soft leather moccasins on my feet. I pulled up my hair and pinned it in such a way that I would appear even taller than I am. The balms and lotions made me feel and smell good. I arranged my tunic so that the muscles of my arms would show.

Finally, I had my brother check my hairline and ears for ticks that we sometimes picked up on the trail. There were none.

Crying Bird did not use the potions or lotions. He said that he smelled good enough without having flowers rubbed on his body. Besides, he said, they attract mosquitoes. He dressed carelessly, without paying attention to detail. When he finished he was handsome and looked better than I did. I was envious.

We were seated to either side of the *niaholata* of Cofahiqui for the banquet and entertainment. Her *inija* was also a woman and very attractive, although many years older than the chieftess, and she sat to the other side of me.

The *paracusi* was Cofahiqui's brother, and he sat next to Crying Bird. Nihoto was nearby to translate for them.

After the meal and dancing, the *niaholata* told us that guests must pay for their meal with stories. Nothing serious was allowed, she said. I raced around my mind for something to say. I finally told the story of the night the Mayacans did not attack. I must have gotten deeply into the story and I found myself on my hands and knees demonstrating how Alobo looked and acted when he got the arrow in his butt.

The story was well told and everyone laughed. I saw the chieftess wiping tears from her eyes, and I knew I had done well.

Then it was Crying Bird's time. He is not a good teller of funny stories, and I was nervous. He thought awhile and then said he would tell another Alobo story, the story of how a coward became war chief. The funniest part of the story, as he told it, was why a person of my nature would want to be *paracusi* in the first place. He ended the story by saying that I was a very kind-hearted human being for honoring a person who had for so long been disrespected.

Gifts were exchanged and pleasant words were spoken to us by all the people.

Cofahiqui spoke last. She said that on the next day she would tell us a different kind of story, one much more painful to tell. The people all sighed, their eyes downcast.

* * *

'I was just a girl,' she said, 'only twelve years of age.'

The five of us stood on a high place looking down on the river. Cofahiqui had only her *inija* with her, along with the interpreter, Nihoto. In this land it was safe for a chief of such great rank to travel without guards.

'They came from the south, and approached that last village you can see through the elm trees. We knew of their coming. They could move quickly with their men on horses, but they were noisy and we could hear them a long way off. We had lookouts and runners and had tracked them for two days.

'We knew of their cruelties. We knew they sought gold and silver and food to eat. They would as easily kill for an ear of maize as they would a bar of silver.

'My mother's sister, who was also called Cofahiqui, was our chieftess. She was not old, but she was ill with fevers that had made her weak in her mind. Our healers said that the

197

illness came to this land with the Spanish, and moved ahead of them like a black cloud killing people as it passed.

'We knew that the Spanish would take her as hostage if they could find her, and she would surely die.' Cofahiqui paused, sighed and took a deep breath.

'We hid her in a village a long way from here where she would be safe.

'I and my sisters met the invaders at the river. We were in a large canoe, like the one you saw yesterday. We smiled, and waved and greeted them warmly as if we were their friends. Our hearts quaked in our breasts. They were ugly, uncultured, rude people without conscience. Their horses snorted fire and they had hounds with teeth larger than those of wolves.

'I smiled all the time, and spoke softly to their leader in order to appeal to his better nature. He was insolent and insulting and said that he required slaves, and precious stones and metals, and the contents of all of our granaries, and if we resisted our men would all be killed, our women used as concubines and our children made slaves. Every village would be burned.

'I told him that we are a poor people. I told him, truthfully, that most of the men had become ill from the Spanish disease, and we had barely enough food for ourselves to survive the winter.

'He called himself de Soto. He cursed me in his language. I still stood in his way, smiling and trying to explain that we, ourselves, needed his help. He shoved me aside roughly and asked where he could find our *niaholata*. I told him she was dead, and he wanted to see where she was buried so he could dig her up and speak to her.

'I approached him with a gift, a necklace of pearls, and placed it around his neck.

'His men went through each village seeking the hiding place of our chieftess. Only a few of us knew, and no one would admit he knew where she was. De Soto knew by now that I had lied about her death.

'He seized my cousin who was the son of Cofahiqui and tormented him with the dogs, and required him to take them to

198

his mother. When he had been tortured he agreed to show them where she was hidden.'

We had been walking all the while as she told her story. She stopped talking until we reached a glade of trees where flowers of many colors bloomed.

'My cousin had them follow him for a long way while he decided what to do. He stopped just there, under that tree and told the soldiers that they should rest for awhile, because they would soon be climbing a steep hill to where Cofahiqui was hiding.'

The chieftess paused again in her story. Then she said 'My cousin pulled out a dagger and stabbed himself in the throat. He died under that tree. The flowers grow where his blood soaked the earth.'

She did not speak again for a long time. We walked through a forest that led to the top of a hill. They called this place Tolomeca. There was a religious temple on top, as large as any council house. It was not round. It had straight sides and the roof was supported by large pillars carved to resemble chiefs and warriors and noble people.

She took us inside, and on each side there were boxes containing the bones of the ancestors, and behind each box the image of the person carved on wood. At the foot of each box was a tribute basket of fine pottery and jewelry and tanned leather hides and more pearls than I knew existed.

We were all silent and prayerful in this holy place.

'De Soto's men robbed the temple. They took everything of value. They spilled the remains of the dead on the ground looking for anything hidden. For twenty five years we have worked to restore the dignity of our ancestors. We trade everything we produce and do not eat, for pearls and tribute.'

Later, when we were outside in the sunlight, her mood also brightened.

'What did you think of the quality of our carvings?' she asked Crying Bird.

'I have never seen anything more beautiful,' he said.

'Then I have something to show you,' Cofahiqui said. We followed her to the other side of the temple which looked out upon hills and the tops of low blue-topped mountains.

'This is the finest carving,' she said, gesturing to a large pole erected at the opening.

At the top of the pole was the figure of an eagle, with wings stretched as far as a man could reach his arms. The eagle's body was of cypress, and weathered gray. The wing feathers were of hickory, and translucent in the sunlight.

'Do you know the name of the craftsman?' she asked, a smile causing small creases beside her mouth.

'I do know,' I said.

'It is the work of the Chief of Ibitibi,' Crying Bird said in a strong voice.

Cofahiqui clapped her hands together. 'Of course it is, the great Ibitibi!' She was very pleased we knew the artist.

'Is he still alive, the Chief of Ibitibi?' she asked.

When we said he still lived, Cofahiqui said she had gotten the best of the trade, giving only a little copper and lower grade pearls, and had worried about it for many years. She had a gift she wanted us to deliver to make things fair. We told her we would be happy to deliver her gift to Chief Ibitibi with her kind wishes.

That evening in the council house all the elders were present. Chieftess Cofahiqui told us the rest of the story. When the Spanish could not find the *niaholata,* they took the younger girl, the future Cofahiqui, as hostage and moved toward the north. After three days she complained that she needed to relieve herself, as she had done several times before. She simply walked into the woods. Then she ran until she could run no more.

She carried with her a bundle which held half the pearls the Spanish had stolen from Tolomeca.

'This is that bundle. It has never been opened. These pearls have been touched by the Spanish and would not be acceptable tribute for our ancestors.

'You are to use this wealth to bribe warriors to fight, to trade for weapons or information, or any other use to kill the Spanish or the French.'

She presented Crying Bird with enough pearls to fill an arroba. They were wrapped and sealed in a water-tight bundle of animal skin.

'I have one other gift. For your uncle, the Chief of Ibitibi, I have this copper breastplate with an inlaid precious red jewel. If he is as valiant as his nephews he will need it to protect him while he slays the enemy.'

My brother thanked her people for their generosity and said we hoped to kill all the foreigners so they would never again be seen by the people of Cofahiqui.

* * *

The next day we were honored by attending a religious ceremony honoring the autumnal equinox. The people of Cofahiqui are as spiritual as we in Acuera, and I would not dishonor them by telling you what we learned in confidence of their beliefs.

They are also very smart, and they may know more than we do of the movement of Father Sun, and the moon and the stars. We went with an elder to the top of a hill a long way from the village. We had with us thirty small children, some as young as three summers. Two women were with us, and they carried food and water for the children.

Games were played and the children were loud and as rambunctious as young wolves. When it began to get dark one of the women, a story teller, started speaking very softly. The children stopped their hollering and gathered around her respectfully, sitting on the ground at her feet.

I also sat on the ground, and before long a young girl was in my lap. One story was very similar to the story told among Acuerans, about the Hummingbird and the Crane. There was another, I don't remember the name, about when the Creator turned a sharp-tongued woman into a crow. I remember most of the stories exactly as they were told. Perhaps some day I will tell them to you.

I was feeling homesick that night. We had left Acuera at the time of the spring equinox and had been gone half a year. Now ancient stories were being told, the same way I had entertained and educated the children of my own village.

Warriors and chiefly people always avoid showing tears, as it is seen as a sign of weakness. Tears spring easily to my eyes and I have never been ashamed. The child looked at my face, and then snuggled close to my chest, which made me even more emotional. I was glad it was dark. The tears ran down my cheeks as they had not for many years.

Crying Bird stood at a distance, and he did not have to be embarrassed by my nature.

When the story time was over, the old man said prayers, then began to instruct the children on what there was to be seen in the night sky. His understanding was the same as our own. He taught the children how to find their way by sighting different stars. He pointed out the homes of the spirits and told of the movement of the moon and how it moved water. The sun's movement around the world was explained more clearly than I had ever heard it said.

I was in for a surprise. Some of the children had been there before and became very excited. When his talk was done, the elder commanded everyone to stand up, and turn around quickly ten times without stopping. Of course, everyone became dizzy and began to stumble around and fall over each other onto the soft grass. Some of the older children acted crazy, as if they had been smoking spirit weed or eating magical mushrooms.

The elder asked who wanted to lead us to the village. Most of the children wanted the honor, but he chose the youngest volunteer, a boy of about six years. The elder ordered the rest to be silent. The young boy regained his senses and studied the stars for a time.

'Follow me,' he said, and struck off down one side of the hill and led us straight to the village."

CHAPTER 23

"Plans were discussed for our return to the south. We would have two large canoes and four braves to guide us all the way to Mocama. If there were threats to our safety, the escort would take us to the house of Satureiwa. The journey was by river, then between the islands and the mainland. It was past the time of the storms and the journey should be pleasant and swift.

The morning we left Cofahiqui there was a chill in the air, and the sun had moved a little to the south.

Nihoto was one of the party that was to accompany us to the village of Satureiwa. His knowledge of the tongues and customs of the people we would meet would be helpful if we were to reach Mocama safely.

Crying Bird asked me if I knew why it was necessary that the two of us have four warriors as our guides for a simple canoe journey down peaceful rivers. He asked the question on the second day, while Nihoto was not nearby.

'It could be that we are being protected against an attack by Utinans, although there has never been an Utinan anywhere in this land,' I said.

My brother made a 'harrump' sound in his throat.

'Then it might be that we carry with us half the wealth of Cofahiqui, and they fear we might be careless and lose it gambling,' I said.

Crying Bird laughed out loud. 'I think our escort will be with us for a long time,' he said.

The river of Cofahiqui wandered for a day before it joined a larger river where a village was located. This village was ruled by another *holata*. Nihoto said the two peoples had always lived as good neighbors and shared the same tongue.

We did not stop. Greetings were shouted between the village and the canoes, but we kept going down the new river. A short distance below the village we pulled the canoes onto a muddy bank to relieve ourselves and to walk around. Two of our guards stayed with the canoes and they took turns getting their exercise.

The third night we did not stop to rest. The villagers in that area were not always friendly, Nihoto said, and sometimes sought tribute from travelers. Crying Bird and I took our turns paddling so two of the guards could rest. The river was swift and there were many snags where old trees broke the surface of the water. The moon was bright and we could see most of them before they were too close.

Once, while I was lookout on our canoe, I began to think of going home to Ibitibi. A floating log scraped the side of the canoe. No harm was done but I was excused from my duty, and one of the guards who had no sleep took my place in the front.

Early in the morning we stopped to refresh ourselves. When we started again we did not go far before the freshwater turned to saltwater, and we passed another village at the river's mouth.

There was a sandbar here, and the tide was out. The water was shallow and we all got out of the canoes and pulled them to deeper water. The sand felt cool under my feet and it was good to walk and exercise my bad leg.

In Mayaca, and I believe in Ais, there is a river that flows southward between the mainland and islands which are strung like pearls on a necklace. It was the same here. We were protected from the ocean waves. Where there were openings between the islands we had to be more careful because the water was choppy and swirled about.

I had to laugh when the guides all began to whistle loudly when the water got rough. We have the same custom among Acuerans. We find it is calming to whistle, and we are less likely to make a mistake and sink the canoe in bad water.

My brother and I were not impressed with the quality of the canoes. They were large enough, and as comfortable as a canoe can be, if a canoe can be called comfortable at all. We had built canoes, or helped in the building under the direction of the master canoe builder, our uncle, the Chief of Ibitibi. These hulls were poorly shaped for both speed and stability. It would have been rude to say this to our hosts.

* * *

On the second day in the saltwater the world looked different than before. We were in the middle of a sea of marsh reeds and grasses, so high we could not see our way out. The channel was narrow and winding like a snake. There were always many ways to turn, and only one was the right way.

Our guides never slowed. They would go to the right, then the right again. Just when the way clearly lay to the right because it was wider, they would suddenly steer to the left into a narrow opening which would soon widen and prove to be the main channel.

Nihoto explained it to us. When we came to a point there would be a clump of reeds near the water edge, tied together with grasses and bent either to the right or left, pointing the way. They were left by traders. The area was so vast, and every place looked just like every other place, so that no one could trust his own memory or sense of direction.

Nihoto said there had once lived here a group of renegade criminals who made false signs, so traders would turn the wrong way and get stuck in the mud. Then they would be robbed and sometimes killed if they had a canoe the criminals wanted.

One of the traders was a great *jarva* and when he was robbed he put a curse on the criminals. They all suffered a terribly rash over their bodies, and the saltwater ate their flesh. Because they were not a tribe and had no *isucu* to treat the disease, they all died painful deaths. Since that time you could believe the markers, Nihoto said.

Several times we had to stop and wait because the tide was out and the water was too shallow. It gave us time to explore the small islands where no one lived but crabs, turtles

205

and birds. Soon the tide would come in and we would begin again.

We watched the sea birds that were always with us. Some would dive for fish just as the osprey and eagle do on the lakes and rivers. Sea gulls made the most noise with their chattering calls. We had no food to spare, but they would gather around us to share even our crumbs. They all seemed to be happy. Many people believe we will live again as birds in the spirit world. I would like to be a pelican if I have my choice."

* * *

"We passed through the land of the Guale in two days. There were villages on some of the islands to our left and on the mainland to our right. At one place where the passage was narrow, two warriors in a canoe hailed us. Nihoto waved to them and told our men to paddle faster. There was no way they could catch us, and they were soon out of sight.

'They were seeking tribute, and would want to search our canoes. We would have to kill them if they found the pearls,' Nihoto said.

We came to the village of Tacatacura, and stopped long enough for two of our guides to get fresh water. They returned with stories of fighting at Mocama. The stories were confusing. One story said the Spanish had returned and been killed by the French. Another story was the opposite, that the Spanish had killed all the French.

We continued our journey and before the end of the next day we entered Mocama and arrived at the main village of Chief Satureiwa.

Nihoto and I were in the same canoe for the entire trip. He taught me much about the language of his people. I am ashamed to say I never used all that knowledge, for I never returned to Cofahiqui.

He could speak the Acueran tongue, but none of the others you would call 'Timucuan.' It was easy for me to teach him the differences with Mocaman, Utinan, Potanan and even what little I knew of the Appalachee. Next to me, Nihoto is the smartest man I have ever known with languages."

When the sun was up and the boy gone to his bed, the Acueran reflected on all he had told de Coya, and what more must be said. He knew his time was short.

* * *

In the early afternoon the priest entered his room. He greeted the old man and sat at his desk, thumbing through the parchments he had prepared.

"Where is the boy?" Marehootie asked.

"We do not require his services any longer. Do you agree?" Pareja asked in an understandable Utinan dialect. "If we can speak directly to each other our work will move faster. I have more confidence in my abilities now."

"No. I do not agree. I need the boy here."

"Juan is a student. Unfortunately, he has neglected his studies and is falling behind the other boys in the memorization of the catechism and other lessons. That is my fault. I asked him to help us, you and I, and at the same time I assigned him responsibilities for the Holy Days."

"Has he asked to be released from his duties with me?" the Indian asked.

Pareja was slow to answer, having some difficulty in expressing himself properly. "It is my duty as teacher to make such decisions for him. He likes you, and he enjoys the stories of when you were young. He has told me of some of your herbal cures, and I do not object. If you were teaching pagan prayers, I would have put a stop to it long ago."

Marehootie sat on his stool, arms crossed over his chest, listening but saying nothing.

"Juan has given me some of your mosquito potion, and it works well. He has taught the others to carve gourd nests for the birds that eat mosquitoes. He even gave me the flower petals you said would help red eyes, and they ease the burning when I have been working too hard.

"You have been a positive influence on the boy. But it is in his interest that you and I go on with our work and let him return to his studies," the priest concluded.

207

"What work can we do, the two of us, together?" the Acueran asked.

Father Pareja sorted his papers and selected one. "I am confused about how some verbs in your tongue are changed by what the Spanish call prefixes and suffixes. I want to know how they are used, and how they change the meaning of the word."

"I do not understand," Marehootie replied.

Pareja tried again. This time he wanted to know how a verb would be conjugated by first, second or third person, and by past, present and future. He was unable even to ask the question with his limited knowledge of Utinan.

With each attempt, the Acueran shook his head in bewilderment.

After awhile Pareja walked outside to clear his mind. *Perhaps such questions could only be addressed to an Indian in the Spanish language, since the Timucuan vocabulary had no words for these concepts*, he decided.

"You have helped me greatly these last few weeks," he said to the Indian when he returned inside. "You have taught me the differences between the dialects and I can use what you have told me in my writings. You have worked hard with the wording of the Confessionario. I should be embarrassed at the clumsy way I expressed myself before you came here. I shall always be in your debt."

"Do you mean you are done with me?" Marehootie asked.

"If I can help you in any way, just ask. I will send the boy to say good-bye tomorrow. I assume you will want to go home soon," Pareja said.

"Do you have the permission of the sergeant to release me?"

"You have been my guest," the priest said.

"I have been his prisoner," the Acueran replied.

Before sundown two soldiers came and removed the desk and returned it to the convento. They locked the door as they left.

Marehootie sat on his pallet, smiling.

When it was dark he moved to the window. Grasping the bars, he pulled himself up, hooking the heal of his foot on the sill. He was so thin it was no problem squeezing his way to freedom. He enjoyed his nightly walks around the island.

As he moved in the shadows around the far end of the garrison he saw the priest and the sergeant sitting on the porch of the convento in animated discussion.

CHAPTER 24

The priest had prepared himself for bed. It was earlier than usual, but the fatigue of the past few days and the disappointing lack of progress with the Acueran had sapped his energy and dimmed his spirit. The sun had set but it was not yet dark. He was kneeling beside his bed when his prayers were interrupted by knocking on his apartment door.

By the time he finished his conversation with God and said his final 'Amen' the knocking had become a rude pounding. Pareja wrapped a blanket around his thin shoulders and pulled the door open and looked out.

The sergeant had never seen the priest without his robe. "I didn't realize you retired so early," he said, making no effort to retreat from the porch. He had brought his stool with him and it sat beside Pareja's chair.

"Could this wait until morning? As you can see, I'm no longer dressed," the priest said, pulling the blanket closer around his body.

"There are matters that must be discussed between the two of us, and they are urgent. I may be taking official actions that you will not understand unless you hear me out," he said.

Father Pareja sighed, closed the door and dressed himself. Presently he re-joined the sergeant on the porch and sat in his chair.

"I want to show you something first, while there is still light enough for you to see," Suarez said. He withdrew a leather pouch from his tunic, and fished his hand inside.

"Do you recognize this?" he asked.

Father Pareja studied what had been handed to him. "I believe I have seen this necklace before. It looks like the one worn by the Acueran. How did it come into your possession?"

"You have seen him wear it, then. Good. Good." The sergeant was smiling.

"Would you say the pearls are unusual?"

The priest held the strand up in the fading light.

"I have never seen pearls of this kind. They are larger than I have seen before. They have a variety of colors, shades of pink, and yellow, depending on the light, and they are not round like most pearls. Some have the irregular shape of large beans, some look like small bird eggs," he said.

"Would you say they are unique?"

"I am not a jeweler, or dealer in such things. I am a Franciscan and I am sworn to a life of poverty. Riches on earth do not interest me. I have no idea whether they are unique. Why do you ask me about these pearls?"

Suarez laid the necklace on his lap, and emptied the remaining contents of the bag into the priest's palm.

"And these? Are these the same as the ones in the necklace?" Suarez asked.

"They are all different from each other, but yes, they appear to be of the same sort. Why do you ask, and how is it you got the strand from around the neck of the old man?"

"Evidence!" the sergeant exclaimed. Now he was smiling broadly in his excitement.

"What sort of evidence? What is it you are trying to tell me?"

"You would have no idea where the pearls you are holding came from, but I shall tell you. One comes from a village of Potano. It was discovered by a patrol in 1566, at the location where twenty-seven soldiers were massacred. They were leading a band of Utinans on a raid against the Potanans when they were ambushed," he said.

"The Potanans left one of their dead on the battle ground, and the pearl was found in his medicine pouch."

"How do you know all this?" the priest asked.

211

"And the yellow one, that one," Suarez said, pointing his stubby finger into the priest's hand, "was found at Santa Lucia, after twenty-three men were butchered by the Ais.

"These two small ones, they were found on the bodies of Indians who attacked St. Augustine when the Englishman Drake burned the town. You see, I know all about these pearls, where they were found, by whom, and under what circumstances."

"How can you possibly know these things?" Pareja asked.

"Records," the sergeant said. "The military writes down everything, every field report, every deployment, and every incident. We have a saying, 'Soldiers kill and get killed. Officers investigate and write reports'."

"You have access to these reports?" Pareja asked.

"And the evidence lockers, also," Suarez answered. "You must remember, I have been commissioned by the Governor to investigate such matters.

.   "These records date back to the time of Governor Menendez, when the French were vanquished and St. Augustine was founded. Of course, the Presidio has burned twice and many reports have been lost over the years."

"Fascinating," Pareja said, "but why are you telling me?"

"Let's see, have we accounted for all the pearls?" Suarez asked. "No, we haven't. Those last three, there, nearest your thumb. Don't they appear to be larger and more beautiful than the others?"

Pareja looked at the pearls. It was almost too dark now to see clearly. "No," he said. "They look just like the others."

"I'm glad to hear you say that. One was found at Santo Domingo de Asao, near the body of Father Francisco de Verascola. Apparently, your 'Catabrian Giant' lived long enough to take one of his killers to eternity with him.

"And do you remember when you were at San Pedro de Mocama, and the Guale attacked the island?" he asked.

"Of course I remember. How could I ever forget that day?"

"Don Juan, the village chief, killed and scalped two of the Guale whose canoe was sunk. Those men died with these two pearls," Suarez said. "Two men, each with a pearl. Curious, wouldn't you say?"

Pareja studied the pearls in his hand but said nothing.

"I believe that it can not be refuted that when Indians kill my people and yours, they are paid for their services with pearls. I am convinced that this old man, the Acueran, with his rich strand of freshwater pearls, is their quartermaster."

"That, my dear sergeant, is preposterous!" the priest exclaimed.

"It may be that these pearls are common, I do not know, but unless you have more evidence you cannot convict the old man just because he wears a necklace of pearls. Even a military court, I think, would require more proof before condemning a man to death."

"You want more proof? I have statements from several Guale that before the killings there were three Indians, two Acueran and one Utinan, who were in the territory stirring up hatred against the Spanish and counseling rebellion. One of the Acuerans was described quite well. He was middle-aged, tall and thin. One witness said he walked with a limp. Everyone agreed that he wore his hair down around his shoulders, probably the only man in the entire Province of Guale who wore his hair in that manner. Do you need more proof?"

"My boy, Juan de Coya, has said that Chief Tacatacura denies that the Acueran is who you say he is," Pareja answered "and Tacatacura probably knows every Guale by sight."

"I knew the boy would tell you. I told him it was official business and he was not to say anything, but I knew he couldn't keep a secret. Did he also tell you that the liar, Tacatacura, has his own pearl that he wears around his neck?"

"So now you also condemn the chief of the crime of wearing a pearl?" Pareja asked.

"It is clear to me now the wisdom of the Governor in ordering me to remove Tacatacura and his people to the south. Had he remained at San Pedro, Tacatacura would have waited for the return of the Guale, and murdered you, Father Lopez and every Spaniard in Mocama."

"Why is it you are so willing to call your own witness a liar when he disappoints you by telling the truth? If you have the authority to convene a court, which I doubt, you will not do so here at San Juan. I forbid it! If you are to try this man, I insist that you do so at St. Augustine. I am sure your superiors will insist on more proof than you have shown me."

Father Pareja was standing now; ready to go back to his prayers.

"I am not an unreasonable man," the sergeant said, "and I have an open mind. I can even agree that it would be better to have someone identify the old man, or perhaps secure a confession. There is one witness who is beyond my authority to produce. You know of whom I speak. If he were willing to come here and tell the truth, perhaps this matter can be resolved," the sergeant said.

Father Pareja covered his face with his hands. "Leave me for awhile," he said. "I will answer you but I need first to think and then pray on it. Half an hour, no more."

Suarez shrugged, then stepped off the porch and walked toward his own quarters in the barracks. Pareja could see him there, through the window. The sergeant had lighted a lamp, and was hunched over his desk, writing.

* * *

When Suarez returned, Pareja was prepared with his answer.

"Father Avila was a slave of the Guale for nine months. He would have full knowledge of the Guale matter. He has refused the Governor's summons to testify against his captors based on the privilege granted to clergy. His faith would not allow him to speak ill of those whom God has put in his charge. My answer would be the same if I were he."

"You priests are all fools!" Suarez exclaimed.

Father Pareja ignored the insult. "It may be, though, that he would be free to speak for the Acuean if he is an innocent man. I will go to St. Augustine tomorrow. I will speak to Father Marron and to Father de Avila. I will return in six days.

Suarez stepped down from the porch a second time, this time carrying his stool. "The Acueran will be alive when you return," he said.

The sergeant walked half-way across the church yard, paused and came back to the convento where Father Pareja was slumped in his chair.

Suarez drew close and spoke in hushed tones. "I don't know if you were aware of it, but the boy, de Coya, stayed with the old man last night. He did not slip back into the convento until it was getting light in the east, according to my guard."

"I will speak to the boy," Pareja replied wearily.

CHAPTER 25

Juan de Coya came early in the morning. He carried corn cakes made with sweet berries, and fresh spring water. The old man thanked him for the gifts. The cakes would make an excellent evening meal.

* * *

"When we arrived we were not granted an audience with Chief Satureiwa. He was an important chief with thirty villages under his rule. He expected our visit long before we arrived and perhaps he felt we had shown disrespect.

We, and the men from Cofahiqui, slept in the council house. For such a large, important village we thought the council house was small.

We met no chiefly person for three days. We were told that Chief Satureiwa was busy with more important affairs. Then we were told that he was away from the town. We knew this to be a lie. Crying Bird and I walked through the village one evening and saw Satureiwa and one of his wives out for a stroll. There were guards all around him.

One morning early we were awakened and told to prepare for a short trip. Nihoto and the men of Cofahiqui stayed at the council house with the pearls.

We got into a canoe, one which bore Chief Ibitibi's mark on the bow, and set off up river. The river was very wide here, so far from shore to shore that you could not call to a man on the other side. We asked the name of the river and we were told it was called the River of May by the French and the San Juan by the Spanish.

'We have always called it the River of the Sun,' our paddler said. It was hard to believe this wide, straight river was the same winding, beautiful river we knew in our homeland.

We traveled a short distance and stopped in a village under the rule of Chief Athore. The chief was there but we were kept waiting for a long time. When we were finally taken to see Athore and his *inija* the chief immediately began to holler and shout at us, insulting us and calling us foul names. He threatened us with a whipping if we did not apologize for coming so late.

Athore was a large man, taller than Crying Bird but not as strong. He wore splendid tattoos on his arms, legs and body. He strutted about, flapping his arms and bouncing up and down on the balls of his feet to look even more fearsome. I was frightened at his display of temper. Crying Bird was not impressed.

At one time my brother looked at me and said in our language 'Have you ever seen such a pompous idiot?'

Athore did not understand the Acueran tongue or did not hear, so I replied to my brother 'He looks like a crane doing its mating dance.'

Neither of us smiled as we spoke, but my chest was heaving with laughter trying to escape.

When Athore's anger was spent, I apologized to him for our delay in arriving at Satureiwa. I told him of the murderous attack by the Utinans, and of the injuries and illness we had suffered. I told him we had discovered the source of wealth to fight a hundred battles. I did not mention the pearls that were under guard at the village of Satureiwa.

He did not seem to listen. It was as if no excuse would be enough, or perhaps any apology was good enough. He opened his eyes wide when I mentioned wealth, and demanded to know more.

I told him the owner of the wealth had instructed that knowledge of it was for the eyes and ears of the great Chief Satureiwa, and no one else. That seemed to satisfy him.

Athore said that he would personally speak to Satureiwa and ask him to talk to us. He said Satureiwa was in delicate negotiations with the Spanish, but might find time for us in a few days.

We said we had been away for many days, and heard only rumors of the things that happened while we were gone. Athore said he had important people to see, but he would send his *inija* to tell us all that happened since summer.

For the rest of the day we were kept in a hut near the council house. There was a guard outside and we did not try to leave. It was strange that in the village of Satureiwa we were given freedom to walk around, but in the village of a vassal chief we were confined.

Late in the day we returned to the council house where Athore's *inija* awaited. He was a pleasant man and answered all of our questions.

He wanted to know the last thing we knew before our journey, so he would know where to start his story. We told him we knew of the coming of the French, and the help given by Chief Satureiwa before they showed their murderous nature

. We said that we knew of the criminal alliance between the French and Outina, and their attack on Satureiwa's friend, Chief Potano. We had also learned of a second attack where even Chief Outina had no stomach for the useless massacre of innocent, unarmed Potanans by the French.

'That is all we are certain of,' Crying Bird said. 'I had a vision of the French moving up the River of the Sun, and when it was confirmed as true we began our journey.'

The *inija* thought for a long time before he began.

'We are well informed of your gift as a prophet, Crying Bird. It is known throughout Cautio that the Spirits speak to you and give you wisdom and courage. With every telling, your fame is even greater.'

Inija looked at me. 'You do not need to interpret. I am comfortable speaking in your tongue.'

This *inija* had been with Athore earlier, and heard the disrespectful things we had said in our language, a tongue *Inija* understood clearly. He smiled at me and he knew that I knew he could have hurt us, but did not. I wondered if this was a man we could trust, or whether he would later try to make us pay for his silence.

'All you think you know is true. The rest of the tale is as hard to believe as the first part,' he said. Then he told us the rest of the story.

During the summer, while we were in Mayaca and Ocale and Potano, the French were starving. They traded everything of value at Fort Caroline for food. Chief Satureiwa was unhappy about the friendship of the French with Olate Quai Outina, and the murder of the people of Potano. He refused to trade under any but the most favorable terms.

Soon Rene de Laudonneire, the French Captain, had nothing left to trade. Soldiers would give their tunic for a poor ear of maize. A chief from a small village wore a metal soldier's hat, and all it cost him was a handful of rotting roots.

Some soldiers deserted the fort. The French turned on their friend Outina and held him hostage for food. When no ransom was paid, they freed Chief Outina and he returned to his village.

The French then lost their minds and locked up their own leader. This was in the late summer. It was what the French called a mutiny. They had two leaky boats and would try to sail back to France.

While they were repairing their boats another French ship came into view. It was a relief ship with food and provisions under the command of a man named Ribault. Seven days later Spanish ships appeared under the command of Pedro Menendez de Aviles, and a war began.

Menendez occupied the village of Seloy, to the south. Ribault devised an attack on the village and led his ships along the coast, leaving only one hundred people at Fort Caroline.

His fortune was bad. A storm sunk a ship and cast another on the shore where its cannons were useless. He lost many men that day.

Within a few days Menendez attacked Fort Caroline by land and killed everyone except a few women and children.

The French who had been shipwrecked were hunted down by the Spanish. When they put up their hands in surrender and dropped their weapons they were murdered and buried in the sand. This was true. It was witnessed by many of Satureiwa's people who all told it the same.

'All the French are dead now,' he said, 'except for a few who escaped and are living in the villages as slaves.'

His story finished, the *inija* sat looking at his own hands. They were cracked and wrinkled with age. 'Do you believe your task is finished, now that the French are all killed?' he asked.

'No,' my brother said. 'We have vowed to die a hundred deaths to rid our land of all these murderous criminals.'

'Well spoken,' the *inija* said.

We returned to the village of Satureiwa the next day. Many of the people worked with metal tools. The woodworkers had awls and knives and cutting edges. Even the field workers had hoes made of metal instead of shell. These were all taken in trade from the French during their last days.

When the French were all killed, Satureiwa's people raided Fort Caroline and found nothing of value, other than metal hats and armor. This metal, when heated and pounded with iron tools, could be fashioned into excellent arrow heads and spear points.

We sat around the fire in the council house after our evening meal. The men of Cofahiqui were interested to hear all we had learned of the war between the Spanish and French. There were two river traders with us and they told what they knew or had heard from others.

Nihoto and his brothers were gentle people, and as honorable as Acuerans. It was hard for them to understand the massacre of innocents. 'Our only experience with this much killing was when we last saw the Spanish twenty-five years ago at Cofahiqui,' Nihoto said.

* * *

The fire wood was of the best kind. It was not wet inside, and was not of pine, so it did not crack and pop, but burned slowly and evenly. For a long time no one had fed the fire. It seemed content to burn all night on the few logs it had.

We were all tired. My brother became quiet and gazed into the fire for a long time. He was no longer listening to the stories told by the traders.

I laid my head on my arm, too lazy even to go to my bed, and went to sleep there by the fire. Later, I heard Crying Bird speak and I sat up. He had not moved, but was staring into the fire. He spoke again in a tongue I did not understand. He was not speaking to me or to any of the men around the fire.

A trader asked me if my brother was ill. I said 'no,' that he was speaking to the Spirits. The traders picked up their coverings and left the council house.

Crying Bird became agitated and began to shout and flail his arms. We were all awake now, and none of us knew what to do. My brother rocked forward and back, looking directly into the fire. He cried out again in great agony and pain. Tears shone on his cheeks for the first time since he was a child.

With a loud 'woosh' sound the flames shot to his face and the tears sizzled and sparked and were gone. Before I could reach to save him, it was over. The fire withdrew, flickered and shriveled and in a moment was gone. There were no burning embers and no smoke, only the ashes of an old campfire.

Crying Bird had fallen to his side and lay sleeping. He did not answer or move when I shook him and called his name. I looked at his face, and it was not burned and the hair of his head was not singed.

I sat with him until morning. He awoke and stepped outside the council house and spoke his morning prayers to the Sun. Then he walked to the edge of the village and relieved himself on a bush.

* * *

Chief Satureiwa was even more impressive than his vassal, Athore. He was not as tall, and slight of build, but he had the regal bearing of a chief. His skin was dark, as if to hide the tattoos that covered his limbs and body.

The first thing I noticed were his eyes, large and spread wide across his face as if he would miss nothing, but take everything in. Where Athore was interested only in himself,

Satureiwa was open and friendly and concerned that he had inconvenienced us by making us wait for an audience.

He stepped down from his seat and clasped our hands, mine and my brothers, then sat down again. He wore a matchcoat of the finest deerskin, with small lifelike figures of animals painted front and back. There was a collar of the pelt of river otter around his neck. The weather had turned cold for the first time, and he wore the coat for comfort and not to impress two poor Acuerans.

This man had been the first to welcome the French, and had been betrayed by them when they sided with his enemy, Chief Outina. Now he dealt with the murderous Spanish for whom death was sport. He spoke of these things in Mocaman, and I helped my brother understand.

He asked what we, as Acuerans, remembered of de Soto. He said he knew of Chief Acuera's stand against the Spanish, and made us promise to tell our chief that the story had been an inspiration to Chief Saturiwa.

Crying Bird was quiet, and told me to answer the chief's questions, as if I were the emissary of Chief Aquera.

I recounted for him what had happened on our journey, of the promises of help from Mayaca and Ocale and Potano. I told him that the Ais could not be depended upon, and that we believed Yustaga would do Potano's bidding.

'And what of your dealings at Cofahiqui, did you find support from a people so far away?' he asked.

I looked to my brother to answer, but he looked straight ahead.

'We carry with us a treasure that is half of the *niaholata*'s wealth, and four warriors who have said their final farewells to their families. The chieftess has said that her fortune is to be spent ridding this land of the Spanish scourge,' I said.

Satureiwa sat quietly holding his chin in his hand and drumming his first finger against his lips.

'You carry pearls,' he said.

'Enough to fill an arroba.'

His eyes widened. 'Who else knows?' he asked.

'Only Chief Athore and his *inija* know we carry wealth.'

A frown crossed the face of Chief Satureiwa. 'What will you do with them?'

'Half are to be left for you and the rest given to Chief Acuera.'

The chief of Satureiwa pondered all that I had said. 'The pearls will not be safe here. The Spanish would kill us all to possess them. You must take them to your chiefs. Acuera and Ibitibi will know how to hide them until they become useful.'

My brother stirred. He looked at me and our eyes met. I saw in his eyes a deep ocean of sadness and pain. He addressed Chief Satureiwa. 'It has been made known to me that Chief Ibitibi will be dead before we reach home, and the village is no longer ours,' he said."

* * *

The old man paused in his story and wet his lips with spring water. Before he could continue a voice was heard from outside.

"Juan de Coya, are you in there? Come out, I must speak to you." It was Father Pareja calling from the churchyard. Juan jumped to his feet and went out. A guard slid the metal latch into place.

The boy followed the priest into the convento.

"I will be traveling to St. Augustine today. It will be six days before I return," Pareja said. "I want you to apply yourself to your studies while I am gone. Your recitations could stand improvement."

"Yes, Father," the boy replied.

"And I want you to go to the villages and find out if any of the old people are dying and will require last rites when I return."

"Yes, Father," Juan said again, as he had been taught. Then he spoke again. "Have I done something that has angered you, Father?"

"No, Juan, you have not angered me. I am disappointed that you would rather talk to the Acueran than get your rest. To stay with him through the night and enter your room when the other students are awakening for the new day is a very bad thing. You showed poor judgment."

The boy hung his head, but did not answer the priest.

"Perhaps it is partly my fault. I encouraged you to befriend him. I hoped he would return your friendship by helping us with . . .helping me with my language studies. It was a poor motivation and a mistake on my part."

"But that is over, now. I have thanked your friend for his help. It won't be necessary for you to visit with him any further. I'm sure he will be gone soon, anyway, after a few things have been attended to."

Within the hour the priest walked out of the village to the south toward St. Augustine. At the sergeant's insistence, he was accompanied by two soldiers.

CHAPTER 26

The Franciscan monastery had burned to the ground three years earlier. Since then the Order of Friars Minor had been housed at the hospital known as Our Lady of Solitude. It was there Father Pareja met with the Franciscan Superior, Fray Francisco Marron.

"I could order Father de Avila to speak to you, Father Pareja, but I will not do so. You know that I counseled him not to speak when he was summoned by the Governor's Board of Inquiry. For him to implicate the instigators of the killings at Guale would violate God's call to all of us that the Indians be protected. He agreed with me, and despite the great privations he had suffered he remained silent.

"It was such a clear choice at the time, but now it becomes more interesting, don't you think? An innocent man, a 'gentle creature of God', as you say, may be condemned to death unless Father de Avila tells what he knows."

Father Marron had been looking out the window, composing his thoughts as he spoke.

"If he speaks out and says the man is guilty, he will be killed by the authorities. If, on the other hand, he does not know the Indian or knows that he is not responsible for what happened, the man will go free, but I fear greater consequences may follow."

Father Pareja cleared his throat, and when he had Marron's attention, he spoke. "What consequences could be greater than the death of an innocent?"

"I fear that if de Avila testifies at all, he will have given up his privilege to remain silent on the subject of what did or did not take place at Guale," Marron said. "Governor Canzo might require him to speak fully about everything, naming everyone involved. Many might suffer and die."

"Man's law would require that he speak," Pareja said.

"And God's law would require that if he speak, he speak the truth," the Franciscan Superior said.

Pareja sat dejected in the wooden chair beside the one occupied by his mentor, the man he followed to this land seven years earlier.

"I look for God's will, and I cannot discern it," Pareja said. "I feel the burden is my own, put there by God. I have no right to ask Father de Avila to violate his vows, yet my prayers for wisdom have not been answered."

Marron reached over and patted the hand of Father Pareja. "There is only one place where Father de Avila may speak of what he knows. It will not be breaking a confidence for me to tell you this. As you know, the privations and cruelties he suffered for nine months have robbed him of his strength, although his faith is as strong as ever.

"His health may never fully be recovered. He is kept busy performing duties in the church here in St. Augustine. He assists the diocesan priest, there. Now, after five years Father de Avila appears to have recovered as much as he ever will.

"I asked him if he was willing to return to the missions. He did not answer me immediately, but prayed on the matter and sought God's will. The terrible dreams he suffered for a year after his rescue have now returned.

"Although he has not said it, I believe his courage is gone. His sufferings have robbed him of his spirit. He has asked me to hear his confession, and I have agreed to do so. He is depressed now and losing weight. I'm afraid the sin he wishes to confess is his lack of strength to do God's will."

"He could not find a more spiritual guide than you." It was Pareja's time to pat the hand of his mentor. "God will put the words in your mouth to heal our brother," he said.

Father Marron looked directly into Pareja's face. "I will not be his Confessor," he said. "You will hear his confession. It is God's will."

"It is surely not His will that I violate the sanctity of the confessional," Pareja answered.

"Of course not. It would be a sin for you to repeat anything he says to you. I'm sure you recall the scripture 'God works in mysterious ways his wonders to perform.'"

"But I don't see how . . ." Pareja started.

"And neither do I, but if God would intercede to save the Indian, he will have a way to do it without either you or Father de Avila violating your vows. Perhaps de Avila will know of some fact that can be established independent of his confession, or some other witness who could tell the truth of what occurred five years ago."

"I will have to pray on this, and I will need to think carefully about the questions I will ask," Pareja said.

"Pray, by all means, but do not give a thought to what you will say. As you have just said, 'God will put the words in your mouth to heal our brother.' Perhaps he will also put the words in Father de Avila's mouth to save your Indian."

Father Pareja prayed for guidance while Father Marron went to the diocesan church in the town to speak with Father de Avila.

It was late in the afternoon when the three priests met at the Mission Nombre de Dios. The chapel lacked a confessional booth, as was available at the church in the town of St. Augustine, but it afforded complete privacy. Father Marron stood guard outside to prevent the others being interrupted. Pareja and de Avila knelt near the altar.

* * *

De Avila cried and prayed for a very long time. When he was ready, he proceeded.

"Forgive me, Father, for I have sinned," he said.

De Avila spoke of his work at the Mission at Ospo, of the failures of his own doing and of the marvelous victories wrought by God. He wept as he spoke of the wonderful people he had brought to God and those who had been baptized. He counted his own sufferings, the loneliness, the near starvation and the freezing winters as badges of honor. He praised God for strengthening his body and spirit to the task.

He confessed his present weakness, his lack of a strong spirit to return to the work God had fashioned for his life. He condemned his own lack of courage to face the privations and dangers that once he counted of little import. When he was exhausted, Father Pareja began to speak.

His message was a simple one. "It is now, and was then, and has always been God's will at work in this land," he said. "He chose Franciscans for this difficult task, and He selected the strongest among them, de Avila, for the greatest test of courage and faith. Martyrs there had been, Fathers de Corpa, Rodriguez, Aunon, Badajoz and Verascola, the Jesuits that were there first and the diocesan priests who had died. Seventeen had died, and possibly more. For the most part their deaths were violent and brutal, yet their suffering was short and they were now with God, where we will all be some day.

"Perhaps God had rendered de Avila weakened in body and spirit for a reason. He was the strongest among them, but had been brought down. Perhaps it was God's will that de Avila not return to the missions. If it were otherwise, he would be there already.

"Perhaps it was His will that his child touch others with his experiences. Perhaps he had been chosen to teach, or write his story, or to return to Spain to serve the weakest and poorest in his own land.

"Whatever God's plan is for you, it is an important task, one chosen only for Francisco de Avila, and He will lead you to it," he said.

The men wept and prayed together.

"You want to know of Guale?" de Avila said later. "I can tell you here in confession and I know it will not be repeated outside this chapel. Father Marron has said that you need information that might save the life of a man you believe is innocent. I will tell you what I know.

"First, as to the cause of the killings. The Governor believes that Fray de Corpa interfered with chiefly succession. He reprimanded a man called Juanillo and forbade him from becoming chief because of the sin of polygamy. Have you heard that?" de Avila asked.

"It is what the Governor's board has published as its conclusion, and that Juanillo killed him for it," Pareja answered.

De Avila sighed. "It is true. That is how it happened. I was a slave. They treated me cruelly. They would neither feed nor clothe me. They took turns humiliating me. It is strange to say, though, that they respected me and wanted desperately that I understand why the killings had happened.

"I knew Juanillo. He cursed the memory of Father de Corpa, and told me how he murdered him. It was the greatest cruelty I suffered; listening to him. Why he needed to tell me about it is a mystery. He did not confess it to gain forgiveness. Perhaps it is an ethic we never discerned in these people. He felt he had to tell me, a slave, and I believed him then, as I do now.

"What you have been told of the deaths of the others is both true and false. The manner of their deaths was as you have heard, although the Indians told me that Verascola fought back and killed one of his attackers.

"The falsity relates to the motives. I have been told by many Indians that they did not admire Juanillo, and some were even pleased to learn he would not be a chief."

Pareja interrupted. "But the deaths all took place in the same week," he said.

"That is true, and Juanillo's act may have caused the others to strike at the same time, but the other chiefs had already agreed to rid Guale of the Spanish and to murder all of us, priests and military alike. It would have happened within a week or a month, but the killing of de Corpa required that it happen immediately, before the military reacted."

"But there was no warning. I spoke to Verascola when he passed through San Pedro on his way to St. Augustine. He was cheerful and optimistic."

"Wasn't he always?" de Avila asked, wiping his eyes.

"The Guale told me that with the deaths their villages had suffered from the pestilence they were no longer able to provide the maize required for St. Augustine. They were threatened by the soldiers. A chief was whipped inside his own council house. At one village the soldiers stole all the maize in the store house, leaving nothing for winter. Not even seed corn for planting.

"And then can you guess what happened? The soldiers burned the corn fields.

"When the soldiers required the young men of the village of Tulapo to carry the maize to St. Augustine, our fate was sealed. They were treated as pack animals. Each boy was loaded with three arrobas. The chief told me that ten young men were taken. Two escaped in the swamp and returned to the village. They spoke of others who died along the trail and were left to rot. Only two of ten, the others dead or sold as slaves."

Pareja shook his head slowly, side to side.

"All because of the cruelties of a sergeant," Father de Avila said.

"Was his name Suarez?" Pareja asked.

"You know of this man?"

"He is the man who threatens to kill the Indian," Pareja answered.

"That man is evil. His sin must be blacker in the eyes of God than a pagan's polygamy," de Avila said.

"Father Marron has told me this Indian of yours is an Acueran, middle aged and thin."

"That would be a fair description," Pareja said.

"I know of such a man, a vagabond Indian. I only know of two Acuerans as far north as Guale. This man lived near Ospo and despite his age he was a religious student for a time."

"This Indian spoke Guale, did he?" Pareja asked.

"Fluently, and he was an apt student. He knew the catechism and might have been baptized had it not been for the killings. It is a strange story. I believe he saved my life. Would you like to hear it?"

Pareja felt a knot in his throat and at the moment couldn't speak. He nodded his head.

"I already knew that Father de Corpa was dead when they came for me. It was a moonlight night, and I attempted to elude them by hiding in the rushes. They found me and I was stuck by arrows in the shoulder and thigh. My hand was also injured.

"The Indian who was my student was nearby, and he told the others I would be a valuable slave or a hostage if the military threatened to attack. They listened to him, an Acueran. I was surprised and grateful. They took me to Tulafina, and I became the slave to all."

"And did you see the man during your captivity? Pareja asked.

"Only one time. It was the day before I was released."

"The day before you were rescued," Pareja corrected.

De Avila reached out his hand and put it on Father Pareja's shoulder. He was smiling for the first time. "This is my story, Francisco. Let me tell it how it happened."

Pareja returned the smile.

"The Acueran came to the village. I was ill from lack of nourishment, and could neither work nor look for food. He said I was no fit slave, and that they should release me. Again, they did what this stranger commanded.

"They took me to a trail that was used by military patrols. I was fearful that I was bait for an ambush. They left me with enough food and water for three days. The Spanish soldiers found me there, sitting against a tree. I was naked, but for the first time in nine months my stomach was full."

"There was no battle?" Pareja asked.

De Avila laughed out loud. It was a laugh full of mirth too long suppressed. "The sergeant ordered the men to fire their weapon into the trees, to scare the Guale. I know those woods. There wasn't an Indian within two leagues."

"I will not ask you the name of the Acueran," Father Pareja said.

"Nor will I offer it," de Avila said, "although I believe we are speaking of the same man. He walked with a slight limp. And he wore the most beautiful freshwater pearls."

CHAPTER 27

Juan de Coya did as the priest instructed. He moved quickly through the villages served by the mission. What he learned was not encouraging. Six people were too sick to come out of their houses, and new fires had been set nearby so they would not be near those who were still healthy.

He had the catechisms already committed to memory and recited them to himself, over and over, as he traveled from place to place. He wondered why Father Pareja would criticize his lessons. Perhaps he would ask the priest how he could improve when Father Pareja returned from St. Augustine.

On the morning of the fourth day after Father Pareja left, de Coya returned to the mission and went to see the old man.

"I left so quickly the day Father Pareja called me you may have thought me rude. *Paqe, Paqe,*" the boy said. "Father asked me to visit the villages in his absence and it took three days to go everywhere, but I have done as he asked."

"You must move very fast. I have never seen you run, but I would gamble on you in a race against a deer," the old man said. "Do you run everywhere you go?"

"Father Pareja said you would be leaving soon. I ran all the way so I could see you again before you go. I would like to hear the rest of your story if there is time."

"We have little time left. I will tell you as much as you need to know," the old man said. He sat on his pallet, his back against the wall, and began.

* * *

232

"In two days we were on the river going south against the slow current. Chief Satureiwa had granted our request to use the canoes of Ibitibi. We were led by four war canoes of Satureiwa's warriors, a total of forty men, in case Outina tried to stop us.

It took three days to pass from Satureiwa territory and through the part of the river controlled by Chief Outina. We saw several well-armed Utinans on the shore and in canoes, but they did not challenge our passage.

By noon the next day we saw smoke rising in the air at a great distance. As we drew nearer we could tell it was not a campfire, and it was not a forest fire. It was a village that burned. It was our home, Ibitibi.

When we pulled our canoes from the water we saw some of the raiders still in the village. My brother ordered that none of us attack them unless they first tried to harm us. I did not understand this order, and argued with Crying Bird for the right of revenge. He left his knife and bow in the canoe, and walked unarmed into Ibitibi, into the midst of the Mayacans.

A cloud of heavy smoke choked the village. One house remained untouched. It was the home of our uncle, Chief Ibitibi.

He lay on the ground outside, his eyes open, staring upward through the branches of a tall pine tree. He had no wounds that could be seen. Crying Bird sat next to him, holding the hand of the dead chief. I squatted beside them and cried until I had no more tears.

Women who had fled into the woods came back when they saw that we were there. They told us the men of the village, led by Alobo, were still in the forest organizing an attack on the Mayacans. My brother sent me to find them and bring them back. They argued with me, but with no leader other than Alobo they followed me.

Alobo did not want to come with me, but cursed and said he would walk to the main village to give the news to Chief Acuera. I said that it would be easier and faster if he came back to the village and used one of the canoes. He followed behind us.

When we entered the village Crying Bird and Chief Mayaca were having a polite conversation, as if nothing had happened.

By nightfall all of the Mayacans had gone, except for a few who remained so it could not later be said they had abandoned the village. Most of the people of Ibitibi had gone to Acuera or to another village nearby. Several women without children remained to collect what little might be salvaged.

Not one person had been killed. Two of Alobo's guards were surprised by the daybreak raid and suffered injuries when they were clubbed by the Mayacans. When our chief awakened and saw what was happening he lay down where we found him. I believe Blind Jarva collected him there and took him to the world of Spirit.

In destroying the village the Mayacans did not pursue those who escaped. They torched the houses but left the granary full and undamaged. The wooden effigies of Chief Ibitibi, the cypress, pine and hickory eagles, owls, otters, bears, wolves, panthers and all the rest were thrown into the river.

For days we heard that those made of hickory and the lighter woods washed up on shore far to the north. The cypress and heart-of-pine animals were heavier and sunk into the mud and muck in the river bottom, and were lost forever.

Crying Bird asked for my help. He wanted the burial of our uncle to be done with the highest honor, and with the dignity due a chief of the Acuera. My brother had already cut off much of his own hair.

In the days that followed the Mayacans lived beside those of us who had lived our lives in the village and had remained. We could stay until the burial was finished. I am sure they knew this might be a long time. The Mayacans take as much care as Acuerans to insure their dead are properly sent to the world of Spirit.

On the night of the day of Chief Ibitibi's death, he was carried on my brother's back to the charnel house of the White Deer Clan outside the village. There had been no death in the clan for a long time, and his was the only body there.

Each day there were prayers said, and each night Crying Bird or I would guard the house against wolves, raccoons or other predators that might consume our uncle's flesh or scatter his bones. We had an early summer and there was much rain. The heat rotted the flesh and I showed my brother how the bones were to be cleaned.

Crying Bird looked for a suitable place for our uncle. The clan burial mound had been desecrated by the presence of the Mayacans and could not be used. He found a high place near the river, close to where Ibitibi had built his famous canoes and wood carvings. The place was blessed and sanctified by the *jarva* of Acuera.

Sand was brought by a barge pulled by three canoes. It was sand from the Wekiva River, and it was a Mayacan barge and Mayacan canoes. Of course, the canoes were manned by Acuerans of the White Deer Clan, as is required under our beliefs and practices.

Three arrobas of ocher were delivered by traders who would accept no payment. The old *isucu* of Ibitibi returned for the burial and brought with him the proper talismans and burial herbs. He said I was too inexperienced for a burial of this importance and he would show me how it was to be done. We had no village *jarva,* as you will recall, and we were honored that the *jarva* of Acuera would be there.

All the time our uncle laid in the charnel house his chest was covered by the copper breastplate which was a gift of the *Niaholata* of Cofahiqui.

For thirty days after his death the women wept, and they wept again in the days following his burial. The men of the clan all bled profusely from the sharp shells and sticks they used to show the suffering of their hearts.

Before the bones were covered in the sand and ocher, Crying Bird claimed the copper breastplate and took it for himself. It would not be proper to bury with Ibitibi an object he had not loved during his life. All of Ibitibi's tools, his awls and cutting edges, were buried with him so he might continue his work in the Spirit world.

My brother and I had handled the rotting flesh of our uncle and *jarva* of Acuera performed the cure ceremony. Without the cure we would be unclean and would suffer agonizing deaths. I learned how that ceremony is done and the herbs and charms that are used. It is like the curing ceremony warriors go through after they have killed an enemy in battle, but it is more complicated.

My uncle was buried properly in the land he loved. Chief Mayaca said any unarmed member of the clan could come and go freely to speak to the Spirit of our uncle forever. Neither Crying Bird nor I ever returned. There was no longer a village of Ibitibi.

* * *

The Mayaca stayed at Ibitibi for five years but found that the soil was not good for growing maize, which we always knew. They could not feed themselves and went back home. They stopped using the fish camp at Wekiva at the same time.

When we left Ibitibi for the last time we went to the main village of Acuera. The men from Cofahiqui and the pearls were still with us."

* * *

Before the Acueran could say more, the door of the cell was thrust open. Two soldiers entered without knocking,

"You are coming with us," one commanded, seizing the Acueran by the arm and pulling him to his feet. The other soldier shackled his hands behind him. A metal collar with spikes on the inside was fitted loosely around his neck. A long iron chain hung from the collar to the floor.

The boy moved to help the old man, but he was swatted down by one of the soldiers. "You are coming, too," he said.

CHAPTER 28

It was mid-day when Father Pareja and the soldiers emerged from the marshy grass trails from the south, crossed the arm of the river by canoe and entered the Mission San Juan del Puerto. A quiet hung in the still air. The mission yard was deserted and the kitchen fires were not lit.

The students who lived and studied in the convento were out of sight, as were the cooks and the gardeners. No one came to greet him. The priest called out and no one answered.

Only one person could be found, only the boy who slept on his cot in the convento. Pareja kneeled and shook the boy and he awoke with a start, one eye wide and fearful, and the other bruised and swollen shut. His lower lip had burst and dried blood covered his chin. His right ear was cut, and blood soaked his pillow.

Pareja wrapped his arms around the boy, held him close, and rocked him gently. "What have they done to you?" he said. "What in God's name?"

The priest brought clean water and a disinfectant, and cleansed the boy's wounds. He gently treated the injury to the mouth. Two teeth had cut through the lip from a vicious blow. One tooth was loose and wobbly to the touch. The other tooth was gone.

The priest had no surgical thread to repair the ear, as would be available at a hospital, and lacked the training to sew wounds. Instead, he cleaned the ear and tore a sheet into strips and fashioned a bandage about the boy's head. He prayed that the cut would heal.

The boy accepted the pain and did not flinch when his wounds were touched.

"The sergeant has beaten the old man," he said. "He asked him questions and when he was unhappy with the answers he ripped at his neck with spikes. Then they trussed him to a pole and they flogged him with a whip. Each soldier had his turn, hurting him as much as he could."

The boy and the priest wept together. When he composed himself, de Coya went on. "A soldier was ordered to beat the tops of his feet with a club until he could not stand." The boy began to cry again.

"Father, the man would not answer them. He spit in the sergeant's face, and they beat him more viciously. He did not speak, not once, and even after they broke his feet he would not say what they wanted to hear."

"How were you injured? Who did this to you"? Pareja asked.

"I told them to stop. I said he was old, and not really a man and they should be ashamed. They laughed at me, and shoved me to the ground. They were jerking on the chain around his neck, making him bleed. I seized the whip and struck the sergeant in the face. He pulled his knife and would have stuck me, but he was slow. He cut my ear off."

"Your ear is still there although it is badly cut, but what of your tooth?"

The boy's hand went to his mouth, and his fingers explored the hole where the tooth had been. "I didn't know it was gone." The boy was no longer crying.

"I awoke here in my bed. I went out looking for the old man but a soldier said I was forbidden to see him."

"Where is the Acueran now?" Pareja asked.

"They still guard his cell and I believe he is there" the boy said. "I am afraid they have killed him."

* * *

Father Pareja did not bother to knock. The rusty hinges screeched as the priest's shoulder struck the door and he charged into the dusty apartment.

"What's this?" Sergeant Suarez shouted jumping up from his desk and knocking the chair over as he backed away. He held a stiletto in his hand, extended toward the intruder backlit against the bright sunlight flooding the room.

When he saw it was Pareja he lowered the knife. "You startled me, Father, entering so suddenly," he said, righting the chair and slipping the thin blade into the scabbard at his waist.

"You best have a suitable explanation for your actions, Suarez," the priest said, "but I warn you I intend to make a full report to the governor and the arch-bishop. If you have killed the Indian Marehootie I will not rest until you have been punished. I know of your kind. Do you believe a pacifist servant of God would not recognize evil when he faces it?

"And your treatment of the boy! If God would forgive, I would gladly say a thousand 'Hail Mary's' for the privilege of punishing you myself," he said. The priest was still advancing, fists extended, shaking with rage.

Suarez moved slowly. He showed his palms and motioned for the priest to calm himself. "I can imagine what you have been told, but until you have heard the truth of the matter I suggest you control your anger. There will be opportunity for threats and recriminations on both sides," he said.

"I shall see the Indian, and I will document his injuries and treat them. May God have mercy on your soul if you have killed him," Father Pareja said.

"He is not dead. You are free to see him, and the boy may see him as well," Suarez said.

A soldier stepped into the room, attracted by the commotion. Suarez waved him away and he left.

Father Pareja saw that Suarez' face was badly scratched and he felt satisfaction in the discovery.

"You swore that you would await my return before further punishment of the Acueran," he said.

"I promised no such thing! I said I would wait until you returned before taking action against the Acueran. You said that without more evidence I should not put the man on trial for the killings at Guale, and I agreed to wait."

"Then I assume that beating the man almost to death is not what you would call 'taking action'?" Pareja asked.

"I merely interrogated him."

"You tortured him!"

"Of course I did. Otherwise he might not have wanted to answer my questions," Suarez shouted back.

"And what did you learn? What did the old man volunteer when you questioned him by pounding his feet with a club?"

"Perhaps I should ask first, what you learned from Father de Avila that would prove the man to be innocent," the sergeant said.

"You know full well a priest can not be compelled to give evidence against a man. Father de Avila stands on that privilege."

"And no priest can be forbidden to speak in behalf of an innocent man. His silence can only mean that the Indian was in Guale, after all. If de Avila had never known the man that would be proof he was not in Guale, that this is just a case of mistaken identity," the sergeant said.

The two men were silent for a time, each lost in thought.

"My every instinct as a soldier convinces me the Acueran is a murderer. Any tribunal could see that. In my mind the evidence is clear. But there is more. There are things you do not know. What happened at Guale is now immaterial."

The sergeant paused. "The Indian has been condemned to death on quite a different matter," he said.

Father Pareja was stunned, unable to speak.

"There is much that I have learned since we last spoke. I cautioned you about the Indian. I told you that the boy, de Coya, had spent the night in his company. You said you would correct him," Suarez said. Then he paused again before going on.

"This is a delicate matter. I have never talked to a priest about such things. Are you familiar with a French term, '*berdache*'?" he asked.

"I speak and write fluently in French. The word is not in my vocabulary," Pareja answered.

"There are other words in our own language, coarse ones, to describe the same thing. To be delicate, let us just say the Indian has the nature of a woman."

"I know what you mean by that phrase," the priest said. "I have heard it before, and we can speak of it without being indelicate. We are not children here. Such people do exist here in this land, as elsewhere. The Moors had the same filthy habits that they tried to import to Spain, as you recall. We Franciscans stand strongly against the practice as pagan and an abomination to God," he said.

"Have you noticed the Acueran's mannerisms, the way he walks and that he wears his hair down to his shoulders?" Suarez asked. "All the other Indian men wear their hair in a knot atop the head."

"And based on that you slander him?"

"That, and the word of one who knows the fact from his own knowledge," Suarez said. "Your own altar boy, who you call Juan de Coya, has pled in the man's defense that the Acueran has the nature of a woman."

"But that could mean many things, to say that he has the nature of a woman. Perhaps it means he has a gentle nature, or that he does not enjoy more masculine endeavors. Such as killing or making war."

"On the contrary, I believe your *berdache* is well acquainted with killing," the sergeant said.

"What the boy said, it has some other meaning," the priest said.

"You told the boy to stay away from the Acueran before you went to St. Augustine?" Suarez asked.

"I forbade him."

Suarez stepped around the desk and placed his hand on the shoulder of the priest. "The two were together when we went to question the old man," he said, "and the boy fought us as if he protected a lover."

Father Pareja shrugged away from the touch of the sergeant, and walked outside. Presently, he returned.

"By what authority do you, a mere sergeant, condemn a man to death on such a flimsy charge?"

Suarez rummaged in the desk and produced a metal insignia of rank which he placed before the priest. "I am a Captain in the Army of the King of Spain. I function as a sergeant because that is the available billet here, but I am a

241

commissioned officer, nonetheless. As such, in this province where no civil government is present I have tribunal powers and I have found the Acueran guilty for his filthy, and, as you would say, his 'abominable' crime."

"But by what authority is the death penalty to be imposed?" Father Pareja asked in a quiet voice.

"Under military justice and with the precedent of an order of Captain Nuno Beltran de Guzman. You have heard his name? In 1530 de Guzman burned an Indian soldier in his own command for the same crime. I have read the order. It is found in the Archives of the Presidio of New Spain. It is well known in the military and it is the law. I can do no less than Nuno de Guzman," he said.

"Is it his nature that condemns him, or is it the filthy act of which you speak?"

Suarez hesitated before he spoke. "In my mind, they are the same," he said. "Guzman had no need for witnesses."

"When will this occur, this burning?"

"In two days. It will be at midnight, so as not to disturb the village, although it might be instructive to these people if they were forced to watch. It will not be in the mission, but beyond the barracks toward the magazine structure."

"I could appeal this action to the governor, but I could not return in only two days." Pareja said.

"If you intend to appeal, I will accommodate you and delay the execution for an additional three days, until Friday midnight. I will even lend you my horse."

"You know full well my vows as a Franciscan forbid me to mount a horse," the priest said.

The sergeant smiled, displaying his tobacco stained teeth. "I am sure God would make an exception to save the Indian's life, don't you think?"

"Very well, I will ride your horse," Pareja said. He moved toward the open doorway.

"It would almost be worth it if the governor ordered the trial take place in St. Augustine," Suarez said, "to hear the public testimony of the boy and his relationship with the *berdache*."

"The boy is in my charge. You have no right to humiliate him."

"You do not understand, Father. If we must go to all the trouble of trying the Acueran in St. Augustine, I intend to charge the boy with the same crime. They will burn together. Together in death as they were together in life," he said.

The priest returned directly to the convento. He instructed the boy to attend the old man and to do what he could to treat his injuries. When the boy was gone, the priest went to his own apartment. He locked the door so he could not be disturbed, and sunk to the floor in prayer.

He prayed for God's forgiveness for his arrogance, and for his display of anger and lack of self control. Lastly, he asked God's direction in his dealings with earthly minions of the devil.

CHAPTER 29

The guard did not hesitate to open the door when the boy approached. He was young, perhaps four years older than de Coya. He had blue eyes which made him different from the others whose eyes were brown, but his eyes were not smiling. Instead, he looked at the young Indian with hatred and revulsion etched on his fresh-scrubbed face.

The old Indian was asleep and his breathing was labored and irregular. His face was hot and flushed beyond what would be expected in the comfortable air. The skin under his eyes was gray and sickly. The wounds around his neck no longer bled, but were swollen and oozed a thick yellow substance.

De Coya rolled the Acueran onto his side. The scourge marks of the whip were encrusted with dirt where he had lain on the ground. His feet were swollen twice their size and looked more like gourds than feet.

The boy left, but soon returned with spring water, clean cloth and an alcohol astringent he was given by the priest.

The boy did what he could, washing the filth from the old man's back.

The Acueran awakened as the boy worked. "Do not put the Spanish medicine on me," he said.

De Coya had thought the man asleep and was startled. "It is all I have," he said.

"Bring my medicine bag."

The boy rolled the old man as gently as he could, and pulled the leather packet from under the pallet. The Acueran withdrew a small carved wooden box. It contained a salve of greenish color.

244

With the man lying on his stomach, the boy was told to scrub his back with a rough stone. "All the scratches that have bled must bleed again," Marehootie instructed.

"Harder, harder," he ordered. "Do I have to do this myself?"

Tears rolled down the boy's cheeks, fell and mixed with the old Indian's blood. The boy scrubbed harder. When Marehootie was satisfied, he told the boy to wash his back with water, and dry it with cloth. The salve was then worked deeply into the wounds.

Marehootie tolerated it in silence.

"I will not die from crippled feet, unless I have to escape a hungry panther," he said. "Clean my feet and do nothing more to them. They will heal as they will heal," he said, "but the neck wounds will kill me."

"Do you recall how I treated my brother's knife wound when he killed the three Utinans?"

"He killed only two. You said you killed the other," de Coya said.

The Acueran smiled, but his eyes were closing. "I'm glad you were listening" he said dreamily." I can't remember now what I did to save him. I have to go to sleep again."

The boy called the old man's name, but he did not answer. He shook his shoulder, but he did not respond.

* * *

The village of Carabay had a respected *isucu* whose knowledge of cures was recognized throughout Mocama. Even the priest tolerated him, so long as he confined his cures to the herbs and other natural substances he collected, and abandoned the pagan prayers and chants used by the other, un-Christian shaman. Rumors persisted that for a price the old cures were still available.

The village was so close to the mission that the boy ran all the way. The *isucu* was there, standing outside his house. With him was a tall man of chiefly bearing. It was Chief Tacatacura, the man who told the sergeant he did not recognize the Acueran.

245

"Give the boy what he needs," the chief commanded the *isucu*. Within minutes the boy was running back toward the mission, clutching a packet of herbs.

* * *

It was now almost dark. Father Pareja came with the boy and carried his oil lamp which was lit and placed on the floor beside where the boy would work. The priest left and returned to the darkened convento.

De Coya remembered the old man had used a poultice of comfrey leaves and spider webs on his brother's knife wound, but the Acueran had not described how it was prepared. He waited, hoping that he would awaken.

Finally, de Coya began to cut the green comfrey leaves in the only way he knew, as if he were cutting myrtle leaves for mosquito lotion. He knew that he should not use bear oil as he had with the mosquito cure.

De Coya ground the green leaf remains under the pestle until the oils separated.. He had found an abundance of spider webs under the eves of the convento roof, and combined them with the oils.

The boy said a prayer before what he did next. He heated a thin-bladed knife point until it glowed. The handle became hot and burned his fingers, but he did not put it down. When it was ready, he seared the inside of a neck wound, then heated the knife again and went to the next wound. The smell of burning flesh was in his nose.

He turned the old man as he worked until he had burned every wound. The boy rested, and then applied the poultice, working it into the flesh. He placed a wrapping of palmetto fiber and moss around the neck and tied it in place when he was done.

The Acuera slept fitfully. The boy loosened the wrapping and the man became quiet.

De Coya stepped out of the cell into the church yard. It was daylight, and the cooks had returned. The air was cool and scented by the smell of roasting yaupon leaves.

The sergeant's horse was tethered to a post outside Father Pareja's apartment at the convento. Later in the day, de Coya watched as a soldier led the horse away.

After the sun set, the old man began to speak in tongues the boy did not understand. He was animated and his arms flew about. De Coya tied his hands together so he would not injure himself. He poured a tea made with dried willow bark into the Acueran's mouth slowly, so he did not choke.

The boy put his fingers in his ears and hummed so that he could not hear what the old man was saying.

When de Coya awoke it was morning again. The old man's eyes were open and unblinking, looking directly at him.

"Are you dead?" the boy asked.

"Untie my hands. I need to urinate," he said.

At mid-day the old man ate a meal of corn cakes and fish broth. The boy changed the dressing on the neck wounds and Marehootie smoked tobacco and herbs. Soon he was strong enough to talk.

* * *

"The death of a village chief and the loss of an entire village were serious blows to the spirit of the people, and all of Acuera was depressed and feeling defeated. The spring rains had not come and it was already summer. Where maize was grown the stalks grew as high as a man's knee and withered.

The chief called for *tacachale* to renew the spirit of the people.

The *jarva* of Acuera asked for my help, since I had experience. I was thankful he did not ask me to do the chants. I trained the dancers and made other arrangements to help.

Tacachale was performed without a single mistake. It was what happened at the end of the ceremony that our people will never forget.

I had seen fire jump from the hearth to dry the tears of Crying Bird when he had the vision of the death of Ibitibi and its chief. This happened in Satureiwa. I never told anyone what I had seen that night, and I never talked about it with Crying Bird.

247

Something like it happened again, that night in the village of Acuera, with the chief and all his principal men looking on. When *jarva* cast the herbs into the fire to make it flash at the end of the ceremony, the fire rose up and left the hearth and swirled around my brother. It was as if his whole body was aflame, and yet he was the flame itself.

When the fire jumped back to the hearth it let out a sigh that moved the air and there was a great wind that extinguished its own flame. Crying Bird was not burned. As before, not even his eyebrows were singed, as can happen to anyone who approaches too close to a campfire.

I saw something then that frightened even me. The reflection of the fire remained in his eyes, though the ashes were already growing cold. I know *jarva* saw it too, and he fell to his knees. The people were stunned to silence. The chief could not speak. My brother's mouth moved as if he would speak, but there were no words. There was only the mournful call of chulufi-yuchi, the crying bird.

Alobo, of all people, was the first to find his voice. '*Atichicolo-Iri*,' he said. '*Atichicolo-Iri*,' the people answered, and those who were still standing fell to the ground.

Crying Bird closed his eyes and his hands covered his face. When he looked out again, the fire had left his eyes. It had burned its way into his heart.

When he spoke his voice was strong and his words were heard by everyone. They were the words spoken a generation before by Chief Acuera. "We vow to die a hundred deaths to maintain the freedom of our land, for the present and forevermore."

It had been made known to my brother that the Spanish were coming to our homeland, they would be there in two days and they were invited by Olate Quai Outina."

* * *

"My story will end with what I will tell you now. It has been long and perhaps clumsily told, but you have been a patient listener. I hope you will remember what has been said and that you will understand what it all means.

There is much more I could say, but for now you need to know only what happened two days after *tacachale*.

The leader of the Spanish was called Menendez de Aviles. He was also called Adelantano, but I do not know what it means. The Spanish give themselves many titles. He is the man who ordered the death of the French.

Menendez was also a liar. He told Satureiwa that he was the Son of the Sun, come to rule and be worshiped. He flashed mirrors in people's faces, and told them that the mirror would betray anyone who tried to deceive him.   Menendez did not know that de Soto had left mirrors here, and every tribe had seen them and knew they were no more magical than a pool of water that reflects a person's face.

Some of Outina's vassal chiefs had met the Spanish and they told Outina that Menendez could make the rain fall. Outina also knew that Menendez was making plans to bring his army to the River of the Sun. To find favor with the Spanish, as he had with the French, Outina sent a man to invite the Spanish to come for a visit.

He also prayed that Menendez would bring rain with him.

When Menendez set out from the village of Satureiwa, it was already raining there at the hottest time of the day. The next day it rained a little farther to the west. Menendez arrived at Matiaca, the main village of Outina, late in the day, and the rains came at the same time.

It was clever of Menendez, and Outina fled into the woods rather than meet the Spanish face to face. He pretended that he feared someone with such awesome power that he could make it rain. I do not believe that was Outina's reason for fleeing. I believe he feared the Spanish would kill him because of his friendship with the French.

Every tribe, even the Utinans, have people who can make the rain fall. They are not people to fear.

We had spies and runners north of the great lake, and they reported that the Spanish would cross in the morning. We hoped they would cross late in the day. Many people had been drowned when afternoon storms hit the lake, but in the morning the water was usually peaceful.

The south end of the lake is shallow. Canoes can pass without a problem, even when the water is low. We hoped that the Spanish boats would be too large or could not find the narrow channel. Our spies told us Menendez' boats were larger than any canoe, but not as large as the ships that the Spanish used in the ocean.

The Spanish crossed the lake and had no trouble finding the river. The sand bar, where it was shallow, hindered their progress. Two large boats were left there, but they continued up the river in a smaller boat.

There were 50 men with weapons on board and eight oarsmen on each side. Menendez stood on a platform near the front, and there was a cabin where he could get out of the sun and rain.

There is a place on the river where the banks are close together. It was there we waited. We had strung stakes across the river, tied together with vines. Beyond, on the east side, forty Mayacan warriors stood, partially hidden by trees. On the other side were the Acuerans, as well as the men from Cofahiqui who had their faces painted red, as is their custom.

A palm tree had fallen along the bank on the Acueran side of the river. It had a large root ball that was tilted up, higher than the bank itself. Crying Bird climbed up and stood on it, above everyone else, and so high he could look into the eyes of the men on the Spanish boat.

We could see the man called Menendez. He had fancy clothing of gold and green and he wore a metal hat that shone in the morning sunlight. He had a bright red plume on his hat. I have never seen or heard of such a large bird of that color.

I knew the man who stood beside him. He was Perchuco, the slave who had been given to us by Oathaqua, chief of the Ais. It was the man we had released to save his life. Now he was dressed with a metal tunic and hat, and he held a musket. He looked very important.

The boat stopped at the stakes and the men rested at their oars. The boat slowly drifted back, as Menendez considered what he should do. He gave a command and the boat moved forward again. Two men with long knives leaned from the boat and chopped at the vines. The snare soon gave way and the boat moved through.

My brother shouted a command that they stop and leave our homeland or they would all be killed. Crying Bird was naked but for his breechcloth and the copper breastplate he wore, a gift to our uncle from Cofahiqui. The red jewel in its center caught the morning light, and glowed brighter than the sun itself.

I was nearby, behind a cypress tree, and I heard Perchuco interpret what my brother had said for the Spaniard, Menendez.

My brother moved his feet to brace himself. He pulled an arrow that he had stuck in the top knot of his hair and strung it on his bow. Menendez gave an order. Perchuco looked to his captain as if to argue. Then he lifted his weapon to his shoulder and pointed it at Crying Bird's heart.

A long moment passed. Then I heard a loud report that echoed down the river. Egrets and ibis and anhinga leapt from their perches in the trees and flew away. The musket ball and the arrow from the bow of Crying Bird passed each other in flight.

Perchuco was pinned against the cabin of the boat, the arrow having easily pierced the flimsy metal tunic. His legs were slack and his chin dropped to his chest and he spat blood. Before he could fall he was struck by an arrow shot by Alobo, and two others from the men from Cofahiqui. He was dead, but his body would not fall to the deck.

Crying Bird did not reach for another arrow. The warriors amassed on each side of the river screamed insults and roared their anger at the Spanish. They awaited only the command of my brother, *Atichicilo-Iri,* to launch their arrows and spears.

A command finally came, but it was from the Spaniard. The oarsmen rested and the boat drifted slowly backward until it came to a wide place in the river. There it turned around and made its way downstream.

A loud cry of celebration went up from the warriors, but it was not heard by my brother. He stood where he was until the boat was out of sight. His legs crumpled under him. My hands reached out and caught him before he could fall. I handed him down to Alobo who laid him on the river bank. His blood mixed with the dark current.

There was a hole in the breastplate the size of a clam shell. When I removed it I saw the hole in my brother's chest.

By the time the sun set we were half way to Wekiva, my brother and I. He had told me many times where he wished to be buried."

* * *

The old man was tired and wished to rest.

"I have a question before I leave you," the boy said. "You told me once you know my uncle who was chief of Coya, and a vassal of Chief Outina."

"There was a falling out. Chief Coya took his village out of the Utina federation and joined Satureiwa, Acuera, Potano, Ais, Mayaca and the rest to fight the Spanish. Chief Coya would not fight Outina because he felt it would be dishonorable.

"Where is Coya now?" the boy asked.

Marehootie lowered his head and paused before answering.

"He died in my arms two summers ago. He had received many wounds in fighting the Spanish, as we all did, but it was the Spanish sickness that killed him. Can you imagine that?"

"Who is Chief of the Coya people now?"

"There is no one left in the line of succession, except you."

De Coya stood and went to the window. He was not tall enough to see anything but the evening sky and the beautiful gold and orange and pink of sunset.

"Do you know they plan to kill you at midnight?" he asked.

"I dreamed that they burned me."

"I can not let that happen," de Coya said.

"When the time comes, you will know what you must do," Marehootie said.

CHAPTER 30

When the boy was gone the old man lay with his eyes closed. From the window he could hear the voices of two soldiers and an Indian. They were gambling behind the barracks, tossing the bones in a familiar game. From time to time the rules changed, as the soldiers cheated the Indian out of everything he had to lose. Then it became quiet again, except for the cicadas and frogs celebrating the rain that had fallen earlier.

Father Pareja rapped softly on the door. There was no response. The guard slid the latch and let him enter.

The priest knelt beside the pallet. He placed the lamp near the man's head, and reached out with his hand to inspect the neck wounds. They had dried, he thought. There was redness and swelling, and the brown marks where the knife had seared the wounds, but no new puss or signs of infection. Marehootie's breathing was slow and steady.

"I wanted to be with you before what is to come," the priest said. "I know now you are not the man you pretend to be." The breathing stopped for a moment, and then the Indian slowly exhaled.

When he spoke his words were soft and rounded. "Are you Spanish the men you say you are?" he asked. "You profess the Ten Commandments yet you kill my people like vermin, your soldiers violate our women and your leaders steal everything we value."

The priest paused. "We have all sinned and fallen short of the glory of God."

There was no answer from the Indian.

253

"Yet with your sin, and I admit I do not understand it, you may yet be redeemed. You know of the sacraments of Confession and of Extreme Unction. I offer both to you now."

"What would an ignorant savage know of such matters?"

"I suspect that next to me, you know more of Christianity than any man in the mission."

The Acueran smiled, his teeth gleaming white from the moonlight through the window. "Is that what the priest of Ospo said to you?" he asked.

"You have done many good deeds in your life."

"I am not ready to confess. At the moment I can think of nothing that shames me," he said. "If I am to die on the fire stake, you can pray over me then."

The priest uttered a prayer for the Indian, and for himself. He crossed himself, stood and prepared to leave. He turned when he was at the door. "If I knew what I could say to save you, I would say it. It is your nature that has condemned you."

"This is not your sin, Father," the Indian said.

The door closed and was locked and the priest was gone.

* * *

Once again there was silence in the room. In time the sounds of the night drifted through the window and he listened to each one. A barred owl called to one of its kind and presently was answered. A cormorant squawked to complain against another crowding onto the same limb in the rookery. The incoming tide hissed onto the beach and a baby in the village awoke with a cry at a bad dream.

Later, when he was near sleep, he heard the sound of a bird usually found in the swamp, seldom on an island surrounded by saltwater. The old man moved from his pallet. He could not stand, so he pulled himself onto his stool. He placed herbs in his mouth between the cheek and gum and sucked the juice to tolerate the pain.

* * *

Nor was the sergeant asleep. He sprawled on his bed dressed only in his undergarment and outer tunic. His boots, freshly polished for the ceremony, stood at attention on the floor. His uniform trousers, pressed and folded neatly, lay across the back of a chair.

The oil lamp on the desk illuminated the room and the Death Warrant he had perfectly worded and neatly inscribed on good parchment.

Before he laid down to rest he had gone to inspect the execution site. His orders had been carried out. Hardwood logs had been laid out, along with dry kindling around the base of the pole to which the condemned man would be chained. Nearby brush had been cleared so the fire would not spread, and a barrel of water was there with buckets in case it did.

He was jolted wide awake by the sound of the church bell, clanging loudly in the mission and echoing through the village and across the island.

* * *

Father Pareja had also found it impossible to sleep, and sat in his porch chair. He was startled at the sound of the bell. No one had entered the church since he closed the door after evening vespers. He jumped to the ground and ran toward the church as soldiers swarmed out of the barracks. He heard Suarez shouting orders.

When the priest rushed into the nave he arrived at the same time as a soldier. They were alone in the church, but the bell continued to toll above their heads. Pareja backed out of the door into the yard, looking up at the bell tower. He could see nothing and no one. All around him excited Indians milled about, attracted by the strange goings-on.

"Fire! Fire!" they shouted, looking toward the woods beyond the barracks where the sky glowed red. Already the sergeant and his men were fighting the fire, and Pareja could hear their profane curses above the ringing of the bell.

The priest ran to the Acueran's cell, just as the boy, de Coya, came from a different direction. The door was open and the room was empty. The guard lay on his back, his blue eyes looking at the sky in astonishment. His throat was laid open and blood soaked his tunic.

"This is too dangerous. Come with me, quickly," Pareja commanded the boy as he ran across the churchyard to the convento. When he opened the door to enter, he looked behind him. The boy had not followed him.

* * *

By now the fire was contained. The hardwood and kindling at the stake had been drenched, but still undergrowth flamed at a distance. Small pockets of fire burst to life, fed by a breeze from the south, sometimes running across cleared ground where there was no visible food for the flames.

While the work went on Suarez stood to the side near the magazine, shouting his orders. He was determined to follow through with the execution. Already, two of his men had been diverted from the fire-fighting to find additional hardwood and kindling.

* * *

The barracks were now deserted, except for the small shadow of one who entered the open door of the sergeant's apartment, and closed it behind him. The door soon opened again, and was closed. From the churchyard, the apartment window reflected the red and yellow of an oil fire.

Behind the church two men huddled in the shadows. The ringing stopped, and suddenly there was a crash as the eve of the roof gave way and sticks, twigs and mortar rained down on them. Then there was a third man, the one who had fallen through the roof. They laughed and embraced each other, then moved away into the woods, one man on each side of the man who could not walk.

* * *

Despite the breeze, acrid smoke hung in the air making it difficult to see. A narrow finger of flame snaked and crackled its way across the ground and almost went unnoticed were it not that Suarez stayed near the magazine.

He shouted to the men, and soon they were with him to help as he stomped and kicked the sand and dirt with his bare feet to extinguish the fuse before it reached the gun powder inside.

When the flame at last died, Suarez saw that the lock on the magazine door had been broken. He swung open the heavy door and peered into the darkness. As his eyes adjusted, he saw that the powder kegs on the floor had been overturned and the black powder was scattered everywhere. The other men crowded into the doorway with their sergeant, congratulating each other that their quick work had averted a disaster.

Looking at the floor, none of them noticed the arrow that had pierced the palmetto roof, or the flame that flickered from its shaft. The draft from the open door licked the flame to life, and live coals of dried palmetto drifted down.

* * *

The four men sat quietly at the embarcadero. "He will come," Marehootie said. The others did not question his judgment. Their canoe was an old one, but sleek and well-made. It bore the mark of Ibitibi on its bow.

There was a sudden 'whump' sound from the woods beyond, and the sky lit as if it were daylight. A wave of heat washed over them, and was gone.

"That was my fuse," Tacatacura said.

"I believe that was my arrow," said the one who was gray haired but powerfully built and heavily tattooed.

Black smoke billowed from the patch of woods where the powder magazine had once stood. Another fire engulfed the barracks, producing a second plume of smoke. Only the church and convento were saved, as Indians from the village carried water to protect them.

* * *

257

"Hurry!" the old Acueran shouted, motioning to a shadow at the edge of the woods.

The boy sprinted across the open ground and stepped into the canoe. In a moment they were gone, lost in the shadow and darkness of the river.

"You have not met my brother, Crying Bird," Marehootie said.

"Atichicolo-Iri," the boy answered. Crying Bird smiled at him.

"The one in the back is Nihoto. He has been deaf for ten years, since he was shot by the Spanish. He is useful for ringing bells," the old man said. The man who paddled in the back cupped a hand behind his ear, smiled, but said nothing.

"These belong to you, Nariba," de Coya said as he handed the leather pouch containing the necklace and loose pearls to Marehootie.

"And I have one other gift, this Spanish paper that demands your death," the boy said, handing him the Death Warrant.

Crying Bird took the parchment from his brother and looked at it in the dim moonlight while Tacatacura and Nihoto paddled.

"I have kept something for myself," de Coya said, holding up the stiletto for all to see.

"And I also have something for you," Marehootie said. He placed a loose pearl in the boy's hand, and he clutched it tightly.

"Will anyone read this paper to me?" Crying Bird demanded. When no one answered him, he tore it into small pieces and scattered it in the waters of the River of the Sun.

* * *

On the third morning, the boy who they now called 'Coya' sat in front, studying the patterns of the trees against the sky, the banks of reeds and the willow trees hanging over the shore.

He wanted to see where the clear waters mixed with the dark.

EPILOGUE

A sure way to encourage debate among historians is to hazard a guess on the population of Timucua-speakers at the time of first contact with the Spanish. That said, most would agree that they numbered between 130,000 and 800,000 when Narvaez stepped ashore near Tampa Bay in 1528.

There is little dispute that only a handful survived until 1763 when they were evacuated with the remnants of the St. Augustine colony to Cuba, and were lost as a recognizable culture. With them went 12,000 years of ancestral memory of life in their homeland.

Yet, of all the aboriginal inhabitants of what is now Florida and south Georgia, theirs is the only language documented in such detail that it can now be studied. Thanks to the writings of the Franciscan priest, Francisco Pareja, we know how they spoke. Thanks to the French artist Jacques Le Moyne who drew their pictures, and to Theodore de Bry who followed up on Le Moyne's work, we have an idea of how they looked.

Because of the work of historians and archaeologists like Jerald T. Milanich, John H. Hann, Michael V. Gannon and John E. Worth we know much about their customs, their beliefs, how they lived and how and why they died.

In the summer of 1955 a dragline operator widening the channel of the St. Johns River made an interesting discovery: an old heart-of-pine log had been scooped from the mucky bottom, to be discarded with the rest of the effluvia. It was a carved owl, standing six feet tall. Two other similar carvings were found nearby in later years.

The carving was carbon-dated to the fourteenth century. The owl is thought to be the largest, single-figure aboriginal carving in the western hemisphere. I asked myself "Who carved it?" and "How and why did it end up in the river?" The rest is history.

The owl carving is now displayed at the Florida Museum of Natural History at Gainesville. A replica stands on the grounds of Hontoon Island State Park, near Deland.

Another replica leans against the wall in the corner of my dining room. It was a gift from my wife, Linda.

The owl watches me as I write. He is my muse. I call him Marehootie.

Fredric M. Hitt
2005

8/25

Printed in the United States
102048LV00002B/290/A

9 781589 397590